The Levelled

Jon Bryant

Dedicated to Karen
for being the spark

Note from the Author

The description of rough sleeping in this book comes from the imagination, not first-hand experience. The Levelled is more about possible routes towards detachment from society than it is about being homeless. I am conscious that appropriating the grim realities of life on the street in pursuit of being published might be questionable. I have tried my best to capture an approximation of the truth and reflect that the underlying issues are extremely complex.

All author royalties from sale of this paperback/e-book will be donated to local homelessness charities.

We late-lamented, resting here,
Are mixed to human jam,
And each to each exclaims in fear,
'I know not which I am!'

The Levelled Churchyard, Thomas Hardy

Chapter 1

Jez had read more novels than ever before since living on the street. Having found a way to tolerate the physical discomfort of hard surfaces, he settled into a routine and books became his emblem. It began with a single volume that unexpectedly fell into his hands and served him well in the early days by giving protection from eye contact; *Jude the Obscure* in paperback, by chance, not that he was bothered to start with. Throughout his life Jez had steered clear of proper literature, assuming it to be dreary and weird, like church and hymns. However, when taken to leaf through the pages out of curiosity, a moment of surprise occurred, almost an awakening. Against expectation he was drawn in, discovering a sympathetic voice revealing plausible lives and situations, in a world he could relate to. He had not anticipated being so absorbed in the stories, let alone for time to pass more agreeably, it was almost like watching TV. He welcomed this new dimension and chastised himself for missing out before.

From that beginning, maintained by long hours of daylight and other people's cast-offs, a steady stream of books followed. Despite the tendency for the homeless to go unseen, Jez became recognisable to observers as '*the book guy*'. He soon latched on to the type ... his regulars ... essentially good-hearted people who refused to take a diversion to avoid the pavement dwellers, but who rarely gave money. Their default response was an apologetic, slow shake of the head, serene in the knowledge they were protecting the poor souls from the addictions that no doubt plagued them. But the option of donating a book was appealing. Anyone doing so would be placating their conscience, as long as they remembered to fish out a redundant one before leaving home. It felt especially appropriate in response to an individual like this, seemingly intent on self-improvement and redemption … and much better for his health than a handful of pound coins. Through this form of charity, a small pile of fiction often accrued. Jez would work his way through, some volumes being swiftly discarded if the characters started to mess with his head.

*

He hated making eye contact. Jez fell into a strategy of understated begging, with a unique selling point of subtlety. The books were not a conscious affectation, but they did help cultivate an air of civility and break down barriers. Still … he hated the eye contact: the pitying looks of people who wished he would disappear, resentful that the dregs of society could intrude upon their field of vision, glancing sideways as they passed, against their better judgement but for as long as they dared. He wanted money and collected money, while blocking the connotations of begging in his mind. He never actually asked. Having slipped out of all conventional ways of living, Jez willed there to be a base level of financial movement that could sustain life, like dust at the edge of tarmac enabling the growth of weeds. He unwittingly played the percentages of folk who understand the argument against providing cash, but who only live by that rule nine times out of ten. A barely perceptible 'Thank you,' at the moment they averted their gaze made them think differently next time. In general, a natural order held sway: the more grey-faced and malnourished, the more likely that instincts would be ignored with a 'just this once' gesture of loose change. A self-regulating feedback loop in which resistance to give is suppressed when confronted with palpable distress. Through these mechanisms of the gutter he collected enough to survive.

Lack of income was a constant worry but was not his primary concern – greater jeopardy lay in the other street life … and the increasing cold to come.

*

Some of his comrades bristled at the relative refinement, aloofness even, of Jez's modus operandi. Nevertheless, by and large he got along, being happy to sit and talk indefinitely about life stories with his fellow downtrodden. He had no answers but was a good listener, gaining strength from the knowledge that others too found the journey of life to be an itinerary of no through roads. A few of his regulars would also stop to chat. Others would march by with a steely determination not to acknowledge his presence at all, let alone pause for conversation. He noticed one chap in particular sidling past a few times. A timid-looking man, shoulders hunched, but giving the impression of wanting to communicate. As if intent to understand why Jez was there, perhaps envying the romantic idyll of life on the road, an existence free from the strictures of normality. While the lifestyle was liberating to a degree, Jez wanted to discourage this stranger from such thoughts, but the stride was never broken long enough for a connection to form. Still, it was a peculiar exception to sense something other than commiseration or disdain from one of the frequenters of his patch.

His patch. Jez reflected that it could be a lot worse, relatively speaking. The town was a good size for his needs. In a smaller place a rough sleeper would be spotted and attract so much unwanted do-goodery, it would be impossible to remain unsaved. Anywhere larger, one would completely vanish in the ocean of outsiders. Jez was optimistic the right balance prevailed here. Here he was part of a sufficiently substantial and uncontained problem that kind gestures were spread too thinly to have any chance of persuading him to confront reality – which suited him. To remain unsaved was exactly what he wanted. Yet by retaining a trace of identity – by becoming a recurring minor character in the swirling stage play of the street – he could stay afloat, buoyed by that background level of compassion in the local inhabitants that flowed past him each day, while rarely having to look anyone in the eyes.

He concluded it was possible to get by. Having adapted to the material challenges, having established a pattern, having controlled his fears to those he could manage, Jez told himself that the cold, sixteen-hour nights that approached perhaps might not be insurmountable after all, for better or worse.

Chapter 2

Christmas 1998 was the first one Bevan had spent completely alone. He wished he could return, to hide there. In retrospect, it was probably the easiest Christmas for him to think about than any other before or since. That year had not required him to spend days with people whose relatively functioning lives made him feel alienated and whose half-hearted enquiries about his wellbeing put him on edge. There had been no need to guess, through tortured yet random deliberation, what gift choices might prevent each recipient wanting to scream *idiot!* inside, on removal of the wrapping paper. No need to disappoint. No need to join in. For one or two years thereafter, he had seen the familiar trappings anew. The frozen breath, twinkly lights and unaffected bonhomie of strangers reviving memories of a time when the mysteries of life held promise and a sense flickered of his existence having some trajectory and purpose. Now, twenty years on, as advent ticked down once more, Bevan was looking back across the decades trying to string together some sonar specks ... the few peaks of contentment he could recall that had left an imprint. Certain occasions had been enjoyable at the time, but subsequent events now tainted their recollection. The decadence of that first Christmas Day free from all pressure of expectation was probably the most fondly remembered blip on the screen that he could see. He wished there had been more.

For the ten years preceding that high spot, Bevan had reluctantly accepted the invitations of his brother or sister for the darkest week. They were trying to help, in response to his unsuccessful attempt to kill himself at the age of twenty-nine. They felt duty-bound to offer him somewhere to go, so managed to put animosity on hold and reach out a hand. Back then, in the immediate aftermath of his failure to die – having experienced the sheer exhilaration of knowing he had done everything right, his method correctly researched, the outcome assured, the possibility of his actions being dismissed as merely 'a cry for help' nullified – waking to the reality he had screwed up again and was still alive felt like the dawn of an even more desolate world. An altered state in which he was barely engaged at all. Something *had* died that night, although regrettably he was still breathing. Bevan was unable to process the wide-eyed dismay and grudging empathy displayed by his relatives in response to his bid to disappear … and he was left desensitised to his own emotional incompetence from that point onwards.

At least until that episode he had trusted enough in the importance of life to conclude his own should no longer be endured. It had never been right. There had been the golden period with Fiona, his most cherished days, but when she disappeared all his fuses tripped. From that blow he could never lift himself up. Eventually, having joyously inhaled moments of knowing he was about to expire, only to be thrown back into the fray with yet more cause for self-loathing, his aspirations became cauterised for good. He stopped yearning for better things – apart from a simple passage to the end of days, without challenge or shame, burying himself in work. A path of least resistance, like a fallen seed carried by river all the way to the sea, to oblivion, indifferent to any lost prospects of taking root. He would never risk seeing those looks again, the unsaid stupefaction of: *how could you?*

*

Over those ten years his sense of needing to atone gradually faded. Bevan's guilt transferred from the shock caused to his siblings by his act of self-destruction to the discomfort inflicted upon them by his continued presence in their living rooms. His brother and sister were both older and had always resented his odd personality. The youngest child of three was supposed to bring comedy, act as a foil, leaven the family hubbub. However, while the infant Bevan could not exactly be described as a malign influence on their own childhoods, he consistently surprised them with his degree of remoteness. He occupied his own bubble and gave the distinct impression of wishing for an alternative set of blood relations. From the earliest age Bevan was hopeless at translating internal thoughts and feelings into his outward demeanour. People assumed this frowning boy was perpetually unimpressed by everything around him – in reality, sometimes he was, sometimes he was not – and had to acclimatise to the oppressive aura that surrounded him.

His brother Keith and his sister Anne soon concluded that little Bevan was not to be their plaything. They mostly allowed him to plough his own furrow and came to accept his apparent disinterest in their own personal milestones and achievements. They progressed into conventional lives, each fashioning a cocoon of house and family, self-contained and snug. Bevan's detachment as a child was given free rein once he embarked upon adult life. He set his own boundaries. He did not feel the imperative to keep in touch and his inner voices gave absolution from responsibility for anything but his own needs. Had he asked to be born? Accepting that burden was enough. He saw little need to broadcast news about his affairs and exploits, thus he survived while hardly leaving a trace … indeed it was only by chance the police were able to identify a next-of-kin at the point when Bevan was discovered in his metaphorical ditch.

Upon the realisation that Bevan had gone completely off the rails, an instinctive collusion arose between Keith and Anne to share the task of rehabilitating him. They had become accustomed to his distance and silently shared a sense of relief that he left them alone, which outweighed any regrets about broken ties. Nevertheless, on grasping the magnitude of his despair, they took him in between them, with a minimum of discussion and planning. Having done so, less than a week passed before they were sufficiently convinced it was unlikely to happen again. They coaxed him back into the wild, back to his bubble, reassured by the knowledge their wayward brother was eager to go – although in truth he was simply beaten. Their level of worry and horror diminished and the pattern of infrequent contact was restored; nonetheless the emotional spider's web of Christmas proved inescapable. They found a way to suggest he came, sharing the load year on year, taking turns to make space in their respective homes. And Bevan was too sheepish to decline, for a while at least.

*

Those annual reunions were weathered with awkward conversation and outdoor strolls made bearable only by encounters with the romping of other people's dogs – Bevan wished he had one but feared for its powers of unconditional love in the face of his empty stare. TV, sleep, not enough to drink. He concluded that Keith and Anne were more concerned about the embarrassment and unwanted attention his suicide attempt had caused than they were about his depth of unhappiness. They had never understood what Fiona meant to him. He sensed them mutely intoning to themselves: if he felt so strongly about *anything* why could he not have shown it before, when it mattered? He also sensed their gratitude when he said his goodbyes once the mince pies and chocolates had gone.

By shutting down his life ambitions to the bare minimum – just adequate to maintain some degree of sanity – and giving up any attempts at self-fulfilment, Bevan had come to realise that his one remaining source of consolation was his job. Work became his place to hole up, his niche, his sheep space. Like the accentuated hearing of the blind, during the early 90s his professional life developed and compensated for the closure of a personal one. Despite the sherries being too small, in later winter retreats he felt the urge to start talking about his minor triumphs with office IT, to make the time go faster. On one occasion he overcame his inhibitions – the shackles imposed by the constant thought that nothing he did was worth telling – and ventured a comment:

'You know, they've got me working with computers now. I'm going to build a database.' Bevan felt embarrassed to be pleased about anything, but he need not have worried, Anne was not out to be impressed. She thought this sounded like something secretarial.

'So, you're a typist now?' she scoffed, before adding, 'You could've done so much more with your life with the right attitude.'

'No, it's not like being a typist …' but his voice tailed off. Bevan was reminded that his part was to stay sullen and deferential.

'Look, there's that bullfinch again,' said Keith, seeking to change the subject. He was uneasy regarding anything to do with computers, mistrusting them as good-for-nothing gimmicks lifted from the pages of science fiction and his attention had drifted towards the garden.

Bevan concluded there was no point trying to convey anything about what was really happening to him. Inevitably, as an approximation of self-esteem was restored, he felt steadily more entitled to escape this seasonal ritual and started to invent excuses. He swore that he would be fine, he had made new friends – in reality though, by extricating himself from their hospitality he was merely extending his solitude to fill the entire year. He withdrew back to his own home again and the fractured channels that connected him to his only near relatives began to silt up once more. The novelty of having freedom to do exactly what he wanted at Christmas generated a somewhat twisted version of the traditional glee – in his case, a sentiment based more on release from obligation than goodwill to all men. Predictably though, after a few years that novelty soon ebbed away, and he lost interest in raising toasts to anyone or anything at standard times of festivity. In the years to come, days were differentiated only by their duration of darkness.

*

In that first Christmas alone, Bevan indulged in a modest degree of ceremony. He bought suitably themed food and drink, he consumed it at unusual hours, he nodded the odd smile at people in the pub. He put the small collection of cards he had accumulated on display, including those sent by the unknown to previous incumbents at his address, who presumably were too distant acquaintances to be informed of the change. It gave an illusion of kinship with humanity. He even made a conscious effort not to glower when the office decorations went up, despite the fact it was ridiculously early as usual. Thereafter, a few years passed without him feeling the usual dread of enforced jollity. Fellow workers humoured his aversion to join social activities yet remained genuine in their good cheer, at least while enough of them clung onto their positions to provide any greetings at all. But the passing of time was unforgiving and, as the fabric of his working environment eroded away, the holiday season turned its terrible face. The 'time for family and friends' inverts into a negative when your job is the sole extent of your dreams. Since deciding to concentrate all his energy on office life, Bevan lost any need for daylight and came to prefer times when it was absent. The fact that it was dark when he left home in the morning, then dark again when returning to his car at the end of the day, was a major attraction of winter but the approach of Christmas became a focal point for his loneliness, as those around him spoke of their plans. Fortunately, he could usually volunteer to man the depot in case of emergency over the holiday period, acting as the skeleton crew, alone but at least with a reason not to be so at home while the rest of the world made merry. He always hoped that his willingness to toil while everyone else was off having fun would ensure his survival, but the threat of compulsory severance had loomed since the invasion of the 'boys in suits' and eventually struck before he reached retirement age.

Now, as Bevan paused to survey his past, reflecting on the key incidents that shaped his destiny, that cruel blow of redundancy five years ago reverberated as a final proclamation. He had been cast adrift, with no wreckage to hold and no one watching from the side. After an eternity spent without celebrations or praise, with the last five years spent in nearly total isolation, Bevan had grown inured to all revelry. Reaching this December, he found his second point of no return – and his ability to keep going was again exhausted. As once before, all reasoning confirmed he would be better off dead. He needed plans and this time there would be no mistake.

Chapter 3

Bevan's capacity to see hope in anything – to keep playing the game, to stay on board the boat – had run dry again. All the community structures and mechanisms that existed to help keep a normal life ticking over had confounded him. His thoughts reverted back to an earlier state: the absolute knowledge that his spirit was gone. He was inextricably tangled in the weeds; the seed had failed to reach the sea.

Thirty years had passed since the last occasion of staring into this particular abyss. Then, after the near miss, he managed to find a way to block the inner voice that constantly taunted him: *why are you here, why are you here* and plough on with life, trying to put other people's feelings first for a change – not through a sudden surge of charitable love for those around him, rather on the basis that his own feelings no longer had any import. This time was different: not the slightest shred of motivation remained. His pilot flame was out. Now that he could see, with crystal clarity, not a single soul would give two shits whether he existed or not, the prospect confronted him once more that his number was up.

*

In the fallout from his initial suicide bid, while an element of that determination to put other people's feelings first concerned Keith and Anne and the distress Bevan had caused them, in truth the greater dimension was his relationship with work. In piecing together a raft of reasons for him to persevere, the only thing capable of providing any real purpose to living was his job. Bevan started his working life as an apprentice electrical fitter in 1976 aged eighteen. Through the byzantine contortions of utilities deregulation, by the 90s he found himself stationed in the stores department of Allied Grids, a new conglomerate known country-wide more for their corny ad campaign promoting the benefits of privatisation than for any understanding of what they actually did. Allied Grids was a spin-off from the earlier National Electricity Board and was responsible for the maintenance and expansion of the UK's power generation infrastructure. The original state-run body had represented an attractive choice of employer for awkward youngsters who were at their happiest when heads down, fiddling around with wires and a toolbox.

After leaving full-time education, Bevan assumed he had entered an adult world in which the main objective was the pursuit of pleasure and self-indulgence, with employment merely a platform to make everything else possible. He believed society in general, and the government in particular, owed him a job. Incidentally, he felt no compassion for former schoolmates who remained unemployed; it served them right for wasting their adolescence arranging and attending the parties he had strived so hard to avoid. Bevan felt a sense of vindication that his reluctance to socialise had served him well, however, his lack of social skills still meant he was scared of entering this new arena.

As an apprentice attached to domestic power supply he revelled in the tasks. It was the perfect scenario – solving problems with his hands while lost in concentration, working out puzzles in solitude. He proved a talented engineer but always remained suspicious of the organisation above him and was fully compliant with the prevailing 'us and them' mentality amongst the workforce. Tea and lunch breaks were pushed to the limit. Hours were forged. Impossible assignments were blamed on other parts of the chain. Missed appointments were blamed on traffic. Sometimes he would join his colleagues in the pub and felt a degree of acceptance he had never known before, not because he was the life and soul, but because he stuck to the unwritten rules and liked a beer. 'Lager top Bevsie?'

*

Only when his personal life fell apart, a decade into his career, did his work for the National Electricity Board and its private sector offspring assume more significance. A diversion, capable of alleviating his frustrations and sadness; something to take more seriously. Around this time, he also began to take heed of the wider world around him. Where privatisation had once seemed like a promised land, the harshness soon started to reveal itself. The epidemic of target-setting in the workplace made him much more conscious that *they* were after you. Idiotic management initiatives were propagated by buffoons who had never wired a fuse box or serviced a sub-station in their lives. A new type of clique could be discerned: managers dressing more smartly, talking in corridors about 'process improvement' and forever scurrying to meeting rooms. The terrifying female examples of the new breed – and their shoulder pads – soon became labelled as *The Stepford Wives*. The male ones attracted more vulgar sobriquets. Shiny young graduate entrants appeared – the boys in suits – fast-tracked into senior positions over the heads of the rank and file. New departments at HQ – organisational sub-divisions they'd been able to live without in the past – sprung up as if from nowhere. Human Resources, Marketing Communications, Facilities Management. The privatised organisation rapidly morphed into an alien landscape that felt increasingly cold and soulless.

He had never really taken much interest in global events before but when stories of civil war in the Balkans appeared in the news he was stopped in his tracks. Educated professionals being singled out for execution. Thuggery taking control in a part of the world where he had been on holiday not that long before, where he had bought drinks and swapped smiles with bar owners and local fishermen, where he had felt happiness. Normally, wars and natural disasters occurred so far away, in places that looked pretty much wrecked anyway, that Bevan was content to feel the awe of the spectacle without absorbing the reality and magnitude of suffering. But Yugoslavia was sufficiently close to home to strike a chord. The older lags in the depot cracked observations about the danger of history repeating itself, which he vaguely understood, but did not explore, in case the expectation of a longer conversation arose. Nevertheless, for a few months he avidly sought out current affairs programmes on TV, as the penny dropped that no one is safe from conflict. He could see himself in the faces of civilians who were being interviewed in reports on the latest case of ethnic cleansing, and his outlook changed for good. He started to watch his back and realise that life owed you nothing; you only got what you earnt and everyone was responsible for their own survival.

Bevan became no company lackey but, as levels of job stability and security eroded around him – factors that had once been taken for granted – he felt the shifting sands and began to show more commitment in his approach. This was partly for self-preservation but also took inspiration from a sense of loyalty to his teammates, and immediate leadership chain, who were being screwed by the system just as much as he was. He spent more time thinking about *why* the national power utility did what it did, and what would happen if it was not there. Suspending disbelief regarding Allied Grids' imperfections, he suddenly could see that the tasks he and his colleagues completed each day *did* matter. If they messed up, money was wasted and consequently, somebody, somewhere, would have a bad day. Admittedly only to a small extent, but the impact was perceptible, and Bevan decided it was worth trying his best, rather than idling and doing the minimum. This was no overnight conversion into an ambitious career man, he just became more conscientious and more attuned to ways of making a difference, contributing to the success of the business – having comprehended you only get out what you put in.

*

Fiona's disappearance and the derailing effect it had on Bevan in subsequent years took place against this backdrop. Once he had launched himself back on track, albeit in a diminished state, he picked up the threads again. For several years, ideas had been fermenting in his head that his skiving and playing the system really ought to stop. On returning to work after his meltdown – in truth he was away only for a short time, he got back in the saddle soon after his hospitalisation, while still being tutted over by Keith and Anne – the opportunity to lose himself in his activities at the Electricity Board, especially the prospect of working longer hours, came as a lifeline. Bevan welcomed the suggestion from management that he could swap life on the road as a roving fitter for a less stressful role in the stores section, where a vacancy had recently arisen with serendipitous timing. He knew the stores function inside out, having dealt with them daily in gathering the parts and materials needed for his installation, maintenance and repair jobs. The depot building felt like a second home and the routine of a regular short commute instead of constantly flogging the roads up and down the region was an additional advantage. Bevan did not need a less stressful position as such – the appeal came from being desk-bound, more self-contained responsibilities and a reduction in the number of people he had to talk to. His attitude of dedication became cemented – he grew to embody the ant more than the grasshopper, and colleagues remarked upon the time he spent buried in contemplation, tapping away at a keyboard, oblivious to the boisterous small talk that flew around the room. This peeved them to a degree, but he had always been a bit of a loner and they mostly ignored him. As for Bevan, he had never been afraid to appear detached and was not exactly desperate to join the banter anyway, especially given the threat of questions about the reasons for his temporary disappearance. Whilst he appreciated the ability to hide in a crowd, the social aspect of working for a large organisation still remained a challenge. However, if you did your job, being the odd-one-out never resulted in victimisation, unlike at school. Everybody just assumed he had suffered something of a breakdown over Fiona and the circumstances surrounding her departure and left him alone, not wishing to stir up difficult memories.

Once his analytical powers set their sights on the methods used by the stores team, Bevan soon pinpointed some aspects of local working practice that were less than ideal. Indeed, they talked about this in the group, admittedly mostly in the context of making their own lives easier rather than satisfying the management agenda of increased throughput, but at least when Bevan made suggestions it was not merely met with: 'Oi, don't be such a brown-noser.' If anyone thought he was turning into *one of them* he would rationalise this on the basis that the ones who ultimately benefited from the national power utility performing more efficiently were the general public. It was not just a matter of appeasing the fat cats at the top. The stores team were providing a service that had a measurable impact in the outside world. By keeping the depot always fully stocked, delays were kept to a minimum. There was a risk of parts running out if they did not plan correctly and operate smoothly. Real people would be made happier – or, more realistically, less unhappy, by a quicker fix, a smaller bill, even if the differences were marginal. He knew deep down that this cause and effect was extremely tenuous, but it gave him sufficient enthusiasm to make some suggestions for improving productivity. And, of course, any proposals informed by his own observations and experience on the ground were bound to be better than the shit-for-brains commandments cascading from above (the management group based at the administrative headquarters in the Midlands).

*

Bevan became established as a regional stores controller. He was part of a unit responsible for managing the raw materials used by the engineering function in one of Allied Grids' larger operational regions. This encompassed the full range of items from nuts and bolts through to the massive galvanized steel girder sections used to construct pylons. The engineering depot comprised a medium-sized warehouse, a large yard for the big items with parking spaces for the various vehicles and a small office block. It would have been full when it was first built in the 60s but staff numbers were in decline when Bevan switched to his office-based role and a few empty desks started to appear. His team occupied a small open-plan space with eight desks, and a closed-in office at one end occupied by Martin, the stores manager.

Martin had permanently close-cropped, gunmetal grey hair and beard, with a fixed expression like the wince of someone who has just swallowed a mouthful of neat alcohol. He had done every job in the depot over the years, understood the pressures of the field staff and had the broad respect of his flock of delivery coordinators and storemen. He had been a punk in his day but now came to work in a suit, mostly to be seen with sleeves rolled up, tie loosened, and a fag perched precariously in shirt pocket waiting its turn. When the depot was in its rollicking heyday the offices filled with cigarette smoke while 'Page 3' calendar girls and smutty cartoons adorned the walls. By Bevan's time smoking bans and the anti-sexism purge had cleaned the air, although the fabric of the building somehow held on to a patina of clubroom bar. The imprints of beer-breath, barrack-room humour and the odd carnal act during office parties somehow lingered. The years of half-hearted cleaning had allowed a film to descend upon all the fittings, fixing the dirt and memories in place.

Martin's function had effectively evolved into that of a fall guy, a puppet of the senior management mandarins, tasked with selling the latest decrees to a recalcitrant front-line. That and mentoring the troops through their various hang-ups and grievances – his pastoral role – trying to convince them to make an effort despite the near non-existent possibility of career development or meaningful reward. He had risen to his minor peak of middle management on merit and accepted he had found his level. He was not going to sell his soul to advance further, into the upper echelons of the HQ building, the well-trodden path of staffers getting promoted beyond their own ability. Anyway, the influx of young blood had begun, so the reliance on internal resources being re-skilled was beginning to wane.

Bevan and Martin formed a sound working relationship, each trusting the heart of the other to be approximately in the right location. Bevan was nervous of Martin's hinterland – his activities outside work – suspecting that his most ardent thoughts were fixated on what he would be doing once his standard hours were over, rather than while they were underway. He tried to skirt around the conversations on Monday mornings that began: 'Good weekend?' They each had different definitions of what that constituted. In Bevan's case it was surviving to Sunday evening without a panic attack or prolonged bout of self-criticism.

Martin was amused by Bevan's insistence on pouring scorn on every single utterance from senior management. It was relentless and Martin wished he would give it a rest sometimes. Bevan's personal life was a closed book and even in the obligatory one-on-one performance review meetings – in which Martin was supposed to adopt the mantle of counsellor, teasing out any problems at home that might be affecting his charges' well-being and productiveness – it always felt like walking on eggshells and both felt the sigh of relief when the final 'everything's fine, honestly,' was allowed to stand. But Martin still wondered what Bevan got up to away from the office.

Bevan had inherited command of the T-card board, the wall-mounted panel containing hundreds of slots in rows and columns in which the movement of cardboard flags depicted order progression through every stage of the stores operation. Each individual was responsible for moving the card when a job transitioned from one stage to the next. However, this needed policing and Bevan would spot the anomalies and investigate when something was awry, for example if a batch of components was in the warehouse but the card was stuck in the *Ordered* column. He took pleasure in ensuring strict adherence to the new colour coding scheme he had devised. In later years, Bevan looked back fondly on the T-card board as a design classic: it gave everyone a tactile connection with the outcome of their labour, a ritual moment of feeling things being done, of progress being made through the long queue of tasks. Of course, this was one of the first casualties of office automation once workflow systems started to appear, one of the first types of computer software tools to be rolled out by the embryonic central IT department in HQ.

Bevan started to notice certain trends, especially when log jams occurred, made visible by multiple T-cards being stuffed into the same slot when a column overflowed. He realised that by spreading out the parts ordering process more evenly – smaller amounts but more often – the log jams occurred less frequently, and people no longer found themselves kicking their heels quite so much. In earlier times any attempt to *do more work* would have been held as treasonous by his co-workers. Anyone observed completing more jobs per day than the tacit yardstick recognised within a group was viewed as a traitor and occasionally beaten up. But by the late 80s and the advent of performance management, such that an individual's ratings were dependent on the success of the team as a whole, behaviour that would have once been viewed as contemptible swottishness in school began to be tolerated.

*

Bevan did not regard himself as a computer geek. He was a bystander during the office conversations about the earliest forms of home computer that sometimes erupted –'anyone remember the Commodore?' – with similar frequency to outbreaks of nostalgia concerning children's TV programmes or types of sweets. His introduction to the personal computer coincided with the rise of Windows. Once PCs started to appear on the shop floor, he was sufficiently intrigued to buy one for himself, spending time at home following the instructions for installing software from floppy disks. He became well versed with the fledgling subculture of word processing and spreadsheets. When a PC first landed in Martin's office Bevan was able to show him the ropes and even do basic troubleshooting. He understood what things like printer drivers and serial ports were and soon developed a love/hate relationship with the company IT helpdesk. They were grateful to have someone in situ able to articulate problems in a more forensic way than the usual 'it's stopped working'. However, they were disdainful about Bevan's tendency to fiddle with settings. On Bevan's part he enjoyed the opportunity to show off his knowledge but resented the snide and long-suffering looks he was subjected to by the young IT support guys in their grunge band t-shirts, when called out.

The prevailing mood in this body of men and women was one of predictable dissatisfaction with their lot. The bosses were lucky that they bothered turning up each day in their considered opinion. As far as the stores team was concerned, they were battling heroically to keep the fires burning despite the best endeavours of management to make life difficult and suppress their career aspirations. Morale was constantly low and output levels were sustained through stubborn survival instincts rather than any great company loyalty. The one incentive Martin did have, that had the potential to give at least some of his fold a modicum of job satisfaction, was training. Allied Grids took capital out of its efforts to invest in its people and there was a piffling budget available to send everyone on courses. Each year, as part of the performance management ritual, Martin relied on the conversation about training plans as the only possible offset to the news that a pay rise was unlikely. He would talk through the menu of possible courses knowing there was an imperative to send each team member on one per year as part of his own management targets. In most cases this came down to things like Manual Lifting or First Aid. For several years Bevan tried to dodge any training but as his interest in computing grew, he eventually spotted something that would make sense: Relational Databases. He had created some simple forms and document templates on Martin's PC and had begun to look at a spreadsheet version of the T-card board but he knew what they really needed was a database. Martin said he would investigate the prerequisites.

'It says you need to pass the IT Trainability Test before you can do the database thing Bevsie,' Martin shouted across the room.

'Trainability?'

'Yeah. I think they check you're not brain dead or likely to drool on the keyboard.'

'Sounds a bit like brainwashing. Can I go on it?'

Strictly speaking the cost of the IT Trainability Test alone was enough to blow the budget allocated to one person but Martin realised it was worth it in Bevsie's case. He worried that maybe his penchant for computing might ultimately lure him away from stores into the IT department but in reality there was little chance of that; Bevan needed to breathe the family fug of the stores in order to survive. He would be scared witless if ever re-assigned to HQ.

*

Bevan passed the test with ease; he was delighted to discover it was just like one of those IQ tests you did at school where all you had to do was spot patterns and identify the next in a sequence. Piece of piss. The database course followed. He avidly grasped the logic of tables, fields, relationships and queries and enjoyed the visual aspects of designing forms for data entry and interrogation but got annoyed by the tutor's insistence on following the examples in the handouts. Bevan wanted to branch out and build a database of racing drivers or serial killers and had to be coaxed back to the standard example of insurance policies to stay in touch with the class, which he found deathly dull. The training was run from the Allied Grids HQ building: most of the candidates were either based locally or had travelled from their region and were staying in a hotel nearby. Bevan chose to commute back and forth each day, keen to avoid the situation of being asked to join the group for an evening meal. Plus it was good to have an excuse to journey by train, paid for by the company, because he loved to see the countryside and also the edges of towns with the glimpses they afforded into other people's worlds – their back gardens, their rear windows – viewable from a safe distance. He would lose himself in daydreams on the train. He sometimes worried that by absorbing the constantly changing view from the window, previously stored pictures in his head would somehow be erased as each new frame of hedgerow, rolling farmland and the occasional deer was saved to memory. From time to time he also wondered whether he was mad, identifiably insane. How could that be defined? Bevan doubted his thoughts were normal, and he frequently found them scary, but how could he tell whether everyone else was the same under the surface? He liked the idea of being different but often wished he could switch the weirdness off. And even though he wanted to complete the course, part of him yearned to stay aboard the train all day, despite the eccentricity of his imagination causing moments of alarm, as he peered out from the carriage.

When Martin signed off the expenses, he was surprised to see a weekly season train ticket and not a hotel bill, but his relief about the total being within budget distracted him from any calculation of exactly how long Bevan must have spent travelling, or what times he must have departed in the morning and arrived home at night. Bevan returned to the office with a plan. He knew he could apply his new skills to create an application capable of replacing the current paper-based method they used for tracking goods. He convinced Martin to allow him access to the office PC – soon there would be one on every desk – and to get permission to install the database software. Working into the evening every day for a month, before long his pilot system was ready. He had defined tables for all the equipment types, orders, engineering regions, major projects, job types and staff; he'd built all the relationships and designed the forms. He had even conceived a name: CRUSOE. All computer systems of the day demanded a catchy name based on an acronym. Many of these stretched credulity but Bevan was chuffed with CRUSOE.

'It means the Computerised Record of Utilisation of Stores and Office Equipment.'

'Christ. That really trips off the tongue… I *don't* think. The U is fucking stupid Bevsie. Utilisation Of?' One of the itinerant engineers, who knew Bevan from his previous incarnation, had been passing and listened to the announcement with wide-eyed incredulity.

'At least the name is actually relevant to what the system does,' replied Bevan. 'Most of the other names miss a letter completely.'

'Maybe you could try making it *Unused* Stores. That's what they are after all. By definition, at the end of the day all that stuff in the warehouse is not being used.' Martin was trying to be supportive.

'A database of unused things? That could possibly the most pointless computer system in history, Martin.' Bevan was in his element. 'You're all morons. *Utilisation* is perfect … it suggests degrees of used-ness, it sounds more dynamic. We're sticking with it.'

Bevan was possibly the happiest he had ever been in his professional life, but acknowledged to himself that the acronym was a bit contrived, but only a bit, and there was obvious scope for adorning the front screen with suitable images like desert islands and parrots. CRUSOE was born and Bevan had something to care for.

Chapter 4

Back in the beginning, everyone with any experience to bear on the matter advised Jez to keep on the move. It was not safe to stay in the same place forever and besides it helped relieve the boredom to adopt multiple locations. He planned his days meticulously. His favourite spot was strategically positioned alongside a cut-through, linking one of the town centre's open-air car parks to its best remaining example of medieval thoroughfare, which was lined by an assortment of half-timbered independent shops and restaurants, made over with varying degrees of sensitivity. A neatly-shaped rectangular recess in the side of a modern extension at the rear of one of the stores formed a convenient alcove in which to sit, surrounded by the few desultory possessions he clung onto, with reasonable skywards cover being provided by the building's overhang. There was protection from the elements on all sides bar one, so only when rain was blown in on a northerly wind did conditions become completely untenable. The base of the cavity was concrete but remained dry for a greater proportion of time than did most of the pavements, and with blankets and cardboard it was possible to get comfortable if you really put your mind to it. Which Jez had been able to do – he called it his 'pigeonhole.'

The pigeonhole was not so deep as to appear dark and cavernous. It was accommodating enough for Jez to sit, parallel with the opening, while still being visible to anyone taking the cut-through, unless they averted their eyes, which many preferred to do. Indeed, by placing himself side-on, people walking from their parked cars would see his intent face and the cover of the book he was reading as they passed. He was glad to have found such a serviceable shelter. It required no improvisation to bolster the structure and, by catching the morning sun, it had the benefit of whatever warmth was going first thing. The smell was simply concrete and dust, although the efflux from the extractor fan at the rear of the next-door café added layers of fried bacon at times, despite the emphasis on artisan coffee and vegan snacks in the chalk messages that stood on the pavement at the front. His spot was not quite as good as a shop doorway, but was not disgusting. Unlike the environs of the bus station or the back of the main covered shopping centre where most the town's rough sleepers congregated, it was not routinely fouled. This was not a path typically used by pub or club-goers, it was some way distant from the epicentre of popular entertainment venues, so although it lost something in footfall it was spared the worst extremes of nightly mayhem.

At night Jez would usually have to seek something more substantial. There *were* overnight accommodation options available that afforded more protection – spaces that had actual walls and floors, that counted as being *inside* – and he sought them out. But you could not use them all day. When he settled in his pigeonhole again in the mornings after a stint under proper cover it was usually undisturbed. It was *his* discovery and generally speaking, the other street dwellers would respect the turf of primary claimants. The location was more suited to his style anyway. He was not the type for the busier areas where the cheeky-chappie approach to gaining sympathy held more sway; he was not a youngster; he was not ex-Army and he didn't have a dog. He could not compete in a more mainstream environment. He seemed to strike more of a chord with the conservative souls who gravitated towards his part of town, on the hunt for sourdough loaves, hand-made birthday cards and cheeses of the week. They would notice the book and become trapped in their internal dialogues about whether it was right or wrong to give. He kept an old ice cream carton in sight, with a few coins apparent, so everyone could see the nature of the hoped-for interaction. He never asked, but lost count of the number of times he recognised the same individual pass by without blinking on a few occasions then succumb to the urge to drop some money in at a later date. Jez was never judgemental either way but could not help thinking his regulars had allowed themselves a glass or two of vino for lunch on the days they coughed up. He kept most of the cash hidden to create the impression he had barely enough for a hot drink. His real target was the nightly fee at one of the B&Bs that tolerated homeless customers as long as they could put down a deposit. A couple of B&Bs would accept all sorts for a relatively minimal rate, but the nature of the bargain was plain. They provided token warmth and a roof over the head, but the squalid facilities were hard to stomach, the atmosphere was decidedly unsavoury and, in many ways, his concrete perch was preferable.

Jez had other places to hang around but the pigeonhole acted as his base camp. Sometimes he was stationed just to read, to pass the time, without any expectation of generating income. He would use donated candles early and late if the daylight was too gloomy to see. At other times he would simply rest the book on his knees and look into the middle distance, too tired to follow the text, waiting to hear the clink of coins. Sometimes he offered his: 'Thank you,' as the sound of footsteps peaked in proximity, but he only did so in moderation. He tried not to be annoying. When the weather was fine and dry, he would head for the park to spend a period of respite on soft ground under a tree. The sun was always welcome as a way of keeping warm, but was also one of the major perils. It was difficult to express a desire for sun cream rather than money. Street beggars wearing wide-brimmed hats and sunglasses were not a common sight. And the sun deepened the shadows, adding a further measure of concealment to an already unseeable morass.

*

For essentials like toilets and washing, when the shelters were not an option Jez migrated out towards the edges of his territory. Not the furthest outer rim of urbanisation with its industrial-scale shopping complexes – these were effectively unreachable on foot – but the collection of more modestly proportioned retail parks now bulging from the inner ring-road that choked the town centre like a noose. A couple of these had acquired the label Retail Village, which struck Jez as laughable as they were almost as forbidding to pedestrian traffic as the out-of-town behemoths were and had an air of sterility that not even the most dismal rural outpost could attain. But this anonymity was the attraction. It was possible to access the public facilities of the drive-through fast food joints without challenge or recognition, unlike the smaller places in town – the pubs, cafés and betting shops – that jealously guarded their washrooms for paying customers only. Public conveniences were but a distant memory. Let multinational burger brands pay for the nation's sanitation, *not an inappropriate state of affairs*, he thought. Jez soon learned to time his circumnavigation of the town's core to coincide with these establishments at his moments of greatest need. It was best to arrive when they were quiet but not empty. To be the only customer on site risked attracting attention. He frequently traipsed the ring road full-circle, as new outlets were popping up all the time and it was good to keep abreast of the available facilities. He smiled grimly to himself at the thought of town planners being blissfully unaware of the impact their best efforts had on his daily routine.

The pigeonhole was in one of the prettier parts of town, but the area was not the main visitor attraction in the vicinity. Although the surrounding streets had their share of ancient buildings, the borough council was most proud of its development around the old docks. Every town in the country seems to contort itself to furnish some kind of watery heritage these days, whether by surrounding a canal basin with gastropubs and boutiques, or by integrating its river defence scheme within a pedestrianised heart.

A nation of Little Venices, overlooked by honeycomb banks of studio apartments with their tiny balconies and cacti … and the exterior seating areas of global chain eateries that get heated in winter. They heat the outdoors now; Jez fancied a piece of that. Where the British had spent the last quarter of the 20th century invading the Mediterranean, the early part of the 21st seemed to revolve around recreating the same effect on home soil. This town's waterside was pleasant enough and popular with the local inhabitants for taking time out from the day. Jez and his fellow dispossessed liked it too. There were plenty of arches and covered walkways, formed by restored warehouses reaching out to the quay, in which to seek sanctuary, especially when the rain poured. However, the allure of the maritime quarter had its drawbacks. There was competition for the best pitches and Jez never felt able to fully relax for fear of being usurped. The dockside development corporation employed security guards to harass the itinerants to move along as well, so it wasn't possible to guarantee a period long enough to rest, let alone raise any capital. He never lingered here at night, mindful of the irony that localities favoured by the gentlest and most kind-hearted members of the community by day became infested by the most wicked and dangerous after midnight. The tranquil ambience of swans being fed, and teas being sipped when the sun was shining, transformed into a treacherous void in the small hours, where lone, vulnerable wanderers foolishly tread. Jez listened to the stories of unexplained disappearances and built a finely-tuned risk factor into his mental map of the world.

*

Jez laughed bitterly to himself to see the al fresco bistros and microbreweries, that had sprung up everywhere, offering patio heaters and hampers full of tartan blankets to patrons. There was something obscene about catering for people's comfort outside when they could easily choose to sit inside in the warm. Oh, to have that option. They were paying for the right to breathe cold air – conspicuous consumption of a different kind. Jez could give them the guided tour, the curated experience, if they really wanted to know what it was like.

When his regulars chose to buy him a coffee instead of handing him money, Jez understood the sentiment and sometimes it was nice to be waited on but he had to stop himself from saying *I could have got that myself you know* on occasion. He never wanted the sugar, they always insisted on loading them with sugar. And he was decidedly unimpressed with the modern trends of coffee culture as well – the steamed milk, the foam. What's wrong with a kettle? He could make himself a coffee in 30 seconds using a kettle. Now they stand for hours while monstrous machines whirr away and after all that waiting and bashing, it's still not done. You still must apply the finishing touches yourself. People are mad. At times Jez would rationalise his predicament as a statement of protest against the follies of modern life. He was glad to reside on the opposite side of that virtual barrier separating the vagrants from the rest of society, such that he could deny any responsibility for all the nonsense. He was disassociated from the iniquities, such as the grotesque waste of resources inherent to trade in lattes, mochaccinos and other mutant forms – not to mention all takeaway food in general. The morning citizens rushing to work would queue for their scalding hot milkshakes in non-recyclable cups, then parade them through the streets like Olympic torches. Why not simply wait until they get to work? Jez was sure they all must have kettles in the office. The waste bins overflowed with discarded packaging from 'breakfast on the move', detritus from the race to avoid being late. The rat race. Jez could tell them a thing or two about rats as well.

Generally, the morning rush hour of office and shop workers was not a lucrative time. They were pumped-up on self-importance and sped by, ignoring him completely, attention fixed on opening the shop doors on time or getting the first emails out. Jez tended to adopt his position from mid-morning when the pace had slowed, and the flow of mankind contained a greater proportion of individuals out to soak up the surroundings and people-watch. He soon learned not to classify based on simple stereotypes. There was no great correlation between the people that gave him money and a particular demographic. Young or old, male or female, smart or scruffy; there was no obvious pattern, it was more a question of what they were doing and what kind of mood they were in. Encounters with the public did not always follow a standard formula – on more than one occasion he had been asked for change for the car park. He was surprised to find himself providing a civic service at such moments but was happy to oblige as the exchange usually led to a profit. In one memorable meeting a panic-stricken and breathless man appeared at his threshold, smartly-dressed and well-spoken, but clearly having a bad day.

'Terribly sorry to bother you, old chap … I'd love to give you something but, you see … I need a cash machine urgently … do you know where the nearest one is?'

Jez was good at directions and he knew exactly the turns this well-mannered, panting stranger needed to take to find his own hole in the wall. He relished the incongruity of a person in his own present state, as he sat on the bare ground, being asked for guidance by someone who looked and sounded like a banker and probably owned a mansion, on how to acquire money. The pin-stripe suited fellow scampered off with a: 'Thanks a million my man,' and disappeared through the gap. The favour went unrewarded this time, he must have taken an alternative route back to his overheating car, unpaid bill, incandescent girlfriend or whatever else was the cause of his feverish state. Jez had certainly never expected to assume a role as local tour guide – for most of the of time his presence was merely ignored. As it happened, he consciously steered clear of ATMs, being determined not to make people feel nervous – he sensed the agitation of cash machine users if he ever came near them, wary glances being flicked over shoulders. He genuinely felt guilty about what his life had become, he understood that most right-thinking people would feel uncomfortable within close quarters and he sought to minimise the intrusion as much as he could. But this was the only way he could find to live.

Brushes with the likes of the floundering banker were generally welcome. The boredom of the homeless condition was crushing and Jez appreciated any moments of variety. He was content for people to step through the barrier and acknowledge his existence, if they did not seek to deliver his salvation or look him in the eye. For most he was a thing not to be acknowledged – they chose not to see. He observed that the only other group similarly blanked out were the council street cleaners – the day-glo jackets that highlighted them as hazards in the vision of motorists contrarily also succeeded in erasing their identity in the crowd. Draped in hi-vis they occupy a separate plane, using their special powers of access to fulfil their duties, but somehow subordinate to the rest of humanity; like movable bollards, standing out, but barely observed. Nevertheless, however much they went unnoticed, presumably at least they all had homes to go to. Jez coveted their occupation, to be in the open air, enacting an elemental function requiring minimal mental stress, but which everyone valued. He could still be hidden in plain sight, but as the sweeper rather than the swept. It would have been perfect but even this aspiration was beyond his reach now.

Chapter 5

By the year 2000 CRUSOE had become an established part of the Allied Grids IT estate. It had been officially added to the register of all applications kept by the central IT management team – their system of systems, their database of databases. Bevan's name was listed as the main contact, his only disappointment being that CRUSOE's status was flagged as 'found' rather than 'strategic'. There were hundreds of systems: some had been developed under the guidance of the IT department as part of an overall plan, whereas some, like CRUSOE, had been developed more locally and the central team had to seek them out, to bring them into the fold. He had received some advanced training and acquired the skills to add a data feed from another larger corporate system, for downloading financial information relating to the stores items. CRUSOE was now able to calculate the total value of assets held in the warehouse and also generate data reports which apparently got used by the bean counters in HQ. One of the main reasons for cataloguing everything was to understand all the interconnections. It was important to know which computers spoke to which other computers, in order to understand the root cause when things went wrong. When Bevan built that simple extra interface, CRUSOE became flagged as 'business critical' and he was drawn more closely into a new mysterious world.

Having become embedded within the complex mesh of IT applications used across the organisation, CRUSOE was now included in the enterprise-wide system release cycle. Like the butterfly effect, because of all the interconnections, in theory a change made to the function of one computer system might ripple across the network and have unforeseen effects on one of the others. So, when any software changes were introduced, all impacted systems had to be shut down as one, brought back to life again after the changes had been applied, then tested before deciding whether the release could stand or had to be rolled back. This was extremely laborious and needed careful planning but was vitally important to avoid a major crash. The clock ticking over from 1999 to 2000 was the highest profile moment for system testing that anyone could remember. Bevan was smug – he had ensured his date fields would not overflow. While the rest of the country enjoyed a supercharged instance of New Year's Eve gilded by the fruits of New Labour, Bevan enjoyed participating in the surreal countdown that transfixed IT departments around the globe. For two years previously, projects were run to pore over the code, line by line, variable by variable, of every Allied Grids system, looking for traces of two-digit date fields. Urban myths abounded of nuclear power stations exploding in simulation when calculations were suddenly exposed to an unexpected zero. Experts in programming languages that half the current developers had never heard of were exhumed and brought back to life, to check the most venerable systems. It was rumoured that in fact no changes had been necessary in the end at all. But the frisson across the IT teams that night was as memorable as any end of millennium knees-up. The upshot was: as midnight struck, nothing failed at all … and the general populace concluded that the millennium bug was a hoax, an unwanted sideshow of self-importance from a computing industry that sees itself as Hollywood. But Bevan loved it – especially the sense of history.

System upgrades were inevitable and frequent due to the constant need for new functionality to support an evolving business, along with the sharp practice of commercial software suppliers incrementing their versions for no benefit whatsoever apart from their own profits. (Bevan hated software companies with a passion, likening them to Colombian drug cartels, creating a dependency then feeding parasitically off their customers forever after. 'Version 6.1 is not backwards compatible … blah, blah, blah,' they would whine. *Well make it fucking compatible then you bastards*, he would think. Somehow they were allowed to get away with it.)

Being relatively self-contained, the chance of CRUSOE ever actually being compromised by one of the major releases was minimal, but it still had to be tested, it was on the list. This required Bevan to be on standby overnight on each of these upgrade dates, which were usually planned during unsocial hours at weekends to minimise the impact on daily operations. He had to provide sign-off that his system was still working correctly once all the changes had been deployed across the estate. Releases were his favourite part of the job – the term 'unsocial hours' meant nothing to him. He felt essential – a crucial cog – and the dates were highlighted on his wallchart in bright colours.

*

Some of the vibrancy in the office had begun to fade though. Work in the depot itself was never high on drama but the dark and boisterous humour of the storespeople had always fizzed, stirred up by the rotating cast of visiting field engineers that regularly called by, like emissaries from the front. Grisly anecdotes would abound of management incompetence causing horrific waste, adulterous behaviour with customers, unfortunate incidents with pets being electrocuted and so forth. However, by the new millennium, numbers were starting to fall, and the atmosphere was evaporating away. Staff briefings issued from Allied Grids HQ spoke obliquely of *maximising the potential* of the organisation. In reality this meant reducing staff numbers. Incentives were offered encouraging early retirement and a few from the depot had already taken the shilling. There was always a high attrition rate in the engineering teams due to the harsh nature of the work and not everyone was replaced. New recruits were only placed on short-term contracts and had less time to linger back at base. Targets were set to *develop* the remaining staff, i.e. do the same amount of work with fewer people.

Superficially, the gradual loss of community spirit within the workplace suited Bevan just fine. He never really felt at ease with the jocularity, the constant teasing, the doughnuts on birthdays. He often wished they could keep the noise down while he tried to concentrate. But as numbers began to drop and with the first signs of working from home creeping in, sometimes the periods of quiet and isolation were long enough to leave Bevan exposed to the wrong kinds of thoughts. The voices that questioned his right to exist were never far away.

*

CRUSOE was used by about twenty people in the depot. Bevan's time was split between overseeing the stores ordering process and providing support to his small group of system users. It had not been adopted nationally, the other regions had their own tools or were starting to adopt technology rolled out by central IT. Martin was able to dismiss any suggestion of his region following the same path on the basis that the team were hitting their targets and the alternatives developed in HQ were proving unpopular elsewhere. CRUSOE had been sufficiently good in its day, even pioneering to a degree, that it had established a reputation for being indispensable, well before the IT department started to frown upon local teams developing their own software; the 'hobbyists' as they were dismissively referred to. And with Bevan's attention to detail and his dedication to keep the thing running, it had a very low defect rate, keeping it close to the top of the reliability ratings and earning the grudging respect of the helpdesk.

Meanwhile, the endless chorus of internal corporate communications provided an additional unwanted backdrop of double-speak to their daily lives. Not only was Bevan bombarded with spin from central IT about the need for compliance with all standard procedures, the board of directors maintained a barrage of motherhood statements that drained the spirit of everyone. Weekly briefings tried in vain to project an image of Allied Grids as a compassionate employer, with a committed workforce rallying to the mantras of efficiency and customer service. Martin often likened it to North Korea. You had to be on message. He was surprised it was not mandatory to have a poster of the chief executive on every wall. The emphasis of management initiatives was shifting more towards the middle ranks: the likes of Martin, the sergeant majors. As if they had given up with the pond life at the bottom of the food chain – the ones actually doing the work – and were now fixated on the *behaviours* of their immediate leadership level.

'Bevsie … I reckon I must be part of the most hated demographic in the country. Middle management, pen-pushing, tarred by the brush of ex-public sector being inherently useless. I may as well draw a target on my back and let *Daily Mail* readers run after me with guns. They probably hate tramps less than they hate me. You're all right … you can be as shit as you want, no one's watching you … well, no one's watching you except me, and I don't count.' Martin was starting to lose it in the face of the onslaught of bureaucracy and Bevan made a good sounding board.

Despite the Butlins-red-coat-style propaganda that patronisingly whooped-up examples of employees apparently living the corporate values, the sense increasingly grew that the executive board were washing their hands of the plebeian masses, believing them to be beyond salvation, stuck in their old ways and eminently replaceable by shiny young things from college. As if staying in the same place for a long time was a sign of weakness and loyalty had become a dirty word. Adding to the sense of insecurity, Allied Grids' pension exposure loomed as a threat of apparently cataclysmic proportions, like a dormant volcano in a boy's own story. Articles on the intranet made frequent reference to 'the age profile of the organisation', reading like a threat of disease, the only solution to which was eradication of the organisms responsible. To make the impression of the company as a totalitarian state even stronger, Martin and his own seniors seemed to be repeatedly disappearing on team building away-days as if toughening them up for some kind of military action, or an appearance on *It's A Knockout*.

'It's the poxy role-playing I can't stand,' Martin complained one day. 'Personally I wouldn't trust anyone who is even capable of giving so-called 'negative constructive feedback' in a role playing exercise to someone he actually plays golf with in real life; someone who also happens to be a school governor, but is now pretending to be a poor performing fork-lift driver with a stupid accent. It's just a contest of artificiality. It's just a steaming pile of business school bollocks, Bevsie. I wish I didn't have to go.'

'Sounds hideous.' Bevan was extremely grateful he did not have to go himself, he suspected he might spontaneously combust. 'So, they succeed on the basis of how good they are at being fake? No wonder all senior managers are wankers.'

*

The company mission statement was always a source of hilarity. Bevan wondered how the company could afford to employ marketing consultants at all, when there was no longer enough money to buy decent biros. Approximately every five years a new broom at the top would sweep clean, introduce a new brand identity and proclaim the organisation was fully prepared to tackle the challenges of the marketplace, armed with a new set of inspiring words. The latest incarnation was:

Enabling the UK to shine, Enabling the planet to heal.

'Oh, for fuck's sake, what are they on.' Bevan was unable to refrain from laughing out loud at this one. 'In exactly what way are we *enabling the planet to heal?*'

'Get with the programme Bevsie. It plays to the carbon footprint and corporate social responsibility agenda, don't you know,' offered Martin, doing his best to feign commitment to the party line.

'For fuck's sake … it's utter bloody nonsense. We managed about 0.2% reduction in carbon emissions last year. I don't see the ice caps reforming. I don't see fucking polar bear parties breaking out. If we have to have these sodding statements couldn't they at least be real. I swear I'm going to get my car resprayed with a message on the side just saying: 'driving around', in lower case italics.'

Bevan drew out the extent of this imagined strap line with his open hands in the air.

Martin liked it when Bevan went on one of his rants. He knew he was not the target himself and it was good to see him animated, with a glint in his eye, knowing that it would soon pass and the glint would return to his normal deadpan glaze. Bevan was a strange one. He gave every indication of hating Allied Grids and yet at the same time it seemed to be the only thing he cared about. He wished they had more opportunities to talk but Bevan always had an excuse and never opened up about anything apart from the immediate issues confronting them in the depot.

Bevan could feel the ground was beginning to shift under his feet. The new breed of manager and the stream of idiotic company gobbledegook from the internal thought police made him feel like heavy artillery was lining up over the horizon, with the likes of him in its firing arc.

*

Bevan had lived in a coastal town twenty miles north-east of the depot since 1980. Both locales had their own distinct catchment area, so he was safe in the knowledge that he was unlikely to bump into any of his workmates when he went out shopping. He lived in a rented flat with views across the town centre, not the sea. This was not his first address in the town but was the one with fewest painful memories. He drove to work, the easy curves of the dual carriageway acting as a meditation, organising his thoughts on the way in, winding them down on the way home. This was his favourite time for noticing the changing seasons and chalking them off. He was usually the first to arrive. Originally this was advantageous as there were not enough parking spaces when the depot was full, but latterly there were empty slots at all times of day. As well as changing the company logo with unerring frequency, Allied Grids also indulged in habitual 'redistricting': the realignment of operational area boundaries, along with the resulting office closures as the areas got larger and fewer, to deliver 'efficiencies'. In theory there was a constant threat of the depot being closed or moved, but its strategic location made it ideal to service the cabling needs that would follow the anticipated growth in offshore wind power, so this threat was less than it might have been.

During the working day Bevan spent as much time as possible sat in his swivel chair. There had once been a canteen at the depot but it was now closed, replaced by a mobile van service that arrived around 11:30. Bevan had once been a customer of the van but now preferred to bring his own snacks, making sandwiches provided a task to kill time in the evenings. He ate at his desk, his body clock still religiously demanded food at 11:30 – he was unable to wait any longer, until a more normal lunch hour, when everyone else would disappear to their chosen diversions. His colleagues berated him for not having a proper break … and for making them hungry with the sounds of eating and the rustling of crisp packets.

'It's no wonder he's always nodding off in the afternoons', was the consensus of the team when he was out of the room.

Bevan suspected other reasons, although he generally slept well at night. Having learned to switch off his emotions an unplanned benefit was a lack of sleepless nights. He existed through the evenings listening to the radio, mostly sport, and tinkering with his various databases. The internet annoyed him. Suddenly everyone was a computer expert. His hobby had been overtaken by a cultural revolution and all the things he hated about society as a whole were now infiltrating his pet subject: commercialism, fads, false messiahs, the promotion of technology as an end in itself rather than a tool for a job. Bevan was no gadget boy. It was a toss-up between the internet and mobile phones as the thing he most wanted to dis-invent. Computing needed structure and planning – the anarchic expansion of the web, driven by consumer behaviour rather than careful design, was anathema to him and he tried to ignore it all. Why did the world keep insisting on spoiling the few things he held dear? At least they still needed him for CRUSOE.

Bevan had thought about the possibility of taking early redundancy when the opportunity was first mooted – for about a millisecond. Martin had gathered the team together to convey the news of its introduction and talk through the cascaded guidance notes on how to manage people's concerns.

'Folks, there's something we need to talk about.'

'Hallo … You look twitchy Martin. What's this … the scene in *The Great Escape* where the prisoners are told to get out of the vehicles to stretch their legs?'

The thought of leaving was petrifying. Some said take the money and get another job. But Bevan could not countenance finding another niche, another safe haven. He was banking everything on Allied Grids being the vessel to steer him safely through life. The thought of losing his job was another one to compartmentalise, to deny the possibility of. For all its foibles and frustrations, he recognised there could be many more stressful places to work. He still had the fascination for electrical engineering and although the management bullshit and the targets were driving him mad, he did get some satisfaction from witnessing the power industry evolve, as new types of equipment passed through the depot. Nevertheless, he remained empty inside. In his jousts with Martin it felt like someone else was speaking his words. In the evenings in his flat Bevan was essentially marking time, ticking over in neutral, waiting until his time to sleep, or full-time in the football matches. Relatively speaking, he looked forward to the mornings and the chance to get back on the treadmill. He was grateful to have Martin as his manager, acting as a buffer against the company's worst excesses. Bevan shuddered to think about the prospect of one of the boys – or girls – in suits taking over the stores manager role. He prayed his own heathen prayers that Martin would always be there. And that the heavy artillery would fail to detect them both.

Chapter 6

When passers-by stopped to talk, Jez usually welcomed the interruption, as long as they did so without penetrating him with sympathetic, quizzical looks or questions about his life story. His preferred types of interaction boiled down to three possible alternatives: they walk swiftly past without making eye contact; they hand him some money; or, periodically, they stop for a proper conversation, to pass the time, ideally about tangible matters like the books in his pile, his plans for the day or the weather. In the latter scenario, if they also offered money … all well and good. Meeting random characters and making small talk sometimes brought relief to his gruelling and demeaning lifestyle, provided the discourse stayed within boundaries. Fortunately, it only happened a few times per week – any more often and he would get bored hearing himself say the same things. He could always deter them anyway, with the look in his eyes, if he was not in the mood. A few of his regulars could be relied upon to say the right things and he spared them the cold, vacant stares. They afforded him a level of respect – of which he felt unworthy but soaked up nonetheless – clearly under the impression he must have suffered greatly on his downward spiral. Any enquiries along those lines drew a blank though, Jez successfully changed the subject whenever it strayed towards his past – as far as anyone knew, he might just as well have been born on the street. He got to know the names of one or two – they could not exactly join him in the pigeonhole but could crouch or sit next to the opening and he would swing himself round by ninety degrees to be sociable. The path narrowed towards the street but was wide enough here that two crouching bodies would cause no obstruction.

His highlight in any week was Izzy. Izzy was a spritely fifty-something with cascading scarlet hair and hazel eyes that flashed like emeralds if she materialised during a spell of morning sunshine. She owned a gallery around the corner and, whenever Jez was installed in his alcove as she strode by, an effervescent 'All right my darling?' would be beamed in his direction, lifting his spirits even on the occasions her greeting startled him out of semi-slumber. Izzy did not interfere with his private thoughts and demonstrated her compassion by only giving him money every so often. Usually it was food or coffee. She could see the pain engraved in his soul and wanted to encourage him into a different life but would try doing so only subtly. She pointed out his intelligence and sense of humour but did not berate him for throwing it all away. She teased him about his appearance – 'there's a handsome man in there somewhere, you should get your teeth fixed darling!' – and they swapped their grievances about the council, the police, young people or whatever other party had been most vexing that week. Izzy wished Jez was not there … she did not want to see anyone sleeping rough in the vicinity of her business but was generous enough of spirit to keep her misgivings to herself and dispensed goodwill, realising that precious little was going his way from any other quarter. Jez cherished the moments when their paths crossed. He would catch a glimpse of her preternaturally verdant eyes when she blinked upwards to the light and feel ripples of forgotten primordial emotion, aftershocks from what this splendid woman once had been … and was still. Through sitting next to Izzy, he had finally come to recognise feminine beauty as an essential life force, irrespective of prevailing politically-correct views against objectification. Her warmth always boosted the remnants of his morale and her laughter always rendered a fleshly glow somewhere inside his ribcage … but he would not dig deep into the feelings that stirred in her company ... whatever they might be, they were not to be exhumed. He was just grateful to be in her presence and gossip from time to time.

*

Colin worked for The Caravan Trust, a local charity that tried its best to offer a permanent shelter for the town's homeless during the day. The Caravan occupied a former school building, an unusually subdued Victorian red-brick with the customary separate entrances for boys and girls. The building was ideal, having the advantage of being sufficiently unremarkable to avoid listed status ... and its roof was intact. They were on a continual stay of execution, the tenure being an informal arrangement with the holder of development rights to the site while planning disputes were being dragged through various appeals. A bending of the rules being the closest thing to the kind of philanthropy that led to the school being built in the first place, in 1888, that anyone was likely to see in the modern era. There was no prospect of any kind of restoration, but it provided a place to go for respite, hot drinks and companionship. Volunteers took turns dispensing teas and soup, funded by a second-hand shop situated a few streets away from the alley where Jez spent most of his time. The Caravan was Colin's brainchild, a retired teacher himself, he despaired that people were still living on the streets when supposedly the digital age had brought opportunities for all. In the peak of his evangelical zeal he had tried to reach out to every rough sleeper he could find and convince them to take the first steps towards rebuilding their lives, but now he was tired, worn down by lack of money and the spread of drug addiction and professional begging. Now he was more selective. He tried to spot the ones who appeared salvageable. Those in the early stages of street life; those still holding a trace of incredulity about the way their life had turned out, yet to become inured to the indignity and suffering.

Jez thought Colin looked disturbingly like a scout master and initially blanked him out. However, the former teacher's persistence and knowledge broke through the ice and he was allowed into the exclusive circle. Colin's rounds were decreasing in frequency as his heart for the battle faded, but he still popped up in the cut-through on a fairly regular basis, checking to see if new blankets were needed. Jez kept a backpack for his residue of permanent belongings, which he rarely took off. The home comforts: blankets, sleeping bags and flattened cardboard boxes were acquired and maintained on the fly, from a range of sources. Like feeding stations by the roadside during a marathon, multiple sites – charities like The Caravan and various recycling centres – were on hand to provide the protective wrappings as needed, as long as you knew where to go. Colin called them the 'soft furnishings department'. Despite the dog-eat-dog nature of his environment, when Jez went roaming, the soft furnishings in his nook usually remained untouched if he left them behind for a few hours. The damp, grubby chattels of the vagrant drifters were so pitiable they tended to be off-radar for even the most light-fingered thieves. The biggest threat was kids pissing on them, but Jez's most common haunts were not typically descended upon by the delinquent youth of the town.

A recent phenomenon that left everyone in the sector open-mouthed with dismay – both those channelling and those on the receiving end of donated items – was the sudden glut of sleeping bags, portable mattresses and tents being left behind by festival goers up and down the land. The large open-air weekender events all now employed teams of volunteers to gather up the hoard of discarded camping equipment once the masses had gone, too wasted to bother packing it up, let alone remove the mud upon arrival home for re-use on the next pilgrimage. As though some of the audience had been so transported by the music, dope and mystic vibe – so taken by the 'rites of passage' festival myth – they felt reborn and were moved to shed their skins as in metamorphosis. This latest manifestation of throwaway culture also explained the appearance in the retail parks of huge warehouses full of outdoor-living gear that Jez had noticed in his circumnavigations, amid the more traditional denizens like DIY and sportswear. He wondered where they had come from ... he found it hard to believe the world of patio heaters had also suddenly spawned a profusion of mountaineers and other adventurers in such numbers, amongst the middle class.

Colin had quickly worked out that Jez was not interested in being shown any paths to salvation, but still stopped by to talk. He was used to squatting down in dusty corners and could easily come down to Jez's level by the pigeonhole.

'You don't need to live like this, Jez mate. I know you think you've got no other option ... all I ask is ... don't close the door. Don't accept this as being OK ... *OK*?'

Jez was happy with the blankets Colin had brought so was willing to forgive the preaching. Colin sometimes pushed his luck though.

'This is not an acceptable situation Jez. Eventually it just becomes a state of mind. You deliberately block out all the institutions for whatever reason ... but become *institutionalised* anyway ... by the vacuum you're living in.'

Jez paused before responding. He was mildly irritated now and did not completely understand what Colin was talking about ... he changed the tack of the conversation, as Colin knew he would.

'Why is it called 'The Caravan' Colin?'

'Oh God ... that name, I wish we'd thought of something else. When we started it was all about trying to create a sense of movement ... the caravan as a growing body of men ... er, and women ... er, a growing body of *people* on a journey to a better future, like on a caravan trail.' Colin looked wistful and his voice tailed off slightly.

'A bit like the Pied Piper then?'

'Er ... yes I suppose so, a bit ... but um ...'

'You certainly brought the rats out from wherever they hide. There's millions of them around here now.' Jez cackled at his own joke and forgave himself for cutting Colin off.

He went on ...

'Seriously though Col, it's great what you do, especially for the young ones. Some of them have never felt cared for before in their lives.'

'Thanks Jez, you old bugger. Don't get any ideas I care about you though.' Colin looked at the floor and wished for a moment he had not given up smoking. He knew they did not raise enough funds to help anyone on a journey, let alone one to a better life. Now he thought it may as well be called the Caravan Café, founded in a rusting mobile home with its wheels removed and axles resting on breeze blocks.

Jez was usually jovial with Colin, recognising the toll his efforts to do good had taken. The conversations were like sparring contests, with Colin the ageing boxer, still firing his exhortations against Jez's unmovable mitts, seeking to keep them ready for targets more likely to be swayed. Colin found the calm, philosophical way Jez viewed his life to be almost zen-like. Colin also found him strangely compelling, as if he was learning as much about the emptiness of materialism from Jez as he was spreading the gospel about routes out of poverty and disengagement. Jez started to realise he was almost providing a service of his own – the people who stopped to talk sometimes appeared to take something away from the interaction. Counselling from the perspective of: this is the lowest you can get … this is what can happen if you make the wrong decisions … so think on. He wondered if some of the lost souls that loitered in the neighbourhood were seeking him out like a guru, waiting to find enough courage to approach him. It looked like it sometimes.

'Looking out for you to suck them off more likely …'

This was Ginge. Ginge was a fellow tramp. The word 'tramp' has become taboo but Ginge liked it, he liked the vamp-ish connotations. Of the few people Jez passed the time of day with, Ginge was the most constant. It was unclear whether he had ever been known as 'Ginger' or gone straight to the nickname 'Ginge' in one fell swoop. The label was obvious and perfect, Ginge had the craggy, elfin look of a Scottish vagabond although the redness of his unkempt beard was now muddied to burnt umber smeared with grey. Ginge was a heroin addict with a wraith-like demeanour, flickering to and fro through Jez's orbit, appearing as if from nowhere in whichever part of town was the latest chosen stopping point. If he had Scottish roots at all, they were not present in his rasping Cockney accent, although for some reason Jez could not break the association from his first impression. Discussions with Ginge were often frightening, he could be incomprehensible, but even though he regularly binged on alcohol he was surprisingly never violent, and Jez found it hard to shake him off. Ginge spoke obliquely about having once been to art school and was relentlessly optimistic about the future, listing to Jez the places in the world he wanted to visit and the people he wanted to meet. Ginge had discovered Jez to be a touch more cultured than anyone else he had met on the street – 'not like the rest of us tramps' – and was drawn to him whenever the urge came to ventilate his dreams.

Jez enjoyed the surreal nature of exchanges with Ginge, especially when tipsy. Ginge never lit up in Jez's company but he sometimes brought a bottle. He kept several, stashed away in different hiding places no one else could ever find, dotted around the town like chestnuts buried by a squirrel. In England, there are not many periods, even in high summer, where it is genuinely comfortable to sit outside all night. This was Ginge's favourite pastime though and he would implore Jez to join him on his trips to the park, to look up at the stars. When they did end up sharing each other's company at night the conversation could take bizarre turns.

'That geezer was spooking at you again today, Jez.' Ginge had seen one guy appearing to watch them earlier.

'*Really*? Christ ... it keeps on happening ... for some unearthly reason ... I guess it's because they see me chatting with Colin ... that and the 'alternative lifestyle'... maybe they think I'm some kind of spiritual leader and they are looking to join my cult.' They both laughed.

It was at this point that Ginge made his crude insinuation about potential punters seeking carnal relief. Such propositions were not unheard of, but that was one wealth-generation scheme Jez was not interested in exploring.

'I'll just give them your card Ginge.'

'Yeah, too right. I'll make their earth move. Ruin them for the rest of the cunts.'

They giggled, then fell quiet, hypnotised by the heavens.

'It's so clear tonight. You must get some amazing skies up in Scotland. With all that darkness and heather.'

'Jez mate, why do you always go on about Scotland? I was born Bethnal Green wann'I? And what's poxy heather got to do with anything?'

'Good point. I keep forgetting. Umm … I don't know … I guess it blocks out the light from the valleys.'

'You're a fucking loony, Jezmond old son.'

Jez had never really looked at the constellations before. Not all of them laid out like this. Even when muted by the ever-present background of the town's street lights it was possibly the most beautiful thing he had ever seen. Available for free, with no terms and conditions, no small print. For once it was him suggesting somewhere for a wishlist of destinations.

'We should go there.'

'Where?'

'Scotland.'

'For fuck's sake Jez. I'm more English than you are man.'

'I mean for the darkness. To see the Milky Way.'

Ginge was lost now, not quite believing the Milky Way was actually a thing but was glad to hear his companion getting a bit trippy for a change and agreed to add it to his list. Jez was intoxicated by the vista above. The slowly drifting tableau of a billion pinpricks, perforating the blackout curtain draped across their upward gaze.

'You can see it all moving if you really look. You know that one's Orion, don't you?' Jez pointed at the belt. His pointing hand showed up in silhouette against the starlight.

'Yeah … course. Everyone knows that one.'

'And I think that's the Plough over there.'

Ginge was not really concentrating now but tried his best to see. He stared intently.

'They all look like fucking ploughs to me, man.'

Chapter 7

For as long as he could remember, Bevan had always felt like a misfit, as if he was not really meant to be here. He would swear that his earliest memory occurred one day when being conveyed by pushchair as an infant – a thought crystallising in his head along the lines of: *Oh … this again … really?* As if his first conscious thought had been the realisation that he had walked the earth before in a previous life and had been dragged out for a re-run against his wishes. If he thought deeply enough, he convinced himself it was true, but at other times he wondered if this pushchair moment was merely wishful thinking – his recollection was somewhat indistinct, perhaps it was just a dream, or a vague feeling loaded with too much meaning given the benefit of hindsight. Nevertheless, Bevan had carried a world-weariness from the beginning. He had never been entirely sure that his birth was not an accident. He arrived into an already nuclear family: Mum, Dad, Keith and Anne. The dynamics were set and his introduction made things uneven. He was by no means an unhappy child; he felt the love of both parents and his brother and sister welcomed him into their world of play. But he found too many distractions diverted him away from any real sense of solidarity with what they wanted him to do. If they played a game in the garden, he would worry about the logic of the rules. If they did anything artistic, he would want to use his own colours and characters and shapes; he would not collaborate, he had to be different. He fairly soon showed a preference for playing on his own, inventing games that no one else understood, commentating under his breath. Later he would lose himself for hours in reference books, learning facts and lists, revelling in the order of things whether by date or name or size.

Because he rarely cried and seemed content in his own company, his parents were happy to leave him to his own devices most of the time. The family lived in a new open plan estate at the edge of an average, home counties town that guidebooks of the day would mention only in passing. *Nothing to see here, move along.* (Latterly the place would be granted chocolate-coloured road signs and a heritage centre, but back then it was largely unsung.) Other children his age, theoretically candidates with whom to socialise, were abundant and networks of paths connected an array of green spaces and play areas that would be recalled as an idyll by most who were born there. It was a safe environment to grow up in, but rough boys, flashers and the occasional psychotic dog lurked in the shadows if you took the wrong turn. From time to time the young Bevan would get press-ganged into football matches against his better judgement, if Keith urged him to tag along with sufficient resolve. His skills were minimal – and he tended just to run until losing the ball rather than passing to his teammates – nevertheless, his encyclopaedic knowledge of Football League players and teams and grounds and kits gave him a degree of kudos. But he felt more comfortable in the garden. He collected insects, looked them up and tried to remember their names. He impressed his siblings with the number he could identify, but the scientific Latin names annoyed him, they were prissy and stupid. He wanted the beetles just to be beetles, there was no need to add another poncey name just to complicate things. He read about the lives of great men in wonderment, the men throughout history responsible for pushing back the boundaries of knowledge. He was fascinated by famous scientists but was baffled by their ability to live expansive and successful lives, while extending their learning to such extraordinary lengths. He could understand the desire to get lost in experimentation, tracking down the logic of nature one step at a time. But the thought of having to conjure up grand theories about the world or give lectures to audiences of fellow boffins and unbelievers was petrifying ... better to just keep it all to yourself. And as for explorers ... to set sail in ramshackle boats to unseen destinations without even knowing the shape of the world ... these characters were as mythical and unreal to him as anyone in the Bible.

As a child, Bevan was terrified by the prospect of growing into an adult. Insects were OK, they had a life cycle – orderly stages of transformation in which their changes were managed for them – they were given the tools and a script, and they knew when it would all be over. Insects had nothing to worry about. Bevan was expected to do it all himself and he failed to see how this was possible.

*

Bevan had an affinity with science but doubted he could ever become a famous scientist. If books were given to him, he would read them and he was good at understanding concepts, but he had no drive to seek knowledge beyond his immediate horizon. His parents encouraged him to join various clubs and out-of-school activities, but the idea chilled him to the core. Thinking about his future he pictured it resembling one of the cul-de-sacs of the estate rather than a confident highway stretching out to the horizon. He did not want to make friends with other kids unless it was absolutely necessary. Their ideas always exasperated him and whenever he did try to start a conversation he was usually met with blank looks or playground ridicule. Starting school was torture. Keith and Anne both went to the same establishment and were enlisted to manhandle him to the gates after the initial few trips with Mum. Bevan felt aghast, he could not believe they would really do this to him, and he tried to wriggle free ... but he was effectively dragged in and dumped. Somehow, he managed to overcome the horror. Bevan came to accept that his existence was just going to be a series of painful experiences. He knew that by crying he would be noticed by the hard lads, so he strove to keep it all inside. Eventually the discovery that he was good in some of the lessons made

this enforced time away from home, and the sanctity of his bedroom, tolerable. He was good at tests and looked forward to the
praise of teachers when they handed work back to the class, his
knowledge vindicated in flourishes of red ink.

He was not overtly a swot, was passable at P.E. and by chance
of geography his route to school did not encroach upon the town's
badlands. As a consequence, he was never excessively bullied and
was generally free from the terror inflicted on the poor wretches
that did get singled out for victimisation. The goading, the clothes
soaked in the showers, the physical humiliation. The biggest lesson
to be learned at school was life's cruelty. There was one particular
boy in his class called Kevin who, by having a Pakistani father and
a Scottish mother, was doomed from the start. At that time,
mixed-race kids were few and far between in provincial towns and
matters were compounded by this one being extremely bright and
precocious. He did not look or sound like anything the other pupils had ever seen before and was therefore considered fair game
by those pre-disposed to be evil – of which there were many. A
hard-core of the school population were conditioned to behave
badly … and relentlessly so. Kevin became their number one en-
emy and they took every opportunity to abuse him. He found it
possible to forgive them on the basis they did not know any better,
but what really hurt was the much larger proportion of his classmates who simply stood on the sidelines and watched, giggling
nervously. Casual racism was endemic but lay dormant in the most
part, only revealing itself when the targets were cornered. Bevan
felt a kinship with Kevin, believing himself to be a fellow outsider,
but was afraid of the challenge that would come from the other
kids if he tried to befriend him. Fortunately for Bevan his reticence
in making friends with *anyone* kept him clear from any accusations
of sympathising with the outcasts.

Whenever Kevin would answer a teacher's question there was
stifled name-calling and laughter from the desks at the back, but
he kept on trying. In the playground he was routinely picked on
and pushed about. His life must have been abject misery, and everyone was amazed he continued to turn up each day – his parents
were clearly hell-bent on toughening him up. The persecution

gradually escalated across the school year until culminating one lunch break in the summer term when a gang surrounded the lad and carried him away, to be tied upside down by his bootlaces to a wire fence surrounding one of the more hidden tennis courts. His cries were drowned out by the guffaws of his assailants and the teachers were caught off guard. Some girls in his class raised the alarm and Kevin was finally brought down … but was never seen at the school again. This episode haunted Bevan for years. He had watched the baying mob from a distance and came to realise where he stood in the world. He knew what they were doing was wrong, he wanted to intervene and stop them, but was too afraid to do so. Throughout his life he was never able to deal with confrontation and shied away from it at all costs. When forced into any kind of conflict his reactions were unpredictable … indeed this character flaw would later prove to be his undoing.

*

Having your brother and sister at the same school, in the upper years, was helpful in terms of learning the ropes. It also meant he had an excuse not to spend time with classmates at the beginning and end of each day. Despite these perks, overall Bevan found the presence of Keith and Anne intimidating. He felt like he was being compared to them all the time and their enthusiasm for extramural activities made things worse. When Anne was due to play a violin solo at one of the school evening concerts, Mum, Dad and Keith were like excited puppies, but Bevan did not want to go. If they were honest, each of them hated the screeching noises she made when practising, but the thought of a performance on stage had them all agog. All except one.

'Why don't you want to go and see your own sister play? She's ever so good.' His mum was gently trying to cajole him.

'I don't *know* …' Bevan extended the 'know' inordinately. 'I don't like music … I don't like violins.'

'Everyone likes music, you mong,' was Keith's contribution, but their mother snapped back at him.

'Keith! There's no need for that.'

'I don't care,' said Anne. 'Let him stay here on his own if he wants. I don't want him fidgeting around, picking his nose, putting me off anyway. Just don't expect me to *ever* come and watch you … if you *ever* get picked for something … which you *won't* of course, who'd want *you* for anything. Swear to God, I'll wash my hands with you.' Anne was talking too fast … already feeling nervous enough, she did not want all this extra fuss. Bevan felt confused, but all he could really think about was the peer pressure and he became consumed with anxiety about his own reluctance to learn an instrument, join the choir or go to drama club. He sulked along in the end but did not pay much attention, praying for the thing to finish. Later he asked his mum about something Anne had said.

'She said she'll *wash her hands with me.* I don't know what she means.'

'Oh … yes, um, she meant to say, 'wash her hands *of* you' dear.'

'What does that mean?'

'Um … it just means she was upset. She thinks you don't love her.'

Bevan was unable to think of what to say next, so he shrugged and went to his room. He hated any scrutiny on what he was feeling. Why had they made him go to the concert? It seemed so obvious to him that he should have stayed at home. The sound of the violin was unbearable. His utmost dread was reserved for those quasi-social activities that occurred at the ends of terms, arranged by staff. On one such occasion the pottery teacher organised an extended lesson for which he brought in a record player and encouraged the class to bring snacks. A table was laid with sausage rolls, pineapple and cheese on sticks, Twiglets etc. and after a review of the class's best work of the year what could only be described as a party ensued, in the pottery room. Bevan soon forgot the records that were played, the memory was too traumatising. However, he could never forget the final scene in which the entire class, plus adults from the art department, danced a conga around the room. He sat frozen to his seat, ignoring the cries for him to stop being a baby and join in. This was perhaps the first time he was ever pushed into the state of switching off from his surroundings completely and drowning out the background with an incantation of 'this isn't happening, this isn't happening'. It was possibly the worst day of his life to that point.

Luckily none of the rough kids did pottery, it was too risky to let them loose with the clay, so there was no physical consequence to having his catastrophic lack of social skills revealed so bleakly that day. Otherwise it might have warranted a beating. 'Scaredy-cat! Scaredy-cat!' Bevan did not enjoy pottery anyway. His favourite subjects were maths and science, while he eagerly took to woodwork and metalwork as he got older. He was good with his hands, he built ingenious traps for wildlife in the garden and loved to watch his father wiring a plug. The inevitable electricity kit appeared one Christmas and pretty much the die was cast, it gave him a vocation to take forward. He loved receiving gifts as a rule – and his parents were generous – but the process was too regularly an anti-climax. He sometimes wondered what they thought went on in his mind, based on some of the toys they selected. But the electricity kit captured his imagination more than anything before or since. The circuits, switches, transistors; the identification symbols and the colours that had a meaning. Most of all, the need for order. He was not in thrall of complexity, or the underlying physics of electrons and protons, he just liked simple patterns that made things work. He made home for this new treasure on the desk in his bedroom and became engrossed by its possibilities. In later life Bevan would think back to those spellbound hours spent connecting components together on little boards, under the cone of light from his ceiling. His onward course was fixed from the instant the wrapping paper had fallen to the floor, to show the prize within. If they had chosen a chemistry set for him instead, how different would his later fortunes been? That was pointless to even consider though – at the time nothing could have been a better choice, however profound the long-term ramifications.

Childhood Christmases generally delivered the nuggets of joy most people expect, from the suspense of opening presents to indulgence with lavish assortments of food. He savoured these like any youngster, but also noticed a tendency for the atmosphere at home to turn sour. He started to associate this time with raised voices behind the kitchen door, things being slammed and Anne crying. He chose not to find out why, he could never grasp why people's moods always had to change. His parents had a habit of switching from exuberance and laughter to silence and icy looks at the drop of a hat. His brother and sister frequently seemed to need comforting for some reason or other. When Keith fell out of a tree and broke his leg, Bevan was bribed to join the family excursions to hospital at visiting time by the promise of sweets. His mind went through contortions trying to think of anything to write on Keith's plaster cast in felt-tip pen, when persuaded to do so. He finally settled on *you should of been a monkey*, which struck the nurses as an arresting image but left them disconcerted by the apparent coldness in such a young boy. For the first time in his young life he was scolded by his mother when they returned home. She was beside herself with worry for Keith, being alone, in pain and away from home for the first time. She rounded on his younger brother: 'You horrible little creature, how did you turn out to be so thoughtless and uncaring!' she shouted at him, gripping his shoulders in her hands. She was not intentionally shaking him; she was just shaking with rage. Bevan stared at her in shock, red-faced but without crying. 'I'm sorry Mummy, I'm sorry,' he trembled. He was genuinely sorry to see her so upset but failed to understand what he had done wrong. It made perfect sense to him; a monkey would not have fallen.

*

Overall, Bevan's time at school proved unremarkable. Keith and Anne eventually moved on to their young adult lives, leaving him alone, but by then he could be relied upon to get himself through the gates each morning without coercion. Anne went off to secretarial college. Keith got a job in the local glassware factory. Meanwhile, Bevan was well-regarded and achieving adequate grades. His reports often referred to his quietness in class and how difficult it was to make him contribute to group discussions, but he tried hard with his written work and caused no trouble. He surprised himself in games lessons, there was something about the physical exertion that released him from his usual worries, although he hated the communal showers and spent as little time as he possibly could in the changing rooms. He excelled as a 400m runner, while just about getting by in football and rugby on the basis of his speed. They tried in vain to make him join the athletics team, to compete against other schools, but he had no intention of spending any more time on school premises than absolutely necessary. He resisted all efforts to coax him into extra training but enjoyed those moments of running ahead of the pack during the regular teaching periods.

The one factor that gave everyone cause to rejoice was the emergence of a clear ambition for his next steps. Initially Bevan was so terrified by life, he looked at the prospect of walking out through the school gates for the last time as a young conscript might have anticipated his fate before boarding a ship to the Western Front during World War 1. His parents spoke about university in reverential tones, but the word alone was enough to stir his forebodings. However, when the light shone in his bedroom – both literally and metaphorically – in response to his dabbling with basic electronics, he knew exactly what he wanted to do in the future. He became one of the few pupils able to answer confidently and convincingly about what they aspired to be. Bevan was eagerly pinning his hopes on a career with pliers, bolts and soldering irons.

He was devoid of religion but felt he really ought to give thanks to some form of deity, when it dawned that his favourite pastime might also become his profession. The waves of relief saturated him. He had spent so many hours churning over in his mind how his destiny was going to unfold. Bevan was convinced that everyone he encountered, all the older beings that surrounded him, knew something that he was unable to grasp. They held a key to the allure of being alive that was out of his reach. The imposition of school was bad enough but the mysteries that lay beyond seemed even worse. When he realised a pathway was open – he possessed a skill that brought him pleasure and, through its practise, would enable him to earn a wage – many of his fears evaporated. He was able to see out the remainder of his education with a steely resolve, determined to achieve the minimum qualifications required to begin the climb up his chosen ladder. Bevan moved towards adolescence with at least a plan. He had never asked to be born, he knew he did not think like normal people, everything scared him … but at least he had a plan, a map for the way ahead.

Chapter 8

Teenage years did not strike Bevan as being particularly more troublesome than what had gone before. The changes in his body – and in the behaviour of his peers – just felt like a continuation of what he was already accustomed to: that being alive meant bewilderment by an endless stream of riddles. He successfully steered a course through his latter stages at school, avoiding parties and girls with relative ease. He made no friends to speak of, getting by socially through a knowledge of football, mopeds and how engines worked. With a year to go, he successfully applied to the National Electricity Board for an apprenticeship, provisional on his exam results. This was the summer of 1974. Ahead of their decision, the atmosphere at home crackled with anticipation as Bevan willed the cosmos to deliver the outcome he craved. Rejection would have been a mortal blow. The suspense was agonising as the mornings ticked by and successive deliveries of mail came without bearing the verdict. When it finally arrived, the moment of opening the letter was as nerve-jangling as standing on the top board at the town pool. He handed it to his father.

'I can't do it Dad, please … you open it … tell me what it says.'

'Umm … OK then, let's have a look.' His father fumbled with the A4 envelope before freeing the contents. He made the noises of someone skim-reading before finding the key sentence, the keenly awaited words being preceded by a rapid-fire human snare drum impersonation, then …

'Umm … here we go … umm … *"able to confirm a place on our level 1 craft apprentice scheme, subject to…"*

More drum sounds but Bevan had heard enough. He clenched his fists and eyes tightly shut at the word 'confirm'. More waves of relief. He punched the air and bounced around the room in a rare display of animation.

'Yesss!!! Ace!!! *Ace*!!! Thank shitting *GOD*!!!'

No one in Bevan's family had heard him swear before and there was an uncomfortable silence while his father contained the urge to comment on its ineptitude. Once the bouncing stopped, he just gave a pat on the back and said, 'Good lad.' Bevan was more embarrassed about saying 'God' than any rude words … now he just had to get the right exam results the following year.

*

Bevan's father Robert, known universally as Bobby, worked as a salesman for one of the town's main insurance companies. At home he was always cheerful, always teasing the kids and their mother in equal measure, with a restless glint in his eye. He was just too young for call-up during the war but still inherited the backs-to-the-wall optimism and matey-ness from his National Service days. When the family was younger, he would encourage the children to be active, while at the same time usually being too preoccupied to join their games.

'All right boysies … why aren't you out there playing Spurs or Man Utd, eh?' – a typical rejoinder as he whisked through the living room on his way to the garage.

The house witnessed more laughter than tears and usually held no trace of ill-feeling or coldness. Bobby liked how his youngest son would spectate on his various jobs around the house, like installing a hi-fi or tinkering with the car, but lacked the patience to allow the boy to have a proper go himself.

'No, not like that … hey listen, don't worry, you just watch me, eh?'

And watch Bevan did, then look for things to do in his room, or the garden, that involved actions similar to those his Dad had been performing. His father would frequently try to coax him out of this solitary recreation but one shake of the head in response to a breezy, 'You coming down the shops?' was enough and Dad was off, usually with Keith and Anne in tow. As teenage years fell the teasing shifted to the archetypal milestones. When would he bring a girl home? When would he go out drinking with his mates instead of staying in his room? By then the conclusion had been reached that Bevan was not a *chip off the old block* and the glint had gone from his father's eyes, knowing the wind-ups were futile. Nevertheless, Bobby was proud of his son for having a plan and was genuinely pleased about the apprenticeship – even though, as the last of the brood departed the family nest, his role as clown-in-chief would come to an end.

*

Bevan put everything into that last year at school, but almost came unstuck. Physics was always a weak spot. Although he would never admit it, physics raised the same misgivings he felt about religious education, which happily he contrived to drop at the earliest opportunity. From the very first R.E. lesson, on the role played by religion in the evolution of man, he resented the wasted time, time spent listening to why different ethnic groups around the globe believed in fairy stories. Bevan wanted proof. He scoffed at mankind's weak-mindedness. Unfortunately for him, physics also appeared to involve indoctrination in concepts he could not see and required blind faith to embrace. He could learn by observation the practical effects of what the various particles were up to, when bulbs flickered or speakers hissed, but the theories of exactly how these effects occurred at a sub-atomic level were tantamount to witchcraft in his eyes. He missed the necessary grade in the physics exam but mercifully had the lifeline of a re-take, which he achieved by the closest margin. He managed this by telling himself just to accept what the textbooks said and learn the words by rote, even if he disbelieved them. At the last gasp, he managed to get his foot on the ladder towards a secure future. He had been rescued from uncertainty in a way that reminded him of those TV news pictures showing the final evacuees lifted off the US embassy roof in Saigon by helicopter. He was on his way to safety – his apprenticeship would begin in early 1976, not long before his eighteenth birthday.

The most fundamental implication of the new venture was the need to leave home. The vacancy was based in the eastern region, a relocation of around 100 miles from his parents. Keith and Anne had already both fledged by then, still living within a bus ride, building their own nests not far from the place of their birth. Bevan was relatively self-sufficient and the prospect of moving to a different town was not abhorrent to him, but he knew he would have to share lodgings with other trainees and that made him nervous. His father was sanguine about the disappearance of his little boy, he sensed he was troubled and thought perhaps it might be the making of him. He was more worried that the arguing in the house, which he hoped had always been successfully concealed, would now get worse without the distraction of the children being around. Bevan's mum, Barbara, felt the dread of finally having to surrender all her offspring but her concern was offset by the promise of liberation from the boy's intensity. She loved him but his … his *otherness* … put her on edge and she felt his reclusive nature disrupted the equilibrium of the family. Reluctantly she had to admit, to herself only, that maybe she would be more relaxed once he was away.

*

Barbara and Bobby fell in with each other at the start of the 50s, brought together as a result of their respective clans frequenting the same pubs and social clubs on a regular basis. She was a couple of years older, but his cheeky self-assurance was persuasive. She soon concluded this charming conman had the perfect attributes to make a good living as a salesman and, being passably good-looking, therefore represented the best potential mate she felt likely to find. Barbara was feisty and did not suffer fools. Winning her heart struck Bobby as an irresistible challenge and he pulled out all the stops, but she could keep him to heel – he soon learned from her piercing stares not to call her Babs. After a spell of courtship lasting just long enough to placate their own parents' expectations, they were married. She had once dreamed of becoming an artist or fashion designer and this creative side found an outlet through her job in the drawing office of a chartered surveyor … but raising a family and building a cosy home were her primary motives. To her regret, her days as a draughtswoman had to end when the babies came along. Initially they thought the first two would suffice. As Keith and Anne took shape as individuals, though, Barbara realised she wanted to be pregnant again, so they decided to try for two more, to keep things even. However, the fourth child never materialised so their youngest of three was left somewhat isolated, marooned as a lone outcrop.

Bevan's mother doted on the children and tried to indulge everything they wanted. She encouraged them to be independent but found her youngest's inbuilt determination to set his own agenda quite disarming. She wished he would engage more with the other boys in the neighbourhood but, when they called, he ignored the pleas to come to the door, leaving her to shrug apologetically to whichever gaggle of would-be playmates stood outside, ball under arm. She was frustrated by Bobby's apparent indifference to the problem and could be sharp when she thought they couldn't be overheard.

'Can't you get him off his arse sometimes? He'll grow roots in that bedroom of his.'

'He's all right Barb. He's not doing any harm. He's a bright lad.'

'Bobby love, he needs to get out more … mix with the other children … he needs his rough edges knocking off. And he doesn't listen to me, I'll tell you that much.'

Bobby knew she was right, but he had too many schemes of his own to pursue, he did not want the distraction. His life had been simpler when they only had two to worry about.

As Bevan grew older, he started to notice the air stiffen if he entered a room when both parents were already present. He was grateful to his father for instilling his love of electrics, and to his mother for trying so hard to make a happy home. He appreciated their efforts but they had, after all, brought him into this world without his consent. His gratitude was not without limits. Once the dust had settled after the exams, he began to look forward to getting away, praying in his own godless way to get lucky with the group of housemates his helicopter dropped him into.

*

Bevan's posting was to the eastern region's training centre, co-located alongside its main equipment depot in a medium-sized town forty miles north-east of Greater London. On acceptance of their offer the Electricity Board sent reams of information about the apprenticeship structure and the support provided to recruits, which Bevan pored over as a historian might inspect the Dead Sea Scrolls. The centre had an occupational care team dedicated to sourcing reliable landlords with furnished shared houses to accommodate each year's intake. Bevan looked first for his allocated digs: 14 Sebastopol Road – the name itself suggested adventure and intrigue. The address stared starkly out from the page as he read the details of his enrolment. On the day of his move, a suitcase of clothes plus several boxes of books and assorted indispensable childhood junk were loaded into the car with just enough room for him in the back; his father drove, his mother sat alongside in the passenger seat trying not to get irritated. His parents chain-smoked throughout the journey, the rasping of the lighter punctuating the way like mileage signs. Smoke blew around inside the car as winter drizzle swirled outside – his view from the rear window as they traversed the North Circular Road resembled scenes from a dystopian black and white science fiction film, revealed in fragments as he wiped away the condensation. On arrival, the only free parking space was outside Number 6, the bay window of which was barricaded with dense net curtains that trapped two things against the glass: a table lamp adorned with frilly crimson shade and a sign reading: *Model, please ring.*

'Jesus, it's the red-light district. At least you've got some prozzies on hand son.' His father had to explain to the boy while failing to suppress a chortle. Barbara lit another cigarette and fixed her eyes on the sky through the windscreen.

Number 14 held the same smell Bevan had noticed in other kids' houses back on the estate, on the rare occasions he was dragged into one of them. Walls and floors steeped in the aroma of stale cooking oil and boiled vegetables, only here with an undertone of sick. Sebastopol Road was one of a small grid of terraced streets, now separated from the town centre by roundabouts and underpasses. This was a garrison town and the footpaths and wasteland were etched with the ghosts of drunken one-night stands and brawling. The house had one bedroom downstairs and three upstairs. The best two rooms, at the front of the house, had already been claimed. Bevan was happy to take the middle room upstairs, he quickly calculated that being so much smaller it could never become the social hub of the household – he would be able to escape from the inevitable communal TV watching when the time came. With his stuff now transferred to its new hideaway he stood on the pavement by the car, unsure how to feel with his parents about to leave.

'Let's not hang around then.' Bobby sought to break the awkward silence. Bevan was glad for the intervention and took the opportunity to set them free.

'Bye Dad. Bye Mum. Thanks for the lift.'

'Yeah, see ya later. Don't do anything I wouldn't do.' Bobby gave a dirty laugh and swung around to the driver's door.

'Remember what I told you about what to eat love. Look after yourself. You better come and see us again!' Barbara did her best to sound jolly, wiping a cursory tear away with the back of her hand, as she too got back in the car.

Bevan's eyes were dry. He felt numb, returning the waving hands as his parents drove off, pointlessly sounding the horn while craning their necks for a final glimpse. Were they glad to be rid of him? Was he glad to see them go? The answer *Yes* flickered for a while, for both points, but he would not allow himself to dwell on such thoughts. He was more concerned with the immediate challenge. Laughter sounded ominously from the open door of his new abode. He walked back and stepped into the hallway again. Several lads his own age were milling around the ground floor and on the stairs. He steeled himself and did his best job of making introductions, but lost track of which ones were actually house-mates and which were hangers-on. He managed to squeeze past, reach the sanctuary of his room and set about spending the rest of the day re-arranging the furniture and organising his possessions. Over time, the rituals of sharing bathroom and kitchen forced Bevan into establishing a basic rapport with the three other permanent occupants. The house was shabby and damp, the plumbing and kitchen equipment rudimentary, the furnishings creaky and chipped. The four of them had to bond in order to create any kind of homeliness. None were particularly extrovert; they shared a similar degree of social ineptitude and they all found a way to get on tolerably. Sometimes they ate together in the kitchen, sometimes they went out to the pub. Bevan had not previously acquired a liking for alcohol. There was always plenty around at home, but his parents had tended to shield the children from exposure to it, perhaps out of a sense of shame about their own weakness. Now, alongside his fellow apprentices, booze helped him to hide in the crowd. He started to enjoy the inebriation; it became a badge of belonging. But these were no hellraisers. On plenty of evenings Bevan was able to retreat to his room to pass the time alone, listening to cassettes through his headphones, free from any risk of being coerced into a night out against his will.

*

The Craft Apprenticeship scheme was probationary and included a mixture of learning at the town's technical college along with active experience at the region's main coal-fired power station some twenty minutes away by mini-bus. By the age of twenty-one, unless they were exceedingly incompetent, the recruits could reasonably expect a permanent position as an electrical fitter to follow, although this was not guaranteed. Bevan enjoyed the practical elements but some of the scientific aspects of the coursework tormented him. He had reached the boundary of the theories he could easily grasp – this was harder than school, the textbooks were harder to memorise. He continued to struggle with the underlying physics of electromagnetic force and some of the more advanced mathematics they were expected to learn gave him night-mares. He was almost overwhelmed by anxiety as new exams approached and, on more than one occasion, convinced himself he had to quit, despite the unthinkable consequences that would entail. Nevertheless, he managed to hold himself together sufficiently to keep on the right side of the pass marks, while also becoming well regarded for his hands-on application of engineering knowledge in all of the exercises. An additional factor, albeit an unwanted one, also played in his favour during his first year. Dire events were about to unfold back home. Whatever struggles Bevan may have been facing in establishing himself as a trainee due to the testing academic demands, something much worse was about to knock him completely off his stride. As a result, his ability to stay afloat would be alleviated by the supervisors concluding he needed some leeway. Not long into the scheme Bevan's life was touched by tragedy. The training department would be very understanding – he was given time off and everyone made allowances for the emotional withdrawal and weaker performance that followed. The bombshell came out of a clear blue sky, just as he was finding his feet.

As spring began to simmer gently – before anyone guessed the extent of the heatwave to follow – Bevan reached the point of believing he *had* made the right career choice. Or rather, more accurately, the point of recognising that the *only* career choice he ever thought possible might work out as he hoped. He *was* coping with the course – he was scraping through the written tests but excelling in the practical exercises. The potential future way forward, tantalising glimpses of which he had perceived during the latter years at school, was still in sight. He told himself: *he could make it as an electrical fitter* – the work to come would be close enough to what he was already learning, there would be no insurmountable cliff to ascend in the years ahead. A certain peace of mind gradually formed, erasing some of the fears about the point of his existence that constantly nagged him. He had survived this far. Social situations continued to be terrifying – and he had become reconciled to the presumption he would never have a girlfriend – but at least he had proved to himself he could stay on the ladder during the first few months away from home.

One late May morning, during a lesson on electrical earth connections, the college secretary unexpectedly knocked on the door. After a muffled conversation the tutor spoke across the room. 'Bevsie, there's been a phone call for you in the secretary's office, you can leave the class now if you like.' The urgent look in their eyes convinced him to heed the instruction but he was buggered to think what the matter could be. Bevan wondered why she was called a secretary when she basically seemed to run the place, as he trailed after her clip-clopping heels along corridors suffocating with the odour of floor polish. 'It's your brother Keith … he said you should have his number, but I jotted it down just in case,' she panted, attempting a nervous smile. When they reached the office, Bevan thanked her for writing the number down and stared at the tan-coloured phone. The receiver appeared too heavy to lift. He dialled the number.

'Hello there Keith. I'm at college … they said you called.'

'Something terrible has happened. It's Dad. You better come home.' Keith's voice was trembling.

'What is it? What's happened to him?'

'He was in a car crash. It's really …' Keith broke off for a moment. 'It's just really something awful … he was killed … Dad's dead. Just come home.'

Bevan paused for a while, his brain locked. Eventually he mustered a voice to say, 'OK. I'll get there as soon as I can,' before guiding the handset back to the cradle like a dumbbell. The secretary put a hand on his shoulder, her eyes red and watery. He gave her a limp smile and disappeared to collect his bag from the classroom. His tears came later once he reached his room in Sebastopol Road, and packed what he needed to take home, not that he was able to think properly. He wrestled in his mind about what normal people should feel when death happens. He had no answer to that. Surely it could not be true? Each moment of confronting the idea that his father was no longer breathing felt like an electric shock to the stomach. Each moment of picturing the car accident, the injuries, the pain … made him close his eyes and block all thoughts completely. He was desperate to know what happened ... but was he feeling sad like normal people? Would Mum and Keith and Anne believe he was sad? Oh God, poor Mum. Another thought too painful to bear. And why was she not in the car?

*

On the night of the accident, Barbara was in her bedroom when the police called just before daylight. She was used to Bobby's nights out with the lads from the office, a drinking culture was par for the course, he was a salesman after all. Pub crawls, card schools, evenings in London for football or greyhounds or boxing. 'We'll be getting slaughtered no doubt ... you know what Duggie and Mitch are like ... don't wait up will ya love' – he would seek to prepare the ground as he put on his jacket before setting forth. She assumed he was telling lies up to a point. No doubt his blurry recollections after the event, once he had recovered from the hangover, excluded the strip clubs, flirting and occasional grope. But she thought he was too harmless to play around, so was content to let him off the leash from time to time.

The solemn-looking sergeant asked Barbara if they could sit down somewhere, he was accompanied by a female constable whose bearing was drained of all colour. As they described the scene of the crash, beside a lonely B-road linking the town with surrounding farmland, Barbara thought her heart would stop beating. A car had left the road and collided head-on with a large sycamore tree. The two occupants, neither of whom was wearing a seat belt, were catapulted through the windscreen. The male occupant – identified as Bobby, in the passenger seat – had his throat sliced by the lower edge of the broken glass and bled to death at the scene. The female occupant, who had been driving, was found on the car bonnet with severe head injuries and died soon after the ambulance arrived. The nearest house was a hundred yards away, but the sleeping residents were woken by the horrific sound of the impact and had raised the alarm.

'I appreciate this is an extremely difficult time, but we need to ask you a few questions. Are you acquainted with someone by the name of Sandra Mitchell?' The sergeant already sensed an imminent unravelling of unbearable secrets.

Barbara's shaking became uncontrollable; she dropped her glass, trying to replace it on the coffee table. She was speechless for several minutes, shivering and sobbing. '*Sandra Mitchell?*' Disbelievingly, she could barely force the name from her lips.

Sandra Mitchell was the closest thing Barbara had to a best friend. A few years younger and married to one of Bobby's drinking pals, they always hooked up on the occasions the wives tagged along with the sales crew to a function. The two of them also got together sometimes just for tea, smokes and a gossip. Sandra was one of the few people Barbara ever opened up to. Barbara had shared all her fears about the cracks in her marriage and now she despairingly replayed all their conversations, searching for signs of the deception. Witnesses were eventually found to piece together Bobby and Sandra's last movements. They were seen having a candlelit dinner at one of the more expensive restaurants in the area – La Maison Rouge – with its thatched roof, dark padded menus and waiters wearing ties. A popular venue for romantic trysts, a single red rose on each table. The route they were taking back into town could only mean they were heading for Sandra's house; her spouse being otherwise engaged on the bender that was indeed genuine. They both had alcohol in their blood, but Bobby had much more – 'the bastard must've been on the brandy'. It was Sandra's car and she had been driving at speed, but the investigation could find no explanation for her loss of control, no one had seen the car leave the road. Something must have distracted her.

*

Bevan returned home by train and bus. His bedroom was in the same state as the last time he saw it, with Blu Tack holes in the paintwork remaining when his posters had come down. His mother was still in shock and taking tranquilisers. They told her not to drink but she had one on the go in the kitchen, out of sight of the family. When Bevan arrived his brother and sister were both sitting with Mum in the lounge. They all hugged in different combinations before ending up sitting in silence. It was too soon to grieve. They wanted to cry for their father, but any feelings of pity were instantly snuffed out by the harsher emotions of outrage and betrayal. Bevan wanted to find an innocent explanation. Maybe they had just been friends and there was something private they needed to talk about. Something that only Dad could help with? He got as far as, 'Maybe ...' but stopped himself going further. He was unable to construct a theory that made any sense to himself let alone the others and he was frozen by the haunted look of incredulity his mother flashed him at the first syllable. After staring at the latest cold cup of tea for long enough Barbara suddenly lifted herself and strode next door for another slug from the hidden bottle, hissing anguished pleas for explanation on the way. 'How long were they ... How long were they at it?' Keith and Anne would catch each other's glances, agreeing a vow of silence, silently. On one occasion with just the three of them in the room, Bevan tried to probe:

'Do you know how long Dad was seeing Sandra for? Were Mum and Dad going to split up?'

'That's anyone's guess. It doesn't really matter much now does it.' Keith shifted uncomfortably in his seat, preferring the question not to be asked, speaking in clipped tones that discouraged further speculation.

'Poor Mum. She's lost ... *everything.*' Anne was now looking at the floor.

Bevan could not fathom why Bobby had been spending time with Sandra behind Mum's back ... and why his parents had apparently not been happy together. It was impossible to know what to talk about. His mother was too upset but while she stayed in the kitchen he tried again.

'I had no idea something like this might happen. I knew they had some arguments ... but that's normal isn't it? I thought Mum and Dad were rock solid ... didn't you?' Bevan looked at his two siblings in turn, but they closed ranks and stayed mute, as if to suggest the answer was obvious. Ignoring the fact his father was dead he continued to ask about the build-up.

'I wonder when it started to go wrong? How could he end up wanting to be with someone else and risk hurting Mum so much?'

'It might've been *better* if you hadn't …' Keith started to snarl before Anne urgently glowered *not now* with her eyes and cut him short. She was afraid he was going to say, '*if you hadn't been born*'. The pair had discussed many times how Mum seemed less tense when only they were around her and that having a third child had perhaps sown the seeds of friction between their parents in the first place. Now was not the time though. Keith tried to backtrack.

'Er … it might've been better if you hadn't … gone away. At least Mum wouldn't have been alone when she found out. Not that that's your fault. None of us were there.'

They all sat motionless. Bevan was not convinced that was what Keith had originally intended to say; he doubted his being there that night would have made things any better, but he let it go. Words were pointless now. He soon started to feel his presence was not helping anyone. He stayed at home for two nights out of a sense of duty but leapt at the first suggestion that he should get back to work. Barbara sounded spiritless as she encouraged him to go: 'Don't worry love … there's nothing you can do here … better to keep yourself busy.' She was inconsolable and having the kids around only intensified the painful memories of a time when the whole family was together, making her wonder when the lies had started. There was nothing to do yet, nothing to plan. The funeral was delayed by the police investigation. As soon as Keith uttered the words: 'You may as well go, we can sort out what needs to be done,' Bevan was off. He was glad to be free of the feeling that his reactions were being judged. And the reality of what he was leaving behind – 'what needs to be done' – he was oblivious to. Keith was annoyed but not surprised about the lack of protestation. It would be better if he alone took responsibility for sorting through all the stuff left behind from Bobby's life, in case any more clues emerged that needed to be buried. But some acknowledgement of the difficult tasks ahead might have been appropriate, he reflected, when dropping his younger brother back at the station.

*

The loss of his father in such a violent and shocking manner left Bevan feeling that his own senses had been smashed as part of the same accident. The images from the front-page story in the local paper were seared into his brain; he kept the clipping much to the dismay of his family. The headline read: COUPLE DEAD IN CAR HITS TREE TRAGEDY. He was unable to stop himself toying with the preposterous syntax of the sentence. The absurdity of convoluted and life-shattering events being condensed into those seven idiotic words. And how the real tragedy could only be deciphered by what was *not* said in the article: the reasons why those two occupants were not supposed to be where they were, on that section of B-road; the namelessness of the loved ones left behind to pick up the pieces. He was fascinated by the casual inaccuracies in the story but there was no point writing to complain – if these journalists were any good they would be working somewhere better than a crappy small-town rag in the first place. A photographer had managed to reach the site in time and capture an image of the twisted wreckage before it was towed away for forensic analysis. Bevan tried to picture the terror in the seconds before impact. He flinched at the thought of his father suffering but at the same time hoped there had been a moment of realisation that his treachery was about to be uncovered, as the car left the road. As for Sandra he hoped she had been conscious of everything throughout.

He felt guilty about trying to continue with his life but was grateful to be away from the undercurrents and scrutiny of home and for once felt no embarrassment in wishing to be alone. His housemates, co-workers and the training staff all left him to occupy his own space, without challenge. Seeing his mother so devastated was hard to endure and before the funeral the thought of returning tied him in knots. But he made it back again when the time came, and the family steered each other through the day. Barbara was still all but speechless and not the least concerned that hardly anyone turned up – she just wanted the day to be over with. Bobby's drinking gang chose not to attend, as an act of solidarity with Mitch. This was Bevan's first funeral. The ritual formalities made him cringe and he had to concentrate on the sombre sight of the coffin when the priest was delivering a potted history of Bobby's life, in order to keep a straight face. Half the details were wrong. Keith and Anne were frowning but their mother was impervious. In the tense atmosphere Bevan made the mistake of considering how awful it would be to laugh out loud. Once that idea had popped into his head, he tensed up even more and had to pinch himself hard to avoid a nervous giggle. He tried to describe this moment in the living room later but was met with further blank looks. Despite its many failings, Bevan could not get back to 14 Sebastopol Road fast enough.

*

The Electricity Board supported Bevan in resuming the course and allowed him time to catch up. For the rest of that sweltering summer he gradually returned to an even keel, outwardly at least. He felt a part of himself had died inside Sandra Mitchell's car, along with the illicit lovers: that part of his make-up he had inherited from his father, the moments of catching himself pausing to imagine what Dad would have done or said in a given situation. In a way, the allowances he was given came partly as a release, in that he felt less obliged to behave in a certain way to gain approval and could just be himself, for better or worse. The jolt of the car crash had forced him back into the fold, to be reminded of his awkward family relationships, to re-open dialogues that had begun to freeze over. Now that his distant proximity was restored, communication started to tail off again. He made regular trips to the nearest payphone to call home but as the months passed after the funeral his mother sounded increasingly remote during their conversations. Bevan convinced himself she was not really interested in what he was doing, and she never said much, other than, 'Yeah, I'm fine,' when he asked how she was. She took more and more time to answer and sometimes failed to hide her tipsiness once finally picking up. The gaps between his calls got longer and his head became filled by the training centre once again.

The vocational element of the apprenticeship was primarily conducted at the power station. The trainees learned about maintaining the generators along with field trips to understand the distribution network, the sub-stations and domestic supply. Bevan found the work of the pylon gangs totally awe-inspiring, like pioneer railway builders spinning their webs across the full extent of the nation, but doubted he had the necessary head for heights to attempt to join their number. The power station was known colloquially as *the Docks* by everyone in the region. It was situated by the sea to satisfy its ravenous appetite for coal, which was fed by the shipload. On the Docks days the young recruits would be ferried by mini-bus from the training centre. For Bevan, the wait by the loading bay for the shuttle to arrive was always a source of apprehension. Somehow the normal levels of reserve dropped off and the lads – and isolated lass – would assume the need for a degree of performance that left Bevan praying for the driver to turn up as quickly as possible. Jokes were told, impressions were attempted, arms were punched. He looked forward to the moment of arrival and a return to the sober behaviour demanded by the trainers.

Bevan had a lean and slightly stooping posture. He was unremarkable to look at, had been teased about acne at school and his heart generally sank every time he looked in the mirror. His self-esteem was so far off the bottom of the scale that if ever exposed to evidence of his contemporaries getting off with each other, he simply noted that *getting off with* members of the opposite sex was a pursuit enacted in a parallel universe inaccessible to him. He was OK with that. Living a solitary life was hard enough … getting involved with someone else's problems as well struck him as a frightening prospect and no one would want to kiss him anyway. He guessed he must love his family, but stress hummed in the background whenever he was with them, like white noise. It was the same with everyone though – other people always put him on edge. He would clam up completely in the presence of girls, he felt their suspicions penetrate every facet of his being with contempt. He was yet to work out that women were not a homogenous army of the unattainable and were equally capable of idiosyncrasy and surprise as the weirdest of men.

*

There was only one girl in Bevan's cohort of rookies. She had a short wiry frame and spiky coloured hair of various hues. She looked like someone with attitude – consequently he strove to avoid sitting next to her at all costs on the runs to the Docks. He figured she would soon be hooked-up in the regular company of one of the more oafish Jack-the-lad types, that's what usually seemed to happen with females in his experience. Against his expectation, over a year had passed and she still appeared to be maintaining her independence, which drew his grudging admiration. However, such was his timidity towards women, he always made sure to time his boarding of the mini-bus not to coincide with her, until one day she slipped in behind him, as if from nowhere.

'All right Bevsie, budge up you lemon.'

'Oh hi … umm … it's Fiona isn't it?' Even this was a breakthrough for Bevan – actually speaking to a girl. He knew very well she was called Fiona; her name had been mentioned during classes and on the plant room floor on countless occasions. But having never been officially introduced he did not feel entitled to address her directly.

'Er … yeah. As if you didn't know.' Fiona gave a gurgling laugh but refrained from calling him a plonker, which she wanted to. She got a notepad out of her bag and started drawing stars with a lime green pen.

Fiona was the sole female in that whole year's intake. She had only been accepted because her father had worked at the Docks himself before retiring early due to ill health. Her mother was an American by birth and had recently fled back to her homeland for reasons that were not fully understood. 'She joined a cult or something.' Fiona brushed off all adversity, she was a tough little nut.

Bevan was too flustered to say anything else for the rest of that journey. When they reached the Docks she turned to speak, returning her doodles to her bag, but he was concentrating hard at the window and pretended not to notice. Fiona rolled her eyes, gave a slight groan and got off the bus. But she was not giving up – she wanted to find out more about this queer fellow who never spoke. On the way back that evening she got on first then faffed with her bag on the adjacent seat until Bevan got on board. He was trapped. Her eyes smiled as he approached the empty seat she had secured, and a sense of obedience compelled him to sit beside her again.

'Don't worry I'm not going to bite. Don't look so scared! You don't say much do ya … what do you normally get up to in the evenings Bevsie?' Fiona was not seeking a date; she was just trying to make him open up.

'Not much. I usually just listen to music or read up on stuff.'

'Coh! No wonder you're such a brain box. Not out on the town then?'

Brain box. It had never struck him before that someone might hold him in any kind of regard. Bevan certainly had an excellent understanding of the engineering tasks and was always good at solving problems. If the other trainees were ever stuck on something and there were no supervisors on hand, they would often seek his advice on which type of tool was needed to unravel a given type of equipment. He usually knew the answer, but he never felt they respected him for it. And here was Fiona … an actual girl … almost giving him a compliment. From somewhere he was inspired to continue:

'Brain box … me? Ha ha … not likely. How about you, what do you get up to?' He felt safer echoing her words back to her, to reduce the chances of saying the wrong thing.

'Oh … I'll just go and see my dad, then go home. I like reading too.'

They both liked reading. Admittedly, in Bevan's case, this mostly meant magazines. But he was quite astonished to discover this energetic soul who looked like she went out dancing in pubs every night was also a home bunny like him. She too lived in a shared house, but not one of the regular apprentice hovels – it was a larger detached red-brick villa in a leafier part of town, containing ladies from various walks of life. Fiona would have preferred a mixed house, but she promised her dad. She had always liked competing against boys and was determined to follow in her father's footsteps. She was not impressed by the arseing around of the other apprentices and saved her appreciation for people who really knew about machines. She had noticed Bevan from the beginning, being impressed by his economy of words, and wanted to understand the reason for his tortured demeanour.

*

Bevan sustained a conversation with Fiona all the way back to the training centre. He could barely take in what was happening. He felt strangely relaxed. When he made a comment about the day's experience at the Docks she was nodding and smiling in agreement as he spoke. No blank looks. No uneasy hesitation. This had never happened to him before. A pleasant sensation, reminiscent of goosebumps, prickled down his spine as they dismounted the mini-bus and Fiona suggested he accompany her home for a cup of tea. Now he did hesitate. Being so completely taken aback to find himself in this situation he reverted to type and instinctively fired off a reason for why he needed to get back to Sebastopol Road.

'All right mate ... see you tomorrow,' she chirped, seemingly undaunted. Bevan walked home in a stupor. For the first time in his life he had enjoyed talking to someone. His thoughts were not about physical attraction. More fundamentally they were doing backflips at the recognition that he had *been himself* – and this sparkly-eyed girl with punk hair had wanted his company. This was too much to take on board.

After several sleepless nights and a few more conversations on the shuttle, Bevan started to realise this new development might be something more than just a fleeting interlude. A subtle change in his approach occurred – for once he was not running away from his feelings and he even joined the conspiracy to ensure they found adjacent seats after a while. They were both oblivious to the inevitable joshing that came from their fellow passengers and, after repeated invitations at the end of the homeward journey, Bevan finally found the courage to accompany Fiona back to her lodgings. And they talked. Fiona made tea, they sat and talked, they watched TV. After a few rounds of meeting like this they found they could simply hang out together, spend time reading whatever they wanted to read, then slip back into conversation. They concluded that each of them must be wired somewhat differently from the norm, and they were grateful to have found each other. Bevan tried to explain the difficulty he had relating to people.

'I can never think of what to say … anything that would be interesting that is … until about half an hour after the moment's gone. So I panic … and people think I'm an idiot. It's so different with you Fee. I don't know why you latched onto me and not one of the others, you'd be having much more fun.'

'They're all dicks that's why. I like being with you. You're not a dick.'

Fiona had indulged her wild side in her mid-teens, had seen the dangers and stepped back from the brink. Now she was determined to prove herself in a man's world. Bevan was her side-project. She was delighted to have discovered such a rare creature, devoid of all machismo, innocently discovering aspects of life for the first time. She eventually coaxed him onto the bed and despite his initial painful embarrassment they became lovers of a sort. Her playfulness gradually broke down his barriers but at no time was sex the most important thing in their relationship. They loved the togetherness. She hinted at disturbing mistreatment in her past that she declined to elaborate upon, which he gratefully took to mean he was not required to be that good in bed. Whatever they were doing, he felt totally comfortable with her, in a way he never thought was possible. Out of the blue he found a capacity to care about another person's needs and he started to think about her all the time.

Bevan rapidly became consumed by his love for Fiona. The house she resided in was an order of magnitude more salubrious than Sebastopol Road, with much more space, so they spent most of their time there in the early days. Her housemates were not especially enamoured with boyfriends staying overnight so it only happened a few times, which suited Bevan as he still felt extremely self-conscious about doing absolutely *everything* together. But eventually they decided to find a place of their own, swapping the town of the depot for its near neighbour where the Docks were situated, and settled into a bedsit with a partial view of the power station's chimneys. He had spent so much time living half a life, now that Fiona was filling the void, he had little time for anything else. His visits and phone calls home became less frequent, the new joy in his life made him forget the pain of his father's death. Mum was always the same when he did call, she seemed unconcerned by how often he remembered. They were both now thriving in work and successfully made the transition from the apprentice scheme to full-time employment. Fiona was based at the Docks while Bevan had a more roving role in the field. They encouraged each other through driving lessons, made sensible plans for living within a budget and started saving for a holiday. As his vision for the future started to gain shape and colour, his mental picture of life as a cul-de-sac faded away.

*

That fateful bus journey, when they first sat together, was in 1978. The momentum of their fondness steadily grew, and they established a healthy set of mutually agreeable pastimes. Despite a left-field fashion sense Fiona did not hanker for a rock'n'roll life-style – she was just as happy to be swimming at the beach or chasing a frisbee. By 1982 they decided to indulge themselves with a foreign holiday and became giddy with excitement ahead of their ten nights in Dubrovnik, counting down the days and hours to their midnight departure for Luton Airport with goggle-eyes. It looked so beautiful in the brochure. The trip came and went in a flash, but they loved every minute. The beauty of the city and landscape … the sea, the sailing, the food. While strolling through the picture-postcard streets, each turn unveiling a new feast for the senses, Bevan discovered what it was to feel completely carefree. Contrary to his deepest instincts … infused by the sunshine, eye-wateringly gorgeous surroundings and companionship of his beloved sidekick … he allowed thoughts to form that perhaps there was some good in being alive after all. He could tell Fiona shared the glow. He basked in the knowledge that she was equally content … there was no pressure to act in a certain way, they were at home in each other's presence. They relished the warmth shown by locals in the restaurants and bars, in reflection of their evident intimacy and love. It felt like a heaven on earth … the rapture clung to them throughout and still lingered on their journey back to England. If only such euphoria could last. When they arrived home, Bevan noticed an unusual hand-written envelope in their post box. It was from Keith.

I had to write a letter because it appears to be the only method of contacting you. We have been trying to call your number for days. On the few times somebody answers they do not know where you are. Is it a communal telephone?

You might be interested to know that our Mother passed away last Tuesday. She has been drinking too much and it finally went too far. She died at home of alcohol poisoning.

Both Anne and myself have tried very hard to keep her going since the 'accident' but she withdrew completely in the end. She kept telling us how sad she was that you never called any more. Perhaps if you are still around you might care to contact us now. My number is still the same.

Yours

Keith

Chapter 9

The interlude Jez spent in the park stargazing with Ginge was a one-off. He had drifted off to sleep with his thoughts in the heavens, assisted by the balmy air and a night without dew. When he awoke, Ginge had disappeared. Once consciousness kicked in, he instinctively felt for his backpack to make sure it was still there. With relief, he was reassured by the familiar lumps and bumps. Ginge had not robbed him. That they were not out to rob each other was one of the founding principles of their connection. Knowing whom to trust was a key lesson for survival in their circles. Their meetings were usually much shorter-lived. Ginge would not normally linger for as long as he did that evening – typically, just as soon as he showed the slightest sign of settling down, he would be off again … to make a rendezvous with a dealer, alert to whatever was the latest psychoactive agent to hit the area, Jez supposed. Ginge would sometimes descend upon Jez in his alcove, appearing like magic by the opening and perching on the ground with remarkable agility considering the years of being wasted and exposed to the elements. He would snatch hold of whatever book Jez was reading and dismiss it instantly with a: 'That looks shit, what are you reading it for?' On other occasions they would meet by the quayside and swap intelligence about the next expected food bank handout, or discuss the latest schemes for good places to sleep at night. But at night-time they rarely crossed paths.

Night-time. The onset of foreboding associated with the disappearance of daylight repeated in an unforgiving drumbeat, day on day, week on week, month on month. The inescapable approach of nightfall 'Sorts the men from the boys,' as Colin would say, in one of his stock phrases that made Jez cringe. The Caravan Trust did have a few beds in the old school hall, but these were only deployed when its facilities were escalated into the role of emergency night shelter in the coldest weather. The available service providers, including the council, only had enough resources to run emergency shelters when the temperatures fell dangerously low. They were stretched to the limit just keeping the statistic of rough sleepers that freeze to death each winter to a minimum – there was not enough funding across the board to protect everyone throughout the year. The Caravan provided somewhere to go for short spells during the day, nothing more. The volunteers did their best to offer advice and there was power for charging mobile phones, but there were no washing facilities, training programmes or health checks that Colin had once hoped for.

The major national charities ran hostels in the town to support homeless individuals with specific needs: the youngsters escaping physical and sexual abuse, the confessed addicts, those with a mental illness and a clearly defined diagnosis. Jez had his own reasons for choosing this way of life and was determined to contain them inside for now. He was not yet ready to submit himself to a conveyor belt leading to rehabilitation. He did not want to be assessed; he did not want an action plan. He felt able to find his own way, despite being adrift from the conventional structures of society. There were even times when he felt like the streets might be his calling … that his destiny belonged somewhere in this parallel universe and he had to keep on the move to find it. However, like the visitations of Ginge, such thoughts lingered only briefly. Any ideas Jez nurtured that his circumstances might lead to some good were quickly banished by the pitying looks of the majority passing him by.

*

In his mind, Jez pictured himself bobbing and weaving like a boxer, keeping his options open, staying light on his feet, despite the fact they were becoming excruciatingly painful. There were non-emergency night shelters all year round, but you had to pay a nominal fee and, strictly speaking, required referral from one of the official agencies. Jez had established a reputation for causing no trouble so could often get a place if he wanted one, but he only tried when other options eluded him. He did not want to make a fuss and believed that others' needs were greater than his own. Apart from the days he steeled himself for sleeping outside, his preference was one of the low-end B&Bs that graced the town – relatively speaking they were dirt-cheap but would garner zero stars in any guidebook. He had scraped enough cash together early on to afford the deposit that was essential for taking quarters at the most notorious of these: the Viaduct Guest House. His target thereafter was twenty-five pounds per day, if he wanted to room there. Sleep itself was not the most important issue. It was more a question of having somewhere to go that made it possible to switch off after dark, with protection from the weather, to get respite from the hardships of being on the pavement. Jez wished it was possible to walk and sit, walk and sit solidly for 24 hours in the open air … but you may as well ask people to fly. The benefits of a room at the Viaduct were threefold: (1) a key, such that privacy was achievable unless someone kicked the door in, which happened all the time judging by the boot-sized holes in the panels, but not every night; (2) two communal toilet/shower rooms, which were disgusting but just about served their purpose; and (3) simply a space to exist while shielded from the rain, wind and darkness. As for the rest of its qualities, the place was uniquely awful. It became a question of which option was least disagreeable on any given day: were conditions in the open air tolerable? was there only enough money for a shelter? could the mortal hazards and unholy stench of the Viaduct be braved? The negatives had to be weighed up to decide which course of action felt least likely to kill you each time.

The rooms at the Viaduct were squalid beyond all reckoning. The building itself at least had a sense of place, nestling alongside the grey brick spans that carried railway passengers across the flood plain on which the town had grown since the Dark Ages. It had originally acted as an overspill from the main station hotel but, even when newly built, the idea of any traveller ever being delighted by its charms upon arrival was hard to imagine. Now it stood isolated, on the road leading away from the centre towards the most deprived suburbs, pressed against the high brickwork by the overflowing compound of a used car trader. It was an established fixture in the folklore of the town's underclass but went unmentioned in the Where to Stay? leaflets stacked at the tourist information centre – and any favourable online reviews could only be attributable to sadistic fantasists. The main body of the building had been stripped out and now found use as a boxing club, which was represented by the only functioning bell push to the side of the front door. A strip of paper had been appended with tape at some point suggesting: FOR GUEST HOUSE PRESS BOXING, but nowadays that would simply result in a long, nervous wait. You had to walk round to the back, where the accommodation occupied a two-storey annex, adorned with yellowed and torn net curtains stuck to the grimy glass by the vapour from years of demoralised exhalation.

There was an office on the ground floor, alongside a breakfast room with its tiny kitchen. The proprietor – a terrifying man-mountain from Romania who also owned the car business next door – kept the clientele in check through snarling menace, which was reined back simply to contempt for the placid individuals such as Jez, whom he recognised as being harmless. Two oil-smeared henchmen cooked the breakfasts and the place was cursorily cleaned once a week. Access to the first-floor rooms came via a metal fire escape, then a murky central corridor strewn with rubbish and used syringes. Jez would take a deep breath at the top of the fire escape, then push open the usually jammed UPVC door to the inside and scuttle to his own allocated room before letting any air back into his lungs. The smell of the bedrooms alone was bad enough, but it was easier to adapt to just one assault on the senses, rather than endure the full miasmic palette of the corridor and washrooms all at the same time. Mould spread from every corner and seeped through holes in the plastic covers of the mattresses. If at all possible, Jez would have a sleeping bag with him, to protect himself from the ordure imprinted in the sheets, even if only psychologically. Bed bugs and other parasites quivered in every joint of the furniture and every gap in the tiles – he could sense their anticipation of new warm-blooded limbs to assault the moment he came to rest, like greedy shoppers waiting for stores to open before the Boxing Day sales. Animal hair added further texture to the bedclothes – dogs were forbidden, but were frequently smuggled in, scrutiny being less rigorous than at the official shelters. Nevertheless, despite the vile conditions, demand was always high – from other down-and-outs who had raised the cash to the odd misfortunate soul travelling on business, looking to save money and foolishly taking a chance on the place being habitable. As the other guests gradually took their places, bedlam would grow beyond his bedroom walls, with sounds from every angle. It was pointless wishing for quiet, Jez would simply pray for his door to remain unviolated. He listened as the cacophony ebbed and flowed, trying to identify the earliest moment where he might make a break for the toilet, or a shower if really desperate, without encountering danger.

Eventually a tide of exhaustion would override the atmosphere of dread, allowing sleep to engulf him for a while. In the morning the surge of gratitude for having survived the Viaduct once more always came as a fillip and Jez would savour whatever early morning food was served up on the basis that it was the only aspect of the whole experience that rose above the level of degrading. He would head back to his normal daytime beat, entertaining hopes of never having to return … but his reluctance to follow any available path to salvation meant the Viaduct kept luring him back.

*

The need to hit a financial target in order to afford a stay at the Viaduct was a well-established trope among the town's street dwellers. Entreaties about only needing *five more pounds for a bed*

87

tonight' knowingly played on the emotions of would-be benefactors. However, more often than not, their worst fears would be fulfilled: the money really was going to be spent on another fix. But not always … everyone's story was different. Jez steered clear of illegal substances and the money he raised was indeed for his lodgings. He lived by a mixture of the B&B, night shelters on the basis of self-referral and sleeping outside. He had not yet faced the full harshness of winter but told himself not to worry. He would take things one step at a time.

For a few weeks Jez enjoyed the luxury of a small tent, unearthed by Colin from the recycling process. After some stealthy detective work seeking out good locations, he found the ideal spot in the corner of an abandoned churchyard where the thing could be erected on even, grassy ground, veiled from prying eyes by swathes of cotoneaster and ivy. This watertight cocoon was not quite wide enough for Jez to lie fully stretched out, it was necessary to either sit cross-legged or adopt the foetal position for resting, but it acted as an effective barrier to the hazards of the outside world that he could vanish within. He welcomed the opportunity to escape the all-pervasive dampness and initially spent a few blissful nights, out of sight and free from any worries about being set upon by the wildest members of the begging community. There were always a few individuals on the beat it paid dividends to keep away from, in order to avoid being spat on, bitten or knifed. Here he was unlikely to ever come across them, hidden away in the bushes, on ground that had once been consecrated … overseen by God, albeit a God whose congregation had moved on and left the pews empty. When he realised he could pitch the tent relatively close to his pigeonhole, but in a location completely obscured from view, he felt like he had won the Lottery.

There was an innocent and gleeful excitement in sharing living space with urban wildlife, while at the same time knowing the insects, birds and small mammals rustling only inches from his face could not touch him, as he lay enwrapped in the middle of the night. Even though the synthetic fabric was a lurid pink colour the only possible human observers of his camp site were the upstairs passengers on any double-decker bus toiling around the inner ring road. The sole problem was the risk of being seen himself, as he slid between the shrubs, on entry and exit from his secret garden. He told Colin he was pitching in different regions of the park each night, not wishing to offend the supplier of his dream home by admitting to misuse of holy ground. The tent, when collapsed, was easy to carry but just too cumbersome to accompany the backpack on his regular treks around town, so Jez chose not to take it with him during the day. Unfortunately, the inevitable soon came to pass. Whether he had been spotted by one of his comrades sidling out of the churchyard he would never know … but the time came when he discovered his flimsy pink abode had gone from its hiding place, on returning one evening. Jez winced with disappointment but did not ask Colin to find a replacement. Even though his nights under canvas had been a blessed change from the communal horrors of the Viaduct, temperatures were getting cooler and chill was starting to infiltrate every joint in his body. He felt his bones might seize up completely but for the continual shivering. With heavy heart Jez had to concede he needed bricks and mortar in order to survive.

*

'Where've you been lately?'

Ginge had not seen Jez during his camping phase. One day soon after, they found themselves chatting down by the waterfront. Jez explained the story of his portable refuge and its regrettable passing. Ginge was surprised how long he had managed to keep the thing safe, before it was stolen.

'Bummer. Where are you going to go now … back to that shit hole?'

'Yep … afraid so. I don't see what else I can do.'

By convincing one of the outreach teams he was trying to go clean, Ginge had a more permanent hostel placing and rarely reverted to the B&Bs these days.

'You could always try tailgating I s'pose. Mind you … it didn't do that Pavel geezer much good, did it?'

Tailgating was the term used to describe the act of gaining access into the various blocks of flats that proliferated around the old dockside in recent years.

'*Multiple dwelling units* … that's what they call the fuckers apparently. They're really easy to get into, you just have to choose the right ones.' Ginge had considered the options extensively even if he did not have to rely upon them too often himself.

Tailgating involved sneaking through the entry-level security doors that guarded most of the area's apartment buildings, in the wake of a bona fide resident as they made their ingress legitimately, using a combination code or automatic key fob. You had to watch from the shadows until they were in, then pounce before the door became firmly bolted again. Once inside, various options presented themselves, in particular the possibility of bedding down for the night in a stairwell or underground car park. A key attraction was finding warmth. Even in the shared areas there was always an ambient heat, thanks to modern regulations about building materials and insulation. Jez and Ginge could only dream about what the actual flats were like inside.

'You can see the cunts walking around in t-shirts even in the middle of winter.' Ginge found looking through the windows from the outside especially frustrating.

Attempting to tailgate the most up-market complexes was inadvisable – the security mechanisms were more failsafe, the entrances better lit and the occupants more fastidious about watching their backs or calling the police if they suspected an unwanted intrusion. But choose one towards the cheaper end of the scale and the chances were better. The magnetic door locks took longer to re-secure themselves after opening – if they locked at all – and the tenants were less bothered about any comings and goings they saw. Jez asked Ginge to expand on his anecdote.

'Who's this Pavel then? What happened to him, Ginge?'

'Stupid Polish bastard. He tailgated his way into that Coalyard Wharf place … you know that big shitty one down towards the old power station. Got himself into the refuse room and found this old armchair that someone had chucked out. He spent a couple of nights in this chair, getting wasted on vodka until he passed out. One night a couple of kids found him. The little shits sprayed him with lighter fuel and set him on fire.' Ginge looked out across the water before continuing. 'When you're homeless nobody cares mate. Worse than shit. We're sitting fucking targets.'

'Hmm … in his case literally. Jesus Christ.'

Jez tried to get the dreadful image of what must have happened to this poor, wretched soul out of his mind and redoubled his determination to maintain a mental safety map, to avoid going through the wrong doors. He was not going to be breaking into anyone else's home. The Viaduct was execrable but at least everyone was in the same boat … on the same part of the divide … and no one was going to set you on fire, unless they were completely off their faces. Jez was not going to sleep in a refuse room. He had established a routine but was starting to wonder how to continue coping – his body was aching and the need for proper cover was becoming more pressing as the summer months slipped away.

Chapter 10

Keith's letter was so chilling, the news so grotesque, Bevan was rooted to the spot as if struck by lightning. That his mother had also gone was unthinkable. It could not be possible. He knew she had a drink problem but, it was Mum. She was worldly-wise, she always knew what to do. You cannot just die, sitting at home, due to feeling sad; moreover, you do not find out that your mum has died sitting at home by a stupid letter in the post. The abomination was compounded by the way the letter was written. He always knew Keith disliked their association but here it was starkly laid out in the supercilious tone. The fact that Keith coldly pointed out the extent of Mum's disillusionment was also sickening. If Keith had intended to make him feel guilty, it certainly had the desired effect. The positivity in which Bevan had been luxuriating evaporated on the spot. He had been so wrapped up with Fiona it had not even occurred to him to inform the family about the holiday, let alone the other bedsit dwellers in their building. He had been so stupid. Would it have made a difference if he had kept in touch more often? The tendrils of family duty had reached out again to strangle him, to take vengeance for his flight of fancy: the folly of believing he was allowed a carefree existence. Bevan was crushed by the ramifications of the piece of paper in his hand and his knees gave way under the weight.

Barbara had died during the night at approximately the same time the plane was taking off from Luton. She somehow managed to consume more than normal that evening and suffered heart failure due to acute alcohol toxicity, at the age of fifty-four. It was a warm night and she had recently taken a liking to ice in her drink. Maybe she misjudged the amount she was pouring in the glass with the ice in there as well, Bevan later wondered. Ironically there was nothing left in the bottle – on this occasion gin but she was not fussy. It had been just the right amount to kill her.

Fiona helped Bevan into their only armchair and tried her best to console him. She had lived through the bombshell of her own mother's disappearance, but no one had died then, no one shouldered any blame … it was different. She tried to convince him that it could not be his fault. But Bevan had already taken the culpability on board and locked it away. He was overtaken with remorse … and felt a macabre fascination with the contrasting nature of the two deaths – the deaths of both parents only six years apart and so different in timeline. With Bobby it was the scale of all the implications compressed into a single moment, when the car hit the tree, that gripped the heart. Everything changing in an instant, in a sudden tumultuous finale, an earthly big bang. With Barbara it was the scale of anguish over time, the slow build up to her final moment, that cried out for sorrow. Bobby was probably feeling euphoric only seconds before his demise. Barbara suffered a prolonged and miserable decline, like an aircraft with an unconscious pilot gliding grimly back to earth.

By chance they had returned from the Adriatic just in time for the funeral. Bevan's estrangement from his brother was sealed by the antagonism of the phone call once he finally managed to find the right number in an old diary.

'So you found my number. You do have some recollection of your family then?'

'Er … yes … I do have your number Keith. I can't believe it happened.' Bevan was struggling to speak.

'Well you wouldn't believe it, would you. You only ever think about yourself. In actual fact, have you ever really been part of this family at all? I wonder sometimes.'

Bevan was briefly dumbstruck. He ignored Keith's outburst and tried to think practically but was finding it hard to make sense.

'Is there going to be a …'

'Is there going to be a funeral? Funnily enough … yes, there *is* going to be a funeral. It's the day after tomorrow actually. Any danger of you finding time?'

'Of course. Yes … we'll be there.'

'*We?* … oh yes … that girl.'

They did not actually mention their mother at all. Bevan could picture exactly what had happened now, the facts spoke for themselves and he did not want to hear any more of Keith's opprobrium. He confirmed the details for the time and place and rang off. Fiona drove them across, then back again to their bedsit the same day. Fortunately, unlike Bobby's funeral, family friends came out in force and the numbers ensured Bevan's early disappearance from the wake was barely noticed. Keith was executor of the will, the house where the kids had grown up was sold and the proceeds split three ways. Bevan wondered to himself whether any of his insect traps remained in the flower beds, maybe even one with its intended prey decaying inside.

*

Bevan returned to work on the day after his mother's service at the crematorium. She had left no instructions about what she wanted done with her ashes. Why would she? She was too young – and too demoralised – to think about such things. Would she have wanted them scattered near Bobby's or as far away as possible? Six years on, was she still the woman scorned, enraged by his unfaithfulness and deceit … or had the anger faded to uncover more tender emotions of love and regret? Bevan suspected the former, but no one had thought to find out. According to Keith and Anne she had never mentioned her husband's name again. It was hard to think about her sadness but if anyone said, 'At least she's at peace now,' he wanted to karate kick them in the throat. Partly for the presumption they knew what was in his mother's soul and partly because he wanted that same peace himself now – probably more than she did. How do you cope with both parents perishing in such a short space of time, in such heart-rending fashion? He doubted whether she had deliberately tried to end it all. He guessed that her grief at the loss of her marriage and the bitter feelings of betrayal were simply bottomless ... and she had just drunk more to numb the pain, until literally having one too many. His father's demise had been such a stunning shock it was difficult to think past the accident itself, and his errant ways. Bevan never really reflected on his father's life and legacy, just the awfulness of the crash. Contrastingly, in the aftermath of his mother's funeral he got lost in contemplation about the real person she had been inside and how his own personality must have affected her. He was reminded about his sense of being different, an outsider, and Keith's stinging words did not help. He began to realise what a disappointment he must have been and recoiled at the thought of his own weaknesses causing such damage to someone who had loved him. The voices that questioned his right to be alive could be heard once more.

Fiona was concerned that Bevan had changed so much, so suddenly. She did not expect him to be full of the joys, but there was something darker about his distant looks now that made her uneasy. She got the photos developed from the holiday and they leafed through them one-by-one, hoping to be transported back in time, but the sunglasses, thumbs-ups and silly faces were of another couple altogether. The joy they had felt only a short time ago now like an apparition.

'I know it must be hard Bevs. But you've got to try to get your old self back.'

'My old self ... hmm ... I don't think you'd like that.'

'Everyone's mum and dad have to go some time ... you're not the only one it's happened to.'

He let her comment go. She did not intend to sound cruel, she was just trying to find the right words to get him back on track. She feared he might be incapable of ever getting over the upset of reading that godforsaken letter.

As time passed Bevan was more haunted by the hideous irony that his mother had possibly died at the moment of his greatest jubilation, as the jet lifted up through the clouds with Fiona by his side. What ghoulish forces were at play? He appreciated Fiona's efforts to help and he tried to become more upbeat again for her sake, but he could not shake the feeling that he had been reminded of his destiny: he was not meant to be OK.

The workload as a travelling engineer soon started to occupy his mind again and he and Fiona re-established a pattern of walks in the park and day trips at weekends. Bevan was at least glad that switching off from his brother and sister felt entirely warranted now. There was no way back from the harshness of Keith's comments. If Keith did not want him to feel part of the family, that suited Bevan perfectly. Keith and Anne had barely spoken to him at the funeral and blanked Fiona completely. How could they be so rude … what had she ever done to harm them? Fiona was still the best person he knew … she was still his rock … and, although his self-belief was undermined, he could still look ahead to their future. The subject of further holidays was parked for a while and they started to think about their next home.

*

Bevan and Fiona marked time for a few years, they were both working hard and were grateful for a stable partnership to return to in the evenings. They upgraded the bedsit to a proper flat and as their individual interests morphed, like the shifting clouds they had watched in wonder from the plane window, there remained enough overlap that they rarely fell out. Their evolving taste in food and entertainment steered similar courses so there was always something they could agree on to do. Challenges that might have put a strain on many couples were overcome effortlessly. Bevan's mobile role required a great deal of flexibility. The scheduling of work was unpredictable, and he could never guarantee what time he would get home at the end of the day. Sometimes he had to stay away for days at a time, with very little notice, when emergencies arose and other regions needed extra manpower to fix damage caused by storms or snowfall. Bevan never had to worry about icy conditions at home though, Fiona always understood.

One day the morning post included an air mail letter from the USA addressed to Fiona. Whoever was the earliest to get home –

Bevan's timings were much more variable depending on how far he had to travel – collected the mail from the doormat and sorted it into designated places at the dining table.

'What's that then … have you got a new pen friend Fee?'

'Oh it's nothing Bevs, I'll look at it later.'

Bevan was surprised she decided not to open it straight away, he was intrigued to discover who had sent it. He stared at her, hoping for clues, but her eyes had already moved on to the junk mail. Fiona was so reluctant to discuss her mother – and when she did it was always in the past tense – that he discounted the possibility of there being any connection, even though the country of origin was plain to see. Thereafter, more of the same arrived at an interval of approximately every two months, although Bevan noticed that they only seemed to appear on the days he was the first one home. Fiona squirrelled them away and declined any invitation to discuss them. He did not resent the sudden onset of correspondence from an unknown sender, that was none of his business and he trusted her implicitly. However, it was out of character for her to be secretive about anything and the mystery played on his mind.

Fiona knew, by keeping the letters to herself, it showed that her perspective on the relationship had changed since the death of Bevan's mum. She had always wanted to be open about everything with him and felt uncomfortable treating part of her life as confidential, but at the same time wanted to avoid opening another seam of problems for him to brood over. She calculated it was safer to say nothing, despite her conscience warning her that to keep anything private now was a step in a dangerous direction. The possibility of upsetting the harmony that prevailed made her scared. She was proud of how she and Bevan had defied expectations and made a go of things, even though they struck many as a rather odd couple. When their romance started Fiona was single-minded about bucking the trends in every aspect of her life. She was unconcerned what anyone might think about the way she dressed or behaved. She wanted to prove she was just as good as the boys in building a career. She was also determined not to follow the herd and seek conventionally attractive men just for the sake of her image. People pigeonholed her with the epithet 'tomboy' but that failed to do justice to her femininity; she was genuinely pretty, despite hating to be told so. Back then Fiona was an anarchic free-spirit, albeit one bewitched by machinery and having more inner nerd than appearances would suggest. Attaching herself to Bevan was just another example of her independent streak.

Fiona's desire to rescue Bevan from isolation came from an internal light she felt compelled to share. She had experienced her own misfortunes in the past and faced them down. Before meeting Bevan, she had committed to block out all the negatives and launch into life with a sunny aspect, only later to find she wanted to bring someone with her on the journey. Seven years down the line, she had no regrets about her choice of partner. She enjoyed hearing his stories from the front line – from the wild-west of the effort to keep pace with the nation's spiralling demand for electricity. The combination of need – from businesses, civil infrastructure projects and domestic households overflowing with gadgets – cried out for more power, like a nest of giant hungry chicks desperate for worms. The Electricity Board's workforce was stretched to the limit, herself included. Bevan's hours got more erratic but that was never the problem. They had always appreciated their own space and she never complained about being alone for lengthy periods. The only real drawback was that he was increasingly tired, and this was taking the edge off his good humour. She liked his understated pedantry and the dry wit he had cultivated, albeit only in her company. But he was not making her laugh so often and was becoming noticeably more irritable when he got home at night. Fiona told herself this was all just a natural part of living with someone and not to worry, but nevertheless clouds were beginning to drift across her sunny sky.

*

If Fiona was feeling disaffected, her life with Bevan was not the main reason. Her growing restlessness was much more associated with the state of her personal ambitions. She was still the same spiky girl who longed to stick two fingers up at the system and prove her worth, to spite the bastards that doubted her. The burning passion for working at the power station was starting to wane though. She questioned her goals, worn down by the male-dominated environment at the Docks. It broke her heart to admit the fact … but she felt close to throwing in the towel. Despite being extremely competent she had never been fully accepted. By standing up to the constant sexual harassment that was endemic at all levels of the Electricity Board, she stood apart. Most of the other girls turned a blind eye to it. The innuendo, the crude remarks, the expectation of a snog at works parties. 'Too dykey by half that one.' She knew that was the widespread view. 'You can spread them wide for me darling any time.' It made her sick. She loved her profession and was proud of her achievements, but her spirit was being suffocated. Fiona was craving the company of women. 'Aye, aye … we told you so!' she imagined them sniggering to themselves. Not in that way. She was craving a sense of female communion. She ran wild with fantasies of quitting the job and joining the protests at Greenham Common. She still cared about Bevan. He was not like *them*, her gravitation towards him in the first place was consistent with her non-conforming, alternative leanings and she still wanted to be with him and thrive as a pair. She needed some kind of change but was not sure exactly what and how. At the same time, the letters were also making her reassess … but did they hold the answer?

Bevan's alarm bells sounded as soon as Fiona's bubbly personality showed signs of becoming jaded. This was something he had expected from day one. As they spent more time together in the early days, the miraculous took place, as far as he was concerned … her enthusiasm for him remained constant, it never dropped off. She was always there to greet him in the morning with her vivacious smiling eyes, she was always cheerful and full of mischief. He wanted to suppose things would stay the same forever but never lost the deep-seated belief that one day she would tire of him. Her affection towards him and their mutual compatibility were so precious, surely they must also be fragile and impermanent. He chose not to spook her with constant questions about whether she was all right. Besides, he welcomed the peaceful mood that stemmed from the long silences after work, given the days he was having. However, he knew something was wrong, and he guessed what the cause must be. The atmosphere had shifted ever since those airmails started to arrive. Curiosity was getting the better of him and he convinced himself that if he could understand what they were, he would be able to restore the equilibrium. He resolved to find the right moment to investigate, sometime when he was alone in the flat – not to intrude on her privacy but to make sure there was nothing seriously wrong in her life, that he could help her get through. He had an inkling where she was hiding them. He knew she would be outraged to discover his intentions, but he would be careful to leave no trace. He just wanted to make things better again. The first opportunity materialised when Fiona announced she would be late herself one evening, due to a leaving do. Bevan's aversion to parties never left him and he rarely joined her on the occasions she felt obliged to show her face.

A lockable document holder sat on the floor on Fiona's side of the wardrobe. The securing mechanism was minimal and presented no obstacle to someone with Bevan's ingenuity. He did not want to risk any damage though and sought out the key. This was not the most impregnable location to hide her paperwork, Fiona knew that. Her confidence in it staying untouched was based on trusting Bevan never to rummage through her personal things rather than any great attempts at concealment. He found the key in the small ebony and mother-of-pearl trinket box she kept in her knicker drawer, as he expected. He felt sick to his stomach. He knew he was crossing a line in the most despicable way, repeating the sins of his father by acting behind the back of the person he was supposed to love. But if he saw what she was keeping from him, maybe he could find the answer to holding onto the love of his life. He turned the lock and eased the container open, its stiff plastic sides making a disproportionate amount of noise as they parted. He saw the bundle of letters – in greater number than he anticipated – held together by a pink elastic band. The sound of his heart pounding filled his head and he wiped the sweat from his hands to avoid leaving obvious signs behind in the wake of his crime. Before grabbing his intended quarry, his attention was diverted by a bigger bundle of leaflets in the adjacent folder.

For some time, as a result of her misgivings about work and a longing for new purpose, Fiona had been saving information about women's groups, anti-nuclear protests, domestic abuse charities and other movements that caught her eye. She had stored an assortment of material, waiting for a window of time alone to mull over what cause might re-ignite her flame. Her mind was quite open, she was not signed-up to anything in the collection yet … it was just a question of casting the net wide to see what was out there. Bevan detested politics. His deeply-held beliefs concerned the everyday: the idiocy of advertising messages that were stuffed through their door; the fact the trains were always late; the scheduling of TV programmes. He would rant amusingly about the ineptitude of local officialdom but was suspicious of political parties and their activists and spokesmen. He enjoyed dismissing them as *self-publicising arseholes*. He was aghast to discover Fiona was hoarding this type of propaganda. Was she turning into some kind of leftie? He spread them out on the floor trying to make sense of her thinking. Their life together had always been so natural and linear, they were always exercised by the same things. Had she been plotting something different all along? Bevan's imagination ran riot, he was so flummoxed by what he had found that he forgot about the letters completely. He gazed at the array of flyers that surrounded him as if they were an ominous hand of Tarot cards, with a cryptic message he was unable to fathom. Did she believe in all this now? If she wanted to become a muesli-munching radical why had she not said something?

*

The post-work drinks were an anti-climax. The leaver in question – one of the office girls who was about to have a baby – was feeling unwell so the gathering fizzled out within the hour. When Fiona got back to the flat, as she came through the door a familiar grating sound was audible from the bedroom, but she was initially unable to recall where she had heard it before. It was the document holder. Bevan had heard the front door and immediately tried to gather up the leaflets and replace them. Having secured the box he spotted with horror a pamphlet for Christian Aid still on the carpet, just as Fiona entered the room.

'What the fuck are you *DOING*?'

Fiona was so totally incandescent at the sight that beheld her, she was shrieking from the off.

'What the *FUCK* do you think you're doing?'

They both looked at each other in terror. They had never had a massive row before, but Bevan's transgression was so beyond the pale, the nuclear button had been pressed on both sides. All the trust Fiona once felt crumbled into dust. She never thought he would invade her space in this way and was overwhelmed with rage. Bevan had promised himself that the snooping would go undetected. He knew straight away the enormity of his misjudgement – he knew this was the end of his dream, the frustration amplified by the knowledge he was only attempting to achieve the exact opposite. He lacked the emotional depth to apologise or seek appeasement, his brain was locked in defence mode, he wanted to run away but was petrified in position, kneeling on the floor.

'What's all this bollocks doing here?' he said, looking up at her trying to sound indignant, as if she was in the wrong.

'Leave it alone … it's nothing to do with you. *HOW DARE YOU* go sneaking through my stuff?'

Christian Aid was probably the least likely candidate in the pile, she had only picked it up on a whim without much thought, drawn by the pitiful-looking baby on the front page. She was almost as sceptical about the 'God botherers' as he was. He knew this … but any hint of religion put him on edge, he always threw their charity collection bags straight in the bin. He could not bear the thought she held any sympathy towards them.

'Fee I love you … I never said anything about those bloody letters, though God knows what they are … but this stuff is bollocks, I don't like it … only weirdos get involved in this shit.'

'Well you should know all about that. You've always been …'

Even in the heat of argument, she did not really mean what she was about to say. She was unable to control herself and wanted to hurt him back. Bevan saw the words coming and snapped. He had always acknowledged his own weirdness but could not bear to hear it from Fiona. He pounced like a cornered cat and punched her hard on the side of the jaw. They stared at each other even more intently, even more disbelievingly, as Fiona mopped blood from her mouth. She eventually launched a series of kicks and expletives and Bevan just stood there taking them. He could not comprehend what he had just done. He sat on the bed dazed as she hastily gathered a bag of essentials, including the letters, ran from the room and slammed the door. He would never see her again.

*

A few days later she called him – very calmly – requesting a time when she could visit the flat and remove the rest of her possessions. She told no one about the incident. Her condition for not reporting Bevan to the police, or to their employer, was simply that he would guarantee to stay away from the flat for the few hours she needed to package up what was hers. She would blame her facial injury on a stray badminton racket during a doubles match. There was no question of forgiveness. Their bond was broken the moment she caught him red-handed. And while she understood it was out of character, no man would ever get away with physically assaulting her.

He felt incapable of going to work in the following days and blamed food poisoning when the controller phoned to ask his whereabouts. The thought of Fiona disclosing what happened to anyone else had not even occurred to him. He was so transfixed by the fact he had lashed out and destroyed the only good thing in his life, nothing else mattered. When he heard her voice on the phone, he was so mortified with guilt it felt like someone else was answering on his behalf. He complied with her demand for access without question and made no attempt to plead forgiveness. He knew he could never look her in the eye again anyway.

Fiona took her clothes and personal possessions but evidently had no wish to claim any of the furniture or fittings. When Bevan returned to the flat after the agreed time, superficially it looked much the same as always. He spent the next few weekends searching the entire fabric of the place, looking for clues to explain her change in outlook. He turned every drawer inside out and scoured the tops of every cupboard. He lifted the loose edges of the carpet in every room, in case any slips of paper holding crucial evidence had accidentally become lodged underneath. He racked his brain trying to think where she might have left proof behind, like a secret agent searching for listening devices, maniacally possessed to find *anything* to reveal what plans she had made and why their life together had been ruined. He found nothing. Bevan was alone, stuck in the shell of the union he had treasured so keenly, surrounded by reminders of Fiona but unable to decipher the steps leading to her departure. Her father had a form of dementia and his health was so poor Bevan normally left her to it when they visited his nursing home. 'You can leave Dad alone as well,' she had said during the telephone conversation. Bevan consented to that too, not that it struck him as likely to be fruitful anyway.

There was no one Bevan could speak to with any insight into Fiona's intentions. She resigned from the Electricity Board and effectively vanished from view, with the same stealth she had once deployed to corner him when they first met on the mini-bus seven years before. He was devastated by her loss, especially the circumstances that caused it to happen, but the *not knowing* where she had disappeared to was almost equally unbearable. He settled on the assumption that the letters were from her mother, whom she had gone to join in America – perhaps in some kind of cult, his imagination would conclude, in an attempt to post-rationalise her altered demeanour. Maybe he could come to terms with the situation if he convinced himself she had been brainwashed. It was the religious connotations of the Christian Aid leaflet that had particularly unnerved him. If he had accidentally dropped something from one of the other groups he might not have snapped. It instantly gave him visions of her turning to God and, worse, her not being truthful with him about matters of faith. She always swore to him that she too was an atheist and seeing that leaflet made him wonder what else she might have been lying about. He tried to banish the memory of hitting Fiona with the alternative reality of her as a changed person, being lured away from him for some kind of phoney spiritual awakening. He subconsciously created a false narrative in order to airbrush the truth – his own psyche involuntarily providing a structure for self-preservation, albeit a structure built on shifting sands.

*

Bevan returned to work and stumbled on for a couple of years, taking up as many maintenance jobs as he could every day. He started visiting pubs on his own for the first time, when he was not at the depot, in his van or on-site. He had his safety mechanisms – the ability to compartmentalise and block out difficult memories … but if they failed, his thoughts would rumble through the sequence of disasters: Dad, Mum and Fiona. The sudden violence of his father's death; the tragic loneliness of his mother's and his own contribution to her sense of abandonment; the halcyon days with Fiona coming to an end and the unjustified and vicious way he had attacked her. The memories rounded on him: taunting, gurning, baiting him for still being around. He speculated about whether his fatalistic feelings as a child were an omen for the calamities to come … or had he just been unlucky? Had he brought it on himself by being so introspective? What was the point of a life so tortured, so blighted? Bevan's paranoia was exacerbated a few months after Fiona disappeared when he noticed some large withdrawals from their joint bank account. He had not thought to close it down and now his earnings were being stolen, on top of everything else. He refused to blame her, directing his condemnation towards the unseen forces she had fallen in with, but nevertheless swiftly moved his money elsewhere. That was below the belt, a reminder that people were out there in the world who wanted him to suffer. He was running out of reasons to participate in each day that dawned and however hard he tried to seek solace, none could be found, every avenue in his mind was a dead end. Bevan was dashed against the rocks, his enthusiasm cast to the wind. He could see no purpose in trying any more, everything he touched turned to junk, no course of action remained with any likelihood of being productive … until at last the penny dropped:

he knew enough to end his own life and break the cycle of desolation for good. Finally, he had divined the one last cause he could pursue with heart and soul.

As soon as Bevan decided to kill himself, he immediately felt soothed. Why had he not thought of this before? Alcohol had killed his mother; he could follow in her footsteps. He was determined not to take any risks though, failure would be yet another catastrophe, there would be no half measures. Successful suicides and unnecessary early deaths of celebrities always seemed to be attributable to a *drink and drugs cocktail*. Belt and braces. This was obviously the way forward.

Bevan took to planning his escape from the torments of walking the earth with the same zeal he had once applied to catching insects in the garden. He read about the doses required for various chemicals to be lethal. He wanted to proceed unsuspected, therefore prescription medicines were off limits. Paracetamol felt like a suitable choice, its everyday nature appealed to his preference for understatement. He convinced himself of the number that should do the job and doubled it. He bought several boxes one evening, from a series of different supermarkets and convenience stores, delighting in the frisson of subterfuge as he paid the cashier each time – if only they knew his reasons, he thought conspiratorially to himself. He worried about the act of swallowing the pills though. If he took them one at a time, what if the effects started to tranquilise him before consuming a sufficient number? His solution was to grind them up into a powder and suspend them in liquid. That way he could just down a bottle in one go, and oh, it would be the most celebratory bottle he had ever swigged. Even having all the materials in place, he still waited for a night of favourable climate, such that his last moments would not be uncomfortable. A perfect example soon arrived and Bevan set foot from home, heading for a country park on the edge of town. A mild wind blew from the south and patchwork clouds were scudding swiftly across a full moon sky, making light and shadow dance on the streets and trees. He wanted to enjoy that final walk. The sound of the wind became his heavenly chorus. He rejoiced from his deepest core that finally he could retreat, unfurl the white flag and be released from his perpetual hell. If only he could sing it out loud. After an hour he reached an ideal spot. He wanted to die in the open air, but away from any chance of discovery, in case the evils of modern healthcare were able to revive him at the last gasp. He traipsed into a dense thicket, found a comfy-looking patch, cushioned by leaf mould and sat himself down. His heart pounded as strongly as when he broke into Fiona's papers, but now with exaltation. The ground seemed to sway … the absolute certain knowledge that he would never wake to see another day was the most joyous sensation he had ever experienced, and he laughed out loud, like a lost explorer finding water in the desert after days of burning heat. The ground-up tablets still had a few solid chunks – he had mixed the blessed aggregate in water, with some Ribena to take the taste away – and as he shook the bottle it made a soft rattling sound. He imagined it as a maraca, for once he was in party mood and at the height of his reverie the contents were downed. Then the *pièce de résistance* … he also had a half bottle of brandy in his coat pocket. Belt and braces. Delivering his own *coup de grâce* – he was being silly now, thinking in florid language, drunk with joy – the alcohol surely would compound the effect of the drug and hasten his unconscious dying breath. His father had died with brandy in his system, the symmetry granted an additional satisfying dimension to proceedings. Bevan drank from his second bottle. He paused to see if he could feel anything happening. Apart from the acrid taste at the back of his mouth there was nothing so far. He took more brandy and closed his eyes, hoping for one last sleep to envelope him. After several more mouthfuls eventually that familiar feeling of rolling eyes and weightlessness. *Here I come … it's over … oh, thank goodness.* Bevan's body slumped into the leaves.

*

When he came to, Bevan had a brief flash of deliberation about whether or not he felt dead, but any cogent thinking was immediately unplugged as his head began to spin like a fairground Waltzer. Another familiar feeling. From lying on his back, he managed to lift himself onto his elbows before the sickness came. He started to regurgitate in waves. Turning to his side the contents of his stomach continued to disgorge themselves until he was left panting, his last memory – the acrid taste of the brandy in his throat – now replaced by acid that scolded him. Is this what happens when you die? He clung to that thought as his senses rearranged. He was now crouching on the ground, surrounded by the trees in near darkness. The branches still bustled noisily in the breeze. Bevan waited and waited desperate to collapse again, desperate for a sign that his plan had worked. But the only sensations he could perceive from his body were the anger and sadness of a drunkard, once the merriment has gone. He kneeled amongst the debris of the forest floor and sobbed.

Bevan sobbed so wretchedly his head started to hurt. This was ironic under the circumstances, considering the quantity of painkillers he had consumed – and as soon as he became aware of that devilish thought forming in his brain, he knew the game was up. Bevan remained alive – his mental functions were still bubbling away – but he did not understand how. When ultimately deducing that nothing further was going to happen, Bevan reluctantly hauled himself up. He used leaves to brush away the worst of the vomit from his clothes. He hurled the two empty bottles into the darkness with a despairing wail and trudged back to the path. Before he could reach the park entrance he was once more overtaken by tiredness and he lay on the grass to sleep. He knew it was just sleep, he had lost all hope for anything more. A woman out walking her two huskies just after midnight – they were not yet socialised with other dogs, so she exercised them when the park was deserted – found Bevan in his resting place. Having established he was breathing, she scurried home and called an ambulance. Bevan was plucked from the field by paramedics and conveyed to hospital for assessment. He was speaking by the time they arrived and ashamedly confessed his foolishness to the night shift. The fact of his failure was bad enough but now having to recount it to wearied professionals with more deserving cases to attend to made him flinch with embarrassment. They pumped his stomach and placed him in a side room awaiting the police. They told him he had probably vomited in time to avoid absorbing enough paracetamol to damage his liver, and they spared him the lecture on what a stupid choice it had been in the first place due to the unpredictable and slow-acting nature of the effects, in case it gave him ideas for the future. They scheduled him some counselling and a nurse was stationed to keep watch. When the police came, Bevan claimed he had no next of kin, but they insisted on searching his flat anyway in case there were dangerous substances lying around. They found Keith's letter, which Bevan kept in a drawer by the desk as a totem, then dug further until they unearthed a phone number. The junior constable made the call and informed Keith of his brother's predicament. The response was a curt: 'I see. Thank you', then Keith rang off. The nadir was reached: Bevan's suicide attempt had failed in the most humiliating manner possible and now the people he least wanted to see knew all about it.

Chapter 11

Bevan was kept in hospital for a second night, waiting for a duty psychologist to become available for the mandatory counselling. He was in auto-pilot mode again once she arrived by his bed to tip-toe through her routine checklist of questions.

'So tell me … how are you feeling now?'

'Guilty … I just feel very guilty for wasting so many people's time … I don't know what I was thinking … I wish I could turn back the clock.'

'What was going on that became so impossible to live with? Was it work … relationships … illness?'

'Everything just piled up at once … it was too much … sorry, it won't happen again, please don't worry, I'll be fine from now on, honestly, there's no need to worry about me.' Then he added 'I haven't gone mad, honestly.'

His answers were robotic and superficial. He was not going to let the shrink anywhere near the real emotions he was feeling, guessing that major alarm bells would ring if he revealed just how calm and composed he had been throughout what should have been his final hours – and how bitterly disappointed he was now, given that his objective had not been achieved. They probably thought he had lost control of his actions, whereas nothing could be further from the truth. He was fully in command and thinking with perfect clarity on the previous night. His problem was a mis-reading of pharmacological reference material in the research he had undertaken. He wanted to die, he formulated a plan, he thought it was going to happen ... but he cocked it up.

The conviction behind his words 'it won't happen again' was half-hearted when spoken to the medical staff but hardened when his siblings arrived later that day once visiting hours began. The humiliation of his incapacity to contend with life, combined with exposure of his botched efforts to bring about its ending, made him squirm inside like a salted snail. Bevan did not want Keith and Anne to see him at all. Considering their attitude when they had last met face-to-face – holding paper plates of finger food, surrounded by friends of their dead mother at the wake – he shuddered to think what they might be moved to say to him now, as he lay in a hospital bed with a tag around his wrist, in a gown still marked with stains from the charcoal used to pump his stomach. He stammered through their disbelieving questions, delivered intermittently like rounds of sniper fire.

'So, it was all getting a bit much then?' offered Keith, barely allowing any gap between his clenched teeth.

'I guess ... um ... I guess I lost my way a bit, yes. I really didn't want to cause trouble for anyone.'

Keith and Anne raised their eyebrows at each other at Bevan's apologetic turn. As if to say: *if only he could realise just how much they had swallowed their pride to turn up at this depressing place*. His gaze was fixed on the foot of the bed; his visitors formed a jury of two, on plastic chairs to one side, their backs pressing against the curtain. After some silence Anne spoke.

'Was it ... Fiona? That was her name wasn't it?'

'Er ... yes ... that's right ... Fiona was her name. She's not here anymore.'

The look in Bevan's eyes made clear this was not a subject for discussion. Anne waited for the tension to abate before changing tack.

'Can't you manage to just soldier on? Is it really so difficult?'

She was trying to be encouraging but it sounded like a criticism. He ignored her and the intimation that everyone has problems, and that he simply should have been stronger. She had thought about saying *you should have turned to us before, if you were feeling this bad* but it would not have rung true. Bevan knew she resented being there and continued to look straight ahead.

'Well ... please don't do this again. You *mustn't*,' said Anne after another pause. Noticing that Keith was looking at his watch, she felt a pang of guilt. They had swapped notes before coming into the ward.

'Well ... I suppose we're going to have to keep an eye on you for a while. To make sure you *don't* do it again.'

'It won't happen again. Don't worry.'

Bevan knew this was true ... never again could his troubles be allowed to overspill like this, but he did not sound convincing.

'Come and stay with us for a few days. Just until you get your senses back.'

Anne was warming to her task now, visualising herself doing a charitable thing despite instinctively not wanting to, as if bathing the feet of a leper. Keith knew something like this was coming and was primed to nod approval, making abrupt affirmative humming noises through pursed lips while turning his head back and forth between the other two. Bevan shrunk further into horror at the suggestion they should look after him, but equally he found it difficult to contemplate returning to his flat, presumably still bearing the evidence of his doomed endeavour. The empty blister packs and boxes on the counter. The residue of powder where he had bashed the pills with a rolling pin on a chopping board, then dispensed the grounds using a funnel made from a Chinese take-away menu. The Ribena bottle. He pictured the rolling eyes of the policemen as they surveyed the pathetic scene. He did not want to be back in that space again, where escape from his misfit existence had been so close to his grasp; not yet anyway. The offers of refuge from his brother and sister emerged as the lesser of two evils and he succumbed to the idea, knowing full well that their sanctimoniousness would reach a level that would drive him away again before too long. Upon discharge he was ferried to Anne's house and billeted in the spare room, where he tried to pass the time behaving as normally as he knew how, repeating the mantra of *It won't happen again* until he felt they believed him.

The trip back to the estates of his youth began with a quick detour. Bevan needed to gather some clothes, hence the challenge of revisiting the scene of his crime could not be avoided. He did not need much. He was determined not to idle for too many days, with nothing to do apart from agonise over his fate and strain every brain cell to forget what happened – he needed to get busy again quickly. They stopped at the flat en route from the hospital. Anne accompanied him and reluctantly offered to tidy the kitchen before he came in, suspending her own dismay at what she saw, as might a plumber when clearing a blocked drain. Once she gave the nod he skulked inside and hastily packed a bag, pausing to phone the controller to relay hurried excuses about needing time off for an unexpected domestic emergency. His colleagues knew Bevan had been under a cloud since Fiona left and had seen something like this coming, although they were unable to coax any details out of him. The trio then retraced the miles Bevan had last covered on the way to their mother's funeral – back to their shared past of unspoken antipathy.

Bevan spent his time reading the papers, watching TV, going for walks and pretending to be at peace. Keith popped round when he could, but little was said. Any intent to address Bevan's underlying demons had been exhausted at the hospital, now the exchanges reverted to small talk. He saw out his sentence as a temporary lodger, showing penitence for the upheaval he had caused – then, as the measure of shock subsided, the compulsion to work asserted itself and he was drawn back to the solitary world of his flat, the ship he had tried to jump. Keith felt obliged to volunteer as taxi driver for the return leg and the passage unfolded in silence, concluding with awkward farewells and the pledge to reconvene at Christmas. Bevan returned to the battlefield, albeit as a broken man. The proposal of a non-mobile role in the depot soon followed. Bevan had been changed by events in the sense that his bubbling torments were partly sealed over now, like the vent of a volcano plugged by setting lava. The part of his brain responsible for looking forward and indulging hopeful dreams had been switched off. He was not mad, but he now held his emotions in a straitjacket. Ultimately, this was the one lasting repercussion from that night-time walk into the woods.

Bevan took up the suggested desk job and rapidly became grateful for the stability it provided. It was the late eighties and rumours about the possible consequences of privatisation were flying everywhere. The National Electricity Board was eventually broken up and the workforce dealing with core infrastructure was migrated into the new Allied Grids organisation in 1991. The depot was a much safer vessel in which to ride out this storm than the engineer gangs proved to be, and the transition was relatively painless for the stores team. Bevan spent these years establishing his new routine, while adapting to life on his own, apart from the winter breaks with his brother and sister. He had always felt alone, but in physical terms this was his first real experience of solo living. He had gone from the family home to Sebastopol Road and from there to co-habiting with Fiona. Only since the moment she slammed the door on him had he been the sole occupant of any residence. He hated living with the reminders of the times they shared together and the violence of their parting. The drawers that were hers remained empty. He had never properly restored the carpet edges from his fevered attempts to uncover clues to her whereabouts and now the threads kept snagging under the hoover. A year after the suicide debacle he moved to a different flat, further from the Docks with a view across the town – not that he had much time to take it in, being nearly always at the office.

Since his embryonic days as an apprentice Bevan locked into his work with a tunnel vision similar to the obsessive way he tackled mini-projects in his bedroom as a child. His absorption into the intricacies of stores control followed the same pattern, only now he was much freer from distraction. Back in his junior engineering days the periods of dedicated concentration were punctuated by travelling to and from job locations and the vulgarity of the depot coffee room where field guys would congregate between assignments. He endured the ensemble horseplay of these inter-ludes with a nervous smile, always itching to get back on the road, or back to his girl.

'Oi, oi! Bevsie's back already. You must drive that van like James bleedin' Hunt mate.'

'Ha ha … no … it was an easy job.'

'They're all easy to you. In and out like Bevsie bleedin' Gon-zalez.'

'Bevsie … you coming to the Tuns later?'

'Er … no … not tonight, sorry … I need to get home.'

'Yeah, he needs to get home to his boyfriend, I mean girl-friend. It's Scalextric night.'

'Oi … be careful Bevsie … try not to keep slipping out of her slot.'

He might think of a suitably crude riposte on his way home, but it was too late by then. He would slink away as quickly as pos-sible, with a 'See you tomorrow boys.' He knew the mickey-taking was good natured but he wished they would stop. No doubt their ridicule got worse after he made his exit. Bevan pictured them doubled-up, convinced he did not get their jokes. He did … usu-ally. He thought he did anyway, but could never be 100% sure, as the words tumbled around long after the laughter had stopped.

While he was still in training – before Fiona blasted her way into his consciousness – Bevan handled the low-key socialising with his housemates but never made human connections of any substance. Once Fiona had swept him up, there was no longer any need to worry about acting the part as one of the lads. His evening and weekend time were inundated by his new and most adored companion. But both before and during his involvement with her, he floundered at developing meaningful friendships with the other engineers during the working day, even though he did join some of the sessions in the Three Tuns or one of the other local booz-ers. He only felt confident with tools in hand, when the conversa-tions had to stop.

Bevan had always admired – been awestruck by – people who were prepared to be different. Fiona had been the perfect example. Those who could adopt a position apart from the crowd: whether it be their personal appearance, political belief, musical taste or mode of living. That seemingly total lack of fear in relation to the attitudes and prejudices of the majority, that stillness of soul, were things he desperately craved, yet knew were beyond his reach. As he passed through life, day by day, he would imagine countless critical thoughts about him popping in the minds of every person he encountered. He replayed them over and over. He felt perpetually judged, his soul was never still. During training the other recruits thought he was boring. Once qualified as a fitter, the other engineers thought he was soft. Members of the public he had to deal with thought he was creepy. Any looks of disapproval were, in truth, much more likely to be caused by the person concerned having a bad day, or suffering a twinge from a dodgy back, but he read every facial inflection as contempt upon himself. He made up his mind before anyone had a chance to speak. The teasing in the coffee room made him cringe and the voices taunted him afterwards for days, when he was alone. These fears had been held at bay when Fiona was about but as soon as she was gone, they scampered back to him, jumping and yelping like a litter of puppies. Fiona had unknowingly acted as a force field, protecting Bevan from his own self-defeating hang-ups and in her absence, they started to circle around him again as if seeking revenge. They had nearly hounded him to death but now, somehow, he had to find a way to quell them. He chose not to try re-establishing any links with the Sebastopol Road boys; it had been too long, and they had stopped sending messages about meeting up some time ago anyway, but his fondness for beer remained and he now found the wherewithal to visit pubs on his own without feeling awkward.

From the new flat there was no shortage of watering holes for Bevan to frequent. He could count at least ten from his window. There was rarely enough time to go on weekday evenings but catching up with the news over several pints became a weekend ritual. The papers gave him cover, to make himself appear occupied and discourage the notion he was looking for company. If boredom crept in, he could sometimes regress to become one of those archetypal characters, languishing bereft in a corner – he saw them all the time – the sad-looking loner, gazing into a near-empty glass, apparently lost in thought and detached from the universe. He had often considered, on seeing a man or woman alone in a bar, red-faced and pock-marked, with an expression etched by tragedy, the tendency was to generalise. The obvious explanation being that they were drinking blindly, simply to hide the pain of losing an irreplaceable wife or husband. But in reality, there was probably a more nuanced thought process going on than most observers assumed. They were perhaps more likely to be churning away at a tiny specific detail, not just blankly regretting the departure of a loved one. Bevan's own ruminations revolved around how his bond with Fiona had turned sour, but he was not focusing on the basic fact of their parting, he delved into the minutiae. If he had thought to call his Mother from the airport before going on holiday, maybe she would still be alive and therefore maybe the mood in his relationship with Fiona would not have shifted so crucially. If he had refrained from using the word 'weirdos' when confronted by Fiona's rage, she would not have picked up on it, and he probably would not have snapped in response; maybe they could have resolved the drama somehow, maybe she might have stayed. If the final leaflet on the floor had been something else, like Rape Crisis rather than Christian Aid, he would have been perplexed to a similar degree, but maybe he would have just been speechless instead of hostile. He walked through every possible scenario trying to imagine an alternative course of events whereby they could still be together. But it was all futile because he always sensed at the back of his mind that one day she would get fed up with him anyway. Still … he also spent time brooding over who those letters were from and what they meant to her.

The other labyrinth of what-ifs that consumed his attention during his solo drinking sessions concerned his father's infidelity and untimely end. Bevan was stoically unsentimental, even in the tenderest moments with Fiona, but he understood more about romantic love now than he had done aged eighteen. Looking back, he had come to terms with the circumstances of Bobby's death to a certain extent. He recoiled to think about his Mum's feelings of betrayal but equally he could understand the exhilaration in the calculated risk and reward of an extra-marital affair, however unforgiveable. He wondered how many times they had been to Maison Rouge, how many times Sandra had driven them along that road after dark. Was their passion still fresh, was the atmosphere charged with soon-to-be consummated desire? Or were they jaded lovers in the final embers of their adventure? Bevan conjured poignant images of their final meal. The candles, the menu, the liqueurs, the after-dinner mints. Were they laughing or fractious as the bill was paid? What was the nature of the fatal distraction ... crossed words, a heated exchange, a passing fox, a hand up the skirt? Again, he subjected the plot to endless re-writes trying to conceive the tiniest deviation that might have changed the outcome. Maybe without the crash – if the fox had not stepped across the road – the dalliance might have fizzled out, run its course, and with the excitement out of his system Dad might have kept his secret, settled down and strayed no more. Maybe his parents could have been happy. And maybe Fiona could still have been his, maybe she might have stayed.

If he caught his reflection in the pub window and noticed what he was turning into, he would give a shake and return to the paper. He did not want to be one of those types, not least because he did not want people to watch him and make judgements from across the room.

*

Bevan at least could acknowledge one discernible aspect of progress, inherited from his days with Fiona. He had to admit he was slightly more comfortable talking with the folk in the office than he might once have been, before knowing her. He mused on the possibility that we are not solely ourselves – rather, we are partly the product of our interactions with other people. Fiona had disarmed his natural reticence and compelled him to have conversations with her, with a frequency he never thought possible. Her influence had encouraged new neural pathways to open up, making him able to articulate sides of himself that had never been expressed before, like new routes to the Indies discovered by a pioneering seafarer. His confidence had taken a major setback with her leaving but there was still something there, perhaps the only trace she had left behind at all: he was not quite so hopeless at speaking up. Not quite as hopeless as before anyway.

That is not to say Bevan was suddenly a talkative soul. Rather, he found a capacity to develop a discussion, one-on-one, with others in the office if he allowed himself time to gather his thoughts. The formality of being sat at desks helped create a structure for the exchange of comments, unlike the free-for-all of the engineers' bunker. If someone wanted to engage him it would usually be prefaced with, 'er … Bevsie?' by way of introduction, especially since he was stationed facing a wall and they generally preferred not to startle him. If the question was about work, he could reply without being stressed – and this was the essential nature of the change he noticed, nothing more. He had gained the ability to remain composed when talking about subjects inside his comfort zone. This was something new. If the question related to an issue outside work the uneasiness lingered and his responses were likely to be more random. Bevan's co-workers soon understood that any enquiry concerning Fiona or his family – not to mention any probes about *how he was feeling* – were met with a haunted look and a dismissive, 'I can't complain' that closed the discourse. Everyone knew about his father; the accident had been in the papers. They knew his mother had died too, but were unaware of the circumstances, although there were plenty of rumours. Most of them had known, or been aware of, Fiona but no one knew the reasons for her resignation and rapid disappearance. The general consensus was that Bevan was such a miserable bugger it was surprising she stuck with him for as long as she did, but that view was never given voice when he was in earshot. As for trying to kill himself … Bevan was profoundly indebted to the police who resisted the temptation to release any details to the press. He guessed they had some unwritten rule to prevent that, to avoid further anguish being piled on top of the foolish sods that had not got the balls to go on living – not out of compassion, but for the time and resources saved in not having to fish them out again the following week. If the staff at Allied Grids knew what he had done, psychologically he would have been snookered – that would have been impossible for him to face down.

As Bevan was finding his feet in the stores, Martin had recently taken the reins and his management style took some adjusting to. Martin came as a stark contrast to the engineering controllers, who were all of a type: men who took the manner of frustrated sergeant-major on the parade ground, or sadistic P.E. teacher bitter about a sporting career curtailed by injury. They dispensed schedules to the fitters with an air of casual bullying and had a relentless line in derision for anyone naive enough to suggest alterations to the given itinerary. It was taken as gospel that the oiks under their stewardship would not get anything done unless bestowed with strict boundaries, discipline and sarcasm. Bevan expected the same from Martin and was initially disarmed by his more human, collegiate approach. He appreciated the way his new boss recognised his strengths, sought to make use of them for the collective good and seemingly had no intention of trying to expose his weaknesses or change his personality. When Martin encouraged him to pursue IT skills, Bevan was extremely thankful, albeit he never found a moment to say so. That he would proceed to be responsible for one of the company's computer systems was beyond Bevan's wildest comprehension when he first landed in the stores team. By the time CRUSOE was launched the turbulent days of Bevan's early career had partly faded from recollection, although scars remained.

Bevan's rock-bottom, his point of no return – when self-inflicted poison presented itself as the most logical next step – had occurred in 1987, almost two years after Fiona walked away. He had been patched together again by a combination of the measured, yet finite, compassion of his nearest kin, and the good fortune of the vacancy appearing within Martin's body of men and women at the perfect time. Bevan's faculty for blocking out memories also helped. He survived the sweep of privatisation and began to forge his niche in the depot. His interest in computers gave him something to occupy his mind in the same way reference books and lists had done once before, when he was a child. The fact he could bring this enthusiasm to bear in the workplace was a positive boon to his sense of worth, culminating with the birth of CRUSOE in 1995, at which even Bevan allowed himself a glimmer of satisfaction, if not a buzz on the scale of his moonlit walk to the park eight years before. Building something his colleagues were willing to adopt without sneering felt like a genuine triumph.

The resurrection of his ties with Keith and Anne was disconcerting and the yearly December reunions increasingly played on his mind. As a modicum of self-assurance grew, fed by his minor professional successes, Bevan eventually mustered the will to break the pattern. He excused himself from the annual get togethers in 1998, never to see his brother and sister again, much to the relief of everyone concerned. The end of the millennium found him on a relatively even keel ... enthused even, at the prospect of witnessing the date digits rolling over to three zeroes. While it would be a stretch to describe Bevan as happy, the worst things that could possibly happen were now in the past and he had reason to expect the rest of his adult life to be relatively peaceful. These were not hopeful dreams, merely a yearning for an end to misfortune. Maybe the year 2000 would herald a change in his lot. Maybe the company might want to invest in his system and expand it. Maybe, maybe ... The nature of Bevan's meditations when searching for signs in his pint glass had at least become less moribund than a decade before. Nevertheless, given a choice, he still wished for eternal sleep in the leaf mould, as long as he could never be found ... and he wished he could know what the letters were about.

Chapter 12

When Jez first fell into living rough, he had no illusions about it being a rational lifestyle choice, it was simply a last resort. But if challenged, he might have revealed vague romantic notions about the nature of the deal. He knew very well that the sight of beggars on the pavement offended the sensibilities of most normal people but, at the same time, he assumed that a degree of resigned acceptance prevailed – that his predicament would be viewed as an unavoidable side-effect of the way civilisation works, like taxes and queueing in the post office. He pictured the scattering of rootless folk, living on the wing, as a timeless sub-culture that society had become accustomed to. He expected people's standard reaction would either be a blind eye, or a wish to give a helping hand, when coming face-to-face with those off the bottom of the scale, those who own absolutely nothing. Mostly he expected to be left alone. Therefore, he was surprised to discover there were forces at work, intent on making him seek an alternative path, that emerged from nowhere the moment he sat down outside. He could not see what harm he was doing to anyone else, apart from adding minor extra untidiness to the townscape. Which was ironic, since any untidiness he might be responsible for was nothing compared to the mountains of clutter generated by local shops and businesses, without any signs of them being hounded by the police about it.

In his first week Jez was approached by one pair of community police officers and three different members of the council-sponsored, homeless-engagement outreach team. Colin pounced on him in week two. On each occasion his message to them was the same: he was fine, he would not cause a nuisance and did not need any help. He would humour their efforts to take him under their wing, agreeing to a series of assessment appointments that he had no intention of attending. He already understood his needs very well and was blessed with an early stroke of good fortune. Having settled into his pigeonhole and projecting an air of good manners by calmly reading his book, people began to give him donations from the off, without any great conscious effort on his part to encourage them. Almost by accident he instigated a revenue stream from the beginning – far sooner than most others did in his situation, he was later to discover. It had never occurred to him that many fellow derelicts were actually receiving state benefits and chose not to ask strangers for money at all. The police encounter was most informative.

'Good morning sir. I see you have found yourself a cosy little spot. Just so you know … you can't just sit anywhere you like, harassing members of the public for their hard-earned cash,' explained the officer, in a stultified monotone.

'I'm not going to harass anyone. I'm just minding my own business … reading my book, see …' Jez showed her the cover.

'That's all well and good … but it's important you *do* mind your own business, sir. Begging for money is an offence. We are required by law to stop you. You may end up in custody and receive a penalty fine. Just make sure you don't upset anyone, do you understand?'

'Yes officer. Thank you.'

Jez took the inference they would leave him alone as long as he refrained from anti social pestering and so it proved. His subliminal methods caused no one to raise a complaint and the constabulary would simply nod dutifully whenever they saw him thereafter and occasionally ask after his wellbeing. Eventually he even stopped hiding his collection pot. Overt consumption of alcohol was also forbidden, although Jez often wondered how the masses he saw daily quaffing pints of craft ale and sickly-looking cocktails in the open air sections of the nearby hostelries, got away with it, but still.

'If you are caught consuming alcohol in a public space, you will be stopped and moved along, sir. Also, the contents of your can, or bottle, or whatever it is … will be poured down the drain.'

Jez wanted to say *yeah, right … unless you are well-dressed, covered in fake tan and your glass is half-full of fruit and vegetables, in which case it's OK*, but thought better of it. More pressing targets for law enforcement were the 'professional beggars' who stalked the main shopping streets every day. Persistent and aggressive racketeers who pleaded for money from anyone foolish enough to slow down in their path and raise their stare from the pavement at the wrong moment; these operators could all afford a roof over their heads. Armed with well-rehearsed script and urgent, imploring eyes they were a menace to everyone. Jez baulked at the word 'professional'; to him that added an unwarranted veneer of respectability, as if they were revered practitioners worthy of a trade association, an annual conference and letters after their name. He soon came to resent their existence, they were nothing more than petty thieves, giving a bad name to those most in need and he was glad the powers that be wanted to run them out of town.

*

Generally, Jez avoided the haunts of the hard core. By custom, all the demons, all the lords and ladies of misrule, would circle and weave to create their sinister milieu around the edge of the central precinct area each evening, as darkness crept in. An outsider would be oblivious to which of the actors in this diabolical scene were the kingpins – the malefactors preying on the misfortune of others – and which were the pawns. Some were drawn in by the opportunities to steal, some by the sheer fascination of being witness to whatever indiscretions went down that night. In particular, it was necessary to stay connected to the crowd to know where the dealers would be dropping next, especially for those without mobile devices and social media accounts. Jez rarely ventured this way. The first time he did was terrifying. While it may be the case that outsiders were unable to decode the archetypes within the general group of characters that hung around after the shops closed, the players themselves saw through you in an instant. Jez was exploring, looking for the best place to buy cheap spirits. As he turned the corner into the warren of bus stops behind the main stores – where the overhang acts as a dormitory for a large chunk of rough sleepers, nestled amongst the refuse bins and crates of recycled carrier bags and cardboard boxes – a silent exclamation froze the air. He felt a hundred eyes watching, a hundred more unseen in the shadows. They knew who he was, they knew he operated alone … and they knew this was not his patch. Jez reversed his steps and headed in the opposite direction, hoping to be ignored and trying not to panic. Just before allowing another breath back into his lungs, a snaking arm leapt from the darkness of the pavement, pincered around his neck and dragged him towards the wall. The voice came from nowhere, rasping and reeking of ungodly fumes. 'You had a good day today professor? Eh? Have you? Where's your money? Give us it.' Jez did have some cash, but it was buried deep in his backpack and he was too paralysed by fright to delve inside. He managed to tremble 'I have nothing … honestly I …' but was slammed against a metal fire-exit door before he could finish. Now a hand gripped his throat. 'If I find you here again … I'll know you wanna work for me yeah?' The dank voice spattered his face, but he was too petrified to see its source. 'Ha … but you're too fucking old to be any use. Why don't you fuck off?' With that, Jez was pushed hard against the door again then dropped. As he gathered his senses, the assailant loped back into the underworld.

Once more, Jez realised this was just a warning shot. By both police and criminal gangs alike, his boundaries were being drawn. He gave a wide berth to the central precinct from that point on, his aversion magnified by the fact it was also home to the Housing Action Now head office. Housing Action was a charitable body, working in partnership with the NHS and local council to provide a safety net protecting anyone from repeated nights outside. Its outreach teams were the front line in fulfilling government soundbites about the eradication of homelessness. He had been noticed straight away – Jez was spooked by this, being unaware of the network of spotters – and when they descended upon him, he half expected to be ringed, like a rare migratory bird. He did not want their attention but soon came to acknowledge the value of their speedy interventions once they had explained the life expectancy associated with sleeping rough. But that was for others; he knew what he was doing. He listened to the doctrine and when they insisted he attended a 'needs appraisal' meeting he agreed, but only to make them go away. Jez had no intention of having his case reviewed. He wanted to go his own way for as long as possible. After three missed appointments at the Housing Action office their attitude became more forceful. The next time they caught up with him, one of the more timorous volunteers was accompanied by Hazel, the outreach supervisor. Hazel bustled like a pitbull and was hardened to get her own way.

'You're actually being selfish Jez, you know.' Hazel's suit was too tight fitting to allow her to crouch so she stood over Jez, leaning forward like an anglepoise lamp, with one hand on the wall.

'I'm just happy to be left alone. I'm not causing any trouble.' Jez felt the admonishment in her voice and shifted uncomfortably on the ground. He could tell Hazel was a force to be reckoned with – he wanted to curl up like a hedgehog until she ran out of steam.

'You're wrong Jez. You're being selfish. You can sit here, reading your books, letting the middle classes ease their conscience by dropping you a few pound coins here and a few cappuccinos there, that's all very fine for you. But … what you're actually doing is perpetuating the cycle that draws people onto the streets, do you know that? You're collecting money Jez … but you *do* realise we constantly advise people not to give, don't you?' Jez remained mute. He wanted to say, *it's up to us what we spend our money on … and if people want to give … it's up to them*, but kept it to himself.

'Housing Action is *always* campaigning to stop the public giving money to people on the street like you. Do you want to know why?'

'I don't do drugs, if that's what you mean.'

'That's not the point Jez. Do you want to know how many young people – people under the age of twenty-five – have died of overdoses because they get enough money during the day to wipe themselves out? Because of everyone's so-called *compassion* they can disappear from their safe housing and get wasted every night.' Hazel emphasised '*compassion*' with exaggerated hand gestures. 'Who do you think you are Jez? Some kind of gentleman vagabond? The lovable tinker, living the dream ... the romance of the road and the open air? It's all bullshit. You shouldn't be here Jez. You will end up suffering harm ... and you're harming others as well. Are you going to carry on being this selfish or will you let us find a way to get you housed?'

She stared at him fiercely, but Jez continued to put up barriers. Hazel's words were searing but he knew it would be impossible to face the inquisition that would ensue if he cooperated. He could imagine their decision trees, their multiple-choice questionnaires, categorising his weaknesses through structured interrogation, putting him into the right compartment. He was not mentally ill. He just needed some peace. If young people needed help, he could talk to them. He would do his bit. Finally, he spoke.

'I won't be here forever. This is what I need now. I'm grateful for your help but I'll be fine honestly.'

'You won't survive like this. We see it all the time Jez. Sort yourself out and come to the office.'

Hazel did not have time to negotiate all day, there were too many other people to see, so reluctantly she had to retreat. She knew he would not come. His mind was locked – for whatever reason – and he was incapable of listening to sense. Tragically the longer the likes of Jez stayed outside the system the more entrenched their perspective became. She prayed that when his health started to fail he would see things differently, before it was too late ... and she prayed he would continue to stay clear of drugs.

*

There were, in fact, not many people left like Jez. He was something of an anomaly, with his principles and restraint. But the winters had not got to him yet, he could cling to his ideals and remain aloof. He was horrified and bemused by the drug-taking and was adamant about not getting pulled into it, not willingly at least. His only real insight came from his conversations with Colin and Ginge. He knew only too well the unearthly din, the shrieking, the caterwauling, he would hear through the doors of the Viaduct in the middle of the night. He realised this was the sound of the inhabitants getting high but was unschooled in the details – *why so much noise*, he thought, *the chemicals were supposed to calm you down*. Ginge found Jez's naivety endearing.

'They're all doing spice mate ... everyone does it. Well, everyone's tried it. Are you telling me you never? It used to be legal, it should be right up your street.'

'Not me. Not interested.' Jez was slightly miffed at the suggestion his actions were solely driven by subservient obedience to the law and not his own set of values.

'I tried it obvs, but nah ... it drives you nuts. Soon went back to smack.'

Ginge was pragmatic about his own addiction. He spoke openly with Jez about his dependency on heroin, how he smoked rather than injected to avoid the risk of blood poisoning, how he tried to keep it under control but had never managed to give up for more than a month since he started. Ginge was working with his hostel to find new ways to try – but the diversification of the scene due to the flood of synthetic cannabinoids made it easy to deceive the counsellors – and himself – about whether the week's objectives had been met. He could proudly reel off a list of substances he had *not* taken, knowing they might be unfamiliar with the one he had. If there was a drought in supply of heroin or crack there was always something else to take its place for a while. Ginge was just glad his refuge was not one of those enforcing a zero-tolerance regime. He clung by his filthy fingernails to his hopes for going clean.

Jez had never seen Ginge light up. Indeed, he was not sure he had ever witnessed a drug deal on the street of any kind, he was just aware of the pungent aromas of joints being smoked wherever his vagrant comrades congregated. Jez was, however, especially familiar with the unstable and threatening demeanour shown by the regular users – there was always someone causing havoc at the shelters he visited, and it was clear that the volunteers were becoming increasingly nervous about their safety. Colin told him that originally there was hope this new breed of potions would see a reduction in crack and heroin addiction, but now the view among the agencies was very much: better the devil you know. Spice and its various shape-shifting analogues were like a malevolent genie escaped from the bottle. With the unpredictable nature of the different available compounds, using it was like playing Russian roulette with your brain. Ginge promised to get Jez a sample so he could see for himself, but the offers were always politely rebuffed. Jez did wonder if the pharma-induced nightmares might make the real one of staying at the Viaduct more bearable, but he was determined not to find out.

*

The vicarious exposure to drug dealers, as rendered by Ginge's first-hand narrative, was the closest Jez wanted to get. The local gangs had been purged from the area by invaders from London in the last couple of years. Like latter-day Fagins, faceless gangsters in executive cars would recruit teenage foot-soldiers to establish the distribution network in dismal suburban arcades dotting the outskirts of town. Bags of opiates sent east from the metropolis on a new Silk Road would be delivered to inconspicuous safe houses where the young runners laid low. Armed with an array of knives and machetes, they had usually won their spurs by being prepared to threaten, maim or kill the local incumbent gang members, to claim the territory along with the ultimate prize: the mobile numbers of that catchment's user population. Any initial sense of glory soon dulled though, as frequently these juvenile infantrymen would become ensnared into subsistence living, paying off the debt incurred when consignments mysteriously went missing through no fault of their own.

Jez listened to Colin's description of the operation in disbelief. He was stunned to discover that such a sophisticated process took place in plain sight without being stopped by the authorities.

'They're always one step ahead, Jez, that's the thing. They use old models of mobile that are difficult to track and arrange the dealing sites by text at the last minute.' Jez had asked Colin to explain how the gangs worked. 'It's always away from the centre, in one of the estates. Usually near a cash machine ... wherever there's a few shops, sometime after midnight.'

'Have you ever been out there?'

Colin paused before answering.

'Hah ... Yes ... I've been out there. I got 20 stitches for my trouble. That was when I was looking for Melody.'

Melody had materialised on the street a year or so before Jez. When she disappeared Colin was so concerned about her welfare, he had followed one of the regulars at the Caravan on an excursion to buy a fix one night, following a tip off she might be there. When he arrived at the prescribed location Colin did his best to blend in, while scouring the area for signs of Melody. The young bloods did not appreciate the sight of someone sticking his nose into their business. Hooded figures exploded from a car, Colin was jumped, two of them pinned him face down to the concrete while another scored his back with a hunting knife. The dealers and junkies scattered to every hidden corner like insects from a bonfire, as Colin was left to bleed. Knowing who the victim was, one of his flock made an anonymous call and an ambulance soon came to rescue him. The cut was vicious but superficial and the only lasting damage, apart from the terror in Colin's heart, was the dramatic scar.

'I'll show it to you one day, Jez. Maybe. If you're lucky.' Colin gave an unconvincing half laugh and Jez could tell the mental scars were deeper. He re-directed the discussion.

'Who was Melody? What happened to her?'

Colin's expression darkened further.

*

Melody arrived in town on a perfect summer's day, as if descending from the heavens. She was first seen perched on the flagstones of the railway station approach, before soon migrating to the peripheral shopping streets Jez knew so well. Her West Country accent indicated the extent of her displacement; the fragility of her voice suggested she was younger than the twenty-four years she claimed. Her frail form was instantly noticeable, and she was soon swept up by the outreach team – their profiling told of escape from an abusive family situation, but they could not unravel all the details. Melody was reluctant to disclose her story in full. Her hair was short and boyish, turned white most likely by fear. Her skin was so diaphanous, her frame so slight, Colin thought she could have been blown there on the wind, like a dandelion seed. Melody's needs and vulnerability were so obvious she was placed in a women's refuge as soon as a space could be found. Later she was moved on to a small flat, part of the limited array of sponsored accommodation in town set aside for rehabilitating rough sleepers; she was flagged as a high priority and fast-tracked. Throughout this process Melody seemed thankful for the help but always remained unsettled. She found it impossible to hunker down in the flat for long periods during the day and would habitually return to the shop doorways that had caught her, when first coming to rest in this distant land. She was introduced to the Caravan … she formed a bond with one of Colin's volunteers and often came to talk, becoming suddenly more animated and cheerful, while always skirting around her life history. Her confidante later told Colin she thought Melody had probably lost a child somewhere along the line.

For a while Melody was a regular fixture on Colin's rounds until one day her appearances stopped. He immediately knew she was in danger. He searched all the common haunts on his beat and questioned every visitor to the Caravan, to no avail. No one knew where she was. Calls were made to her flat but there was no response. None of the official agencies had the resources to raise a concerted search effort so Colin eventually took it upon himself to follow the lead he had been given, to follow the trail to where the narcotics were sold. In the calamitous aftermath of that mission, when Colin was still being treated in hospital, the full story emerged, thanks to one of the teenage runners who walked into a

London police station, broke down and begged for help and forgiveness, suddenly overwhelmed by waves of guilt. He admitted that he and his associates had spotted Melody in a doorway, won her confidence and persuaded her to let them stay in the flat on the promise of unlimited drugs. She saw an end to the alienation of being stuck in those rooms alone. They saw easy prey. Once inside the door they parasitically consumed their host – they wanted the flat as a safe house. Melody was forbidden to leave and when the gang leaders stopped by on the supply runs, they used her for sex. When anyone rang the doorbell, they held a gun to her face to make sure she stayed quiet. When they went on a drop, one of her captors stayed behind to keep her inside, but as long as she stayed away from the front door and did not make a call, they were not watching. At about the same time Colin was setting off for the outskirts to look for her, Melody was cooking a large dose of heroin and loading a syringe. The heroin was cut with God knows what. She swallowed a variety of pills lying around before locking herself in the bathroom to empty the syringe into her arm. On passing out her head smashed against the side of the bath and she died of respiratory suppression, in a pool of blood, within the hour. When the dealers returned after their abortive drop, they broke down the bathroom door to find her body. Two days later the youngest of the crew, a fifteen-year-old boy whose desensitisation had finally been overcome, slipped his own leash and ran to confess their sins.

Jez was haunted by this story of compounded tragedy. The next time he saw Izzy he asked if she had ever been aware.

'Melody. Oh God yes ... I saw her a few times on my way to work ... that poor, poor waif. You know, she always said to me: "I like your hair, it looks so pretty," she had such a plaintive voice, it really broke my heart.' A tear formed on Izzy's cheek.

'She always looked so pale ... like the ghost of a child. Those scumbags should've been put away for life.'

Izzy looked away, reliving the disgust. She had lit a candle in the gallery for Melody every day since the news broke. Based on the testimony of the repentant runner, six of the gang were convicted of multiple offences, including manslaughter, and imprisoned. The boy was shown leniency by the courts for his cooperation and given a lesser sentence, along with a guarantee of protection in the penal system, that no one really believed could be enacted. His former masters were less forgiving. One week after the trial they raided his parents' home, torched the building and dragged his brother out into the road where he was beaten with steel bars, then stabbed to death. The boy informer must have known this was likely – his was just one of many young lives driven to catastrophic dilemma, through taking the wrong turns in a world infested with evil. An army of children faced with impossible choices, as disposable as razor blades. A new coterie of pushers moved in – the transition astonishingly seamless – and trade in the estates soon returned to normal, as if nothing had happened.

The words of Hazel, the outreach supervisor, echoed into Jez's mind, like church bells, or gunfire. Was he really making it more likely there would be more dreadful cases like Melody, by trying to survive on the streets himself? Should he come in from the cold and sort his life out, as Hazel had implored, to help break the perception that living off the charity of others was a viable alternative? He still struggled with the connection. He thought about what he would have said, if meeting her. If Melody had crouched by his alcove and talked, he would have done his best to encourage her to seek shelter, just as everyone had done to him. But he was different. This was what he wanted. Melody's downfall was her addiction and he could not be blamed for that. Jez turned these thoughts in his head until he could grant his own absolution – the self-administered reprieve he needed to carry on. He gazed at the sky, praying for Melody's soul to truly rest in peace … and felt even more certain it was his destiny to stay where he was and maybe one day help someone.

Chapter 13

From the year 2000 – the advent of which provided Bevan with his favourite moment since the initial adoption of CRUSOE, thanks to the visibility given to the robustness of his software engineering – the depot and its inhabitants entered a period of stasis. Numbers continued to decline but only by natural wastage; no one left without choosing to but, at the same time, the decline in sense of community fermented the urge to leave and that urge was gaining momentum. All parts of the business were targets for cost cutting but Martin's region was a long way down the list due to its strategic importance, or so he would tell his people. In reality, from what he could see, the butchery was becoming increasingly arbitrary and illogical, such that he was beginning to doubt his own words when trying to give reassurances in team meetings.

'Don't worry folks, they can't do without us here. We'll be the last ones for the chop.' This was the usual closing statement on his briefings. Through all the management guff, all the team really wanted to know about was the latest closures. Once there had been social clubs, sports teams, royal visits. Now the internal communications were like the roll call for an executioner.

Bevan distrusted all change with a passion and was especially piqued by the removal of the traditional, tangible building blocks of civilised office life, whenever it happened. While he was partly culpable due to the introduction of CRUSOE, he still lamented the demise of the T-card board and its role as a focal point. He appreciated and depended upon the simple things, the fundamental routines, the familiar landmarks: the sandwich trolley, the monthly team meetings, the fire alarm test … and the stationery cupboard. Since the dawn of time, someone – an actual person – would hold responsibility for maintaining stationery supplies for the office. If he needed biros, post-it notes or paper clips, there was always somewhere to go, and these essential commodities would be present in perpetual abundance. That his needs were understood created the illusion his efforts were valued. There was a social norm associated with the basic sustenance of what he required to do the job properly – you simply went to the cupboard and if anything was running low you knew whom to tell.

The dismantling of this process was an early victim of the corporate slash and burn, a warning shot across the bows, a culling of the low hanging fruit. HQ rabidly insisted that the organisation needed to drag itself into the 21st century and follow the trends of consumer behaviour. Just-in-time ordering from an online portal was made mandatory for all and the idea of having someone responsible for managing supplies on behalf of an entire office was abolished. This struck Bevan as ironic, given the elemental role of the depot in effectively doing the same thing at a regional level, for the engineering materials, but he avoided extending that line of reasoning too far. Now you were made to feel apologetic for using any kind of equipment at all. Everyone was forced to adopt a soulless automated process via the intranet, requiring multiple levels of sign-off by a faceless procurement management chain, the identities of whom were forever changing. Approval requests forever stuck in the inboxes of managers who were either too busy, on holiday, or had only lasted four months in post then buggered off (long enough to fuck something up, then move on with another lie on their CV). The stationery cupboard eventually existed only in folk memory, like ducking stools and highwaymen; and thereafter Bevan bought his own pens as a silent protest.

*

135

Bevan clung onto his niche, his bivouac, as the winds of change gradually blew stronger. Everyone was concerned about the eroding sense of worth as employees but on the whole this was batted away with gallows humour. Bevan laughed at the jokes and occasionally chipped-in with an especially dark one of his own but in general he kept his fears inside. He was always uncomfortable speaking about himself. The quarterly performance reviews with Martin were marked on Bevan's wallchart in black. The intermediate ones were relatively painless, merely acting as cursory checks on progress. But the end of year review, in which Martin patiently asked him to summarise his own opinion on how his contribution should be judged, and worse, the target setting for the ensuing year which followed cruelly soon after, both made his stomach churn. He yearned for a much longer journey to work, preferably by train, on these dreaded days of review meetings.

'So, Bevsie … how do you feel about this year, how do you think you've done.' Martin was duty bound to give a conventional lead-in, he had to be even-handed with his charges.

'Um … about the same as usual I suppose, Martin. I mean … we've delivered everything we're supposed to, and we're within budget. I worked on all the CRUSOE releases without any issues. Um … what else … umm … there's only been one day of downtime on CRUSOE and that's because the stupid IT department cocked up a network upgrade. I guess I've done about the same as usual I would say.'

This non-committal response was exactly what Martin expected and, of course, it was useless to him. He needed deviations. Examples of slightly differential positives or negatives he could slide a cigarette paper between, to tease out his good and bad performers. Marking his whole team as 'meets expected standard', the official equivalent of 'Um … about the same as usual', would not wash with the HR department overseeing the performance management strategy. His problem was simple: his team *were* all operating at the level of 'meets expected standard.' They had all been in the job so long, they had settled into a repeatable pattern. They were not slackers by any means, they were just human beings who had learned a job and were good at it, able to bash out the work sub-consciously at their natural rhythm, like bakers producing perfect loaves at an optimal rate, without having to think. (Unlike bakers however, they received no cheery gratitude from the man in the street.) Their targets had converged around these natural rhythms and any deviations would seem perverse, explainable only on the basis of unexpected personal problems or excessive drug use.

'Come on Bevsie … there must be something you think has gone particularly well this year, something that gave you a feeling of satisfaction … or perhaps something you've been disappointed about?' Martin persevered.

'Not really Martin, if I'm honest … sorry. Nothing I can think of, it was pretty much like last year.'

Bevan was not being deliberately obtuse, for the sole purpose of making his manager's life difficult. He knew the game. He had even been given some training on the conduct of performance reviews himself, in case he ever got the opportunity to manage someone (God forbid) so he understood Martin's dilemma. He wanted to help. However he was not prepared to sacrifice himself, or make something up, when the honest truth was, since his triumph with the launch of CRUSOE, which gave him the only ever 'Outstanding' in his career, each year he had achieved about the same as the year before.

Bevan often thought to himself that the whole structure of performance management was flawed. Reliability was no longer enough – everyone had to demonstrate signs of doing more work, or doing it to a higher degree of quality, or preferably both, year after year. This constant need to be seen to be improving was unnatural. It was like telling Lance Armstrong that winning the Tour de France every year was not enough – he would need to win it next year by a greater margin, while reciting Shakespeare, otherwise he would be considered a failure. A more realistic target for an above-average performer would be simply remaining consistent against adversity, without going insane. In Bevan's view, a better and more grounded description of excellence would be: *stoically continue to turn up every day and meet expected standard despite the Niagara*

Falls of bullshit descending from above on a daily basis. But of course Martin had to pay lip service. He had to find ways of making his team appear as the embodiment of managed progression.

*

Martin did respect Bevan's dedication to the task, despite being unsettled by his monotone intensity. He felt sorry for him staying up all night for the releases without complaint and, after a few years of this, he decided Bevan deserved a morsel of appreciation for once. In his 2003-04 review the dialogue took a new turn.

'Well … I want to tell you Bevsie that I'm going to mark you as 'exceeds expected standard' this year. You can't keep on doing all this extra work without any recognition. I *am* aware of it you know. I can't say that means you'll get a much bigger pay rise mind you, you know what it's like … but it's only fair we give it a go.' Martin knew there would be a battle to get this through, but this year he felt the impulse to try. He was glad to have a rationale for not giving everyone 'meets' but at the same time knew his superiors would rather see people being marked down instead of up.

'OK, great. Thanks Martin.' Bevan was a little embarrassed but appreciated the gesture. He knew it would make little difference to any resulting increase – and he was not exactly craving more money to finance his vestigial life anyway – but he was touched that his boss had actually noticed what went on.

They went through each of Bevan's objectives conspiratorially, identifying where the wording of the acceptance criteria – the definitions of the evidence needed for each rating – could be interpreted in his favour.

'Here we go, look … you've got 'zero downtime' as the evidence needed for Outstanding on your CRUSOE target, matey … that should be enough to bump you up overall.' Martin was relieved to have spotted something.

'I've had 'zero downtime' every year since 1995 actually.'

But they both let that go. The whole thing was a farce anyway. An absurd cottage industry of bureaucracy to give the impression of providing motivation and fairness. Motivation? Bevan did not know whether to laugh or cry. His motivation came from an emptier place than senior management could ever know, not that they would care. Their unspoken attitude was that if the pond life were any good ... if they had the capacity to exceed *anyone's* expectations, they would have found themselves another job ages ago. The fact that so many staff – the 'lifers' – had stayed in the same job for so long was proof that they were beneath contempt. *If they think they deserve more money, fine ... when we give them a quarter of a per cent let's just see if they get on their bikes and look elsewhere.* Bevan pictured them cackling maniacally in the background whenever he read the bulletins about each year's pay settlement.

As for the tortured, futile hours spent composing relevant objectives for what people actually did, and making them measurable in an unambiguous way, he believed this was possibly the greatest waste of human time in the industrial age. The examples distributed by HR to illustrate how these targets should be written were never helpful. The vast majority of staff could not point to a specific quantifiable outcome that could be attributable solely to themselves in any given year. Mostly they were firefighting against events going wrong, that they had no control over. Survival with any trace of sanity for most of them should have been judged as exceeding expectations, in a rational and humane world. But no ... the charade of objective setting persisted in every organisation across the land and it made Bevan want to weep, if he could weep about anything. It was the pretence of fairness that really stuck in his craw. Everyone knew who the favourites were, the bumlickers. Everyone knew who would get the better ratings, irrespective of how much effort was expended crafting one's objectives. Bevan submitted an idea to the staff suggestion scheme that performance reviews should be conducted by public vote, with buttons on the intranet for all staff to select their favourites. The only rule being you could not select the same person more than once. Done and dusted in thirty seconds. It would be no less fair and would probably save the organisation about 20 million pounds per year by avoiding the lost man hours ... but he received no response.

*

139

Martin entered his team's 2004 performance ratings into the HR system with some trepidation – he knew he was going rogue with Bevan's assessment, even if only to a small extent, and might meet resistance. The blue touch paper was lit. No one would actually admit that there were quotas. To mention the word quotas was a cardinal sin. Even the increasingly impotent unions were heard protesting about the threat of quotas. But of course, quotas did exist – in the same way the public sector as a whole has diversity targets, while any attempt to highlight the fact is seen as taboo. When the regional senior managers reviewed that year's provisional scores across the board, they had a problem. They had been directed that there could be no above-average performers and at least forty per cent of staff needed to be rated below average. How else could they explain the fact that the region as a whole had failed to reach its group targets (which, as all the staff believed, were of course written deliberately, by twats, to be unachievable anyway). Review meetings were held to compare the results across all teams. A bizarre game of Top Trumps ensued with the region's top brass, assisted by executives from HR, shuffling the ratings into a profile that matched the available resources, comparing review against review trying to spot flaws in the line manager's reasoning. Bevan was bumped down one, back to what he expected in the first place, while three other members of Martin's team were levelled down to 'below expected standard'.

Levelling. Martin's most hated word. It made him think of carpet-bombing missions over Germany in World War 2. In theory, levelling was the process for making sure achievement against targets was judged consistently in all parts of the business. In practice it was a device for pushing marks down when weak-willed managers failed to do so up front. He had half expected it but tried to push back. When asked to justify his ratings in the levelling review meeting, he explained that the guys were doing their best without any support, but was rebuffed with cold, steely eyes.

'But are they demonstrating they can operate at a level above Martin? Where is the evidence they are pushing themselves?'

'They're all hard-working professionals handling the same number of orders, with fewer people to do the job. None of them have got capacity to be going for night school MBAs at the same time.'

'Where is the evidence though? Marking-time isn't good enough in the current climate. What difference are they making Martin? Everyone needs to be pushing the organisation forward.'

Martin wanted to push them off a cliff. When it came to his own personal review, he feared the worst. He spoke with Bevan in the hour before going in. What Bevan did not realise was that Martin was already on a hit list: the ominously titled Performance Improvement Plan, otherwise known as a PIP. Being 'on a PIP' meant you were under special measures, the equivalent of being on probation in lieu of a more sombre fate, the term having a suitably sinister nursery rhyme quality. Bevan had failed to see the signs and was blissfully unaware. He did notice that Martin seemed more fatalistic than usual on this day though.

'You know what really pisses me off Bevsie? It's all this stuff in the tabloids taking the piss out of middle managers, as if they're all scum, like on a par with child abusers. You see it in the papers all the fucking time … every time there's a report about redundancies it's always offset with some remark like, "It's thought all the reductions will come from middle management, not the shop floor." As if that makes it better in some way! Like the way they sugar-coat stories about plane crashes by saying, "It's OK everyone, no British people were on board, it's nothing to get too upset about." It's so bloody … *unfair*. We work stupid hours, we deal with all the shit, we're the ones actually dealing with reality while the tossers in HQ sit around trying to decide what colour to paint the fucking vans. Nothing would happen without us, not a thing. How would they know how to coax a room full of lazy bastards to pull their fingers out their arses? And you know what … we don't have a voice. No one is going to listen. We're not nurses, we're not police … no one cares about us. We don't count, just because we made it one bollocksing rung up from the bottom. We're like sitting ducks, they're going to kill us all … and when we're gone … they'll be totally fucked, I'm telling you, totally fucked. There'll be no one left that knows what this place is even here for.'

Bevan listened open-mouthed but Martin was not really looking at him through this monologue, his gaze was fixed in the middle distance. He came to with a quick 'Anyway … sorry for going off on one Bevsie … guess I better get going,' and when he walked out of the office door, that was the last time Bevan ever saw him. Martin's major crime had been his poor performances at the management away days. He had done well at strategic thinking tests but his lack of engagement in the role-playing exercises had marked his card as lacking the modern management attitude needed for success in the new economy, in the eyes of the zealots at least. He had been given a warning the previous year. Now his failure to apply appropriate downward pressure on the markings of his team was the final straw. The company were able to sack him for incompetence. He was escorted off the premises. They had kindly arranged for a trained private nurse to be on hand in case the shock caused any medical trauma, but he assured them he was fine. His face winced just that bit more for a moment, then he shrugged and offered them a defeated parting comment.

'Well … thank you very much for that ladies and gentlemen. Good to know the company is in such safe hands, ha fucking ha.'

As Martin rose from his seat, he fired a look of disgust into the eyes of Rowena Harper-Giles, HR director and probably the most partisan devotee of all the new bollocks doctrine in the room, but that was his final act of defiance. He declined the offer of an exit interview; he knew he would be unable to contain his fury. He should have got the unions on his case a year earlier but had failed to find the time and he thought they were useless anyway. It was too late now, and he knew it, as he was shepherded back to his car. A security guard – another irony since the provision of security at all sites had been drastically reduced to save money and none had been seen for months – was on hand to return to the office to clear Martin's desk. Apparently, they could afford security to kick good people off the site but not to prevent terrorists and cable thieves breaking in. Martin did not even get a chance to say goodbye to his team, although in a sense he had already done so before stepping towards his fate.

On hearing from the security guy that Martin would not be returning, Bevan gave a shiver of disbelief. Others in the office seemed to have already known. Bevan chided himself for being so detached from the group dynamic. Maybe he could have saved Martin by sending some good feedback up the chain, if he had understood the situation. He was once more consumed by self-re-crimination – luckily without the extra burden of realising it was Martin's generosity of spirit in Bevan's review that proved the final nail in his coffin. The remaining team in the office sat and remi-nisced about their fallen leader for the rest of the day. Bevan joined them for a while, the bare minimum he felt respectful, then got on with his work, trying to suppress the fearful thoughts swirling in his head. The fact that he had been levelled down himself hardly registered.

*

The following morning Bevan received an email that appeared to come direct from Rowena Harper-Giles, but no doubt was com-posed by some underling.

> *As part of Allied Grids continuing efforts to **enable the UK to shine**, maximise the potential of the organisation and develop our staff we are introducing a new line manage-ment procedure to all areas. At the core of the new policy is the introduction of full-time **People Managers**. People Managers are highly trained, experienced and valued members of staff who understand the needs for staff development and mentoring in a modern business. And with 100% of their time allocated to line management the new People Managers will be able to give you the support you need while ensuring fairness and consistency.*
>
> *For more information please read the briefing pack slides on the Intranet here.*
>
> *People Managers will be assigned to all employees on an in-cremental basis as the responsibilities of your existing line managers are realigned. You will receive more information*

about your transition to a People Manager in the very near future.

I am confident that you will welcome the introduction of People Managers as a positive step towards your own personal development.

Rowena Harper-Giles

'Have you seen this Ange?'

Angie was a transport allocator, a long-standing member of the stores team. She had been one of Martin's fold and was probably the least shocked when he disappeared, as they often went on fag breaks together at the back of the depot, where they put the world to rights. Angie was one of the early starters, so it was often just her and Bevan for a while at the beginning of each day. Bevan liked her soft Scottish accent and her self-effacing wisdom, and, although he would never admit it, he looked forward to her arrival each morning. She showed no outward signs of detesting him and tended to keep the others in check. Also, being one of the smoking circle, she always seemed to have inside knowledge on what was going on, in a way he never did. It was relatively rare for Bevan to instigate a conversation. Even having done so, he still sat face to screen, with his back to the room. Yet to settle down to another day attached to her headset, Angie wandered across and peered over his shoulder, intrigued.

'What's that Bevsie? What's the latest wee bombshell?'

'This email from Rowena Parker-Bowles about … *people managers.*' Bevan stressed those two words with pantomime incredulity. 'What *are* they on?'

Angie read quickly through, muttering the words as she went.

'Oh my giddy aunt! They really are joking now. Poor old Martin, the writing was on the wall, eh. While his seat is still warm from his poor sorry bum.' Angie was as flabbergasted as Bevan.

'That's what I mean Ange. Just when you thought it couldn't get any worse. Mind you, at least it doesn't look like these *people* managers are expected to *help the planet to heal* as well, on top of everything else. Perhaps they're bringing someone else in for that bit.'

Angie laughed her porridge-y laugh and Bevan briefly wished he could talk to her more often, but she needed to start making her calls. He couldn't resist another dig.

'Presumably we'll be getting ours asap under the circumstances. We're in a power vacuum now … who knows what we might get up to … we could form our own religion … start worshipping Prince Phillip … indulge in human sacrifice.' Bevan was on the cusp of a rant but could see Angie itching to move on. 'I wonder if we'll all be lumbered with the same one. I wonder who it will be.'

'Aye Bevsie, I wonder.' Angie plugged herself in and began another day haranguing contractors about the availability and location of various types of vehicle. She shared Bevan's dismay but was happy to wait until the next smokers' confab to find out more.

'Ensuring fairness and consistency, my arse.' Bevan chuntered to himself. 'Ensuring managers don't have the slightest idea what you do, more like.'

*

Sure enough, within days, an email arrived from a Howard Bone introducing himself as Bevan's new people manager. There were four permanent members of the stores team remaining in the office (the rest of what had been Martin's wider team inhabited more far flung parts of the depot building). The other desks were occasionally occupied by itinerants: engineers trying to complete their timesheets but whose tablet PCs were broken; or suits from HQ down for a meeting who needed a hot desk and were resigned to sitting with the riff-raff. But the hard-core was down to four. Of these, each had been allocated a different people manager which left them confused about the stated aim of consistency.

Howard suggested kicking things off with a phone call.

'Hello there … it's Howard here. Is it correct that you answer to the name Bevsie? That's what it says on your notes.' This was Howard's opening gambit at appearing friendly. Bevan flinched at the reference to notes, wondering what else they might contain.

'Yes, that's right, that's what everyone calls me.'

'Super. Good to meet you Bevsie. I will try to come down for a face-to-face as soon as I can.'

'OK, that's great. Can I ask … how many people are you people managing by the way?'

'Er … I've been given a list of sixty names so far.'

'Blimey. I don't envy you that job.' Bevan surprised himself with this display of empathy, but he could already tell Howard was doomed. Sixty was ridiculous. 'Whereabouts are you based Howard?'

'I'm in the North East region, in Sunderland.'

Bevan put his phone on mute briefly to emit some expletives, audible throughout the office.

'Wow! Um … that must involve a lot of travelling. Um … do you mind me asking … what else does it say on the notes you've got about me?'

'Well, obviously I'll be reading all your performance reviews and training records in detail as part of my new role. I've just got some notes jotted down from HR … it says you are a key person especially in relation to something called, er, CRUSOE? I have to say I don't know anything about that, you'll have to fill me in.'

'That's no problem at all. I'll be happy to do that as much as you like.'

'Super … oh … and it also says you are recognised as a single point of failure. So that's something to work on eh?'

Howard was not meant to reveal the contents of the HR notes. The conversation stumbled on for a while, it was only meant to break the ice; Howard promised to arrange a follow-up meeting in person as soon as he could.

*

Single point of failure. Those words rang in Bevan's head for days. What on earth did he mean? Angie tried to reassure him it just meant that he was vital to the organisation because no one else understood how CRUSOE worked and without him, the whole thing would go tits up.

'Single point of failure, you see? It's a good thing Bevsie.'

146

'But what did he mean by *that's something to work on?*'

'I guess he means that they might need to train someone else as cover hun.'

Bevan could see Angie's point and realised she thought he was making a fuss about nothing. But now he felt more threatened than ever. If *single point of failure* was the headline soundbite the seniors had against his name, he must also be on their hit list. If he had to coach someone else to manage CRUSOE, how long before he became dispensable. Looking after the software was one thing. It would be relatively straightforward to show another developer how the forms and queries worked. But you had to understand the data as well. In the same way he used to police the T-cards, now he spent hours at the end of each day weeding out errors in the database after everyone else had gone home. He would step through the data, record by record, scanning for obvious anomalies. He ran queries to identify outlying values that simply could not be true. Supplier addresses with non-existent postcodes; unit costs with minus numbers; lengths of cable over 1000km. (He had incorporated some rules in order to validate the input by users, but they were fairly generous, he wanted to allow for all possibilities. Nevertheless, he could sniff out when an extra zero or two had been typed in by a fat finger.) He even scoured through the *Comments* field, where the storemen could add some remarks for future reference using free text, looking for spelling mistakes. This was not strictly necessary. In fact, the amount of value Allied Grids ever gained as a result of Bevan's fanatical language checking would have been immeasurably small, but he was convinced it was important and that one day they would thank him for it. And, of course, it kept him occupied. He saw himself as a Pac-Man-like superhero, cutting a swathe across the screen of his computer, cleaning CRUSOE's data into a thing of perfection. Stores controller by day, data warrior by night ... and no one knew his secret identity! (While at work, his voices could sometimes be playful.) Bevan's dedication to staying in the office so long was like a self-fulfilling mythology. It gave him vindication against the ungratefulness of his employer. He took masochistic pleasure from the fact that no one knew what he was up to ... and he certainly had no intention of sharing these inklings with his new full-time people manager, they would undoubtedly be beyond his comprehension.

With the loss of Martin, the idiocy of Allied Grids appointing someone as a line manager to sixty unknown people, dotted all over the country, and the revelation that his card was marked even more explicitly that he ever imagined, Bevan began to lose the separation he had established between work and home time. It suddenly became much harder to switch off. In the car driving home and sitting alone in his flat, he turned over in his mind the implications of following in Martin's footsteps out the door, if the Allied Grids' grim reaper ever caught up with him. How would he cope if they made him redundant too? The ground had shifted significantly, and cracks started to show in Bevan's outlook. The line of defence that Martin once represented had been stripped away. Only now did Bevan appreciate the mental pressure his former boss must have deflected from him. Now he was directly exposed to the inhumane workings of the organisation. His doubts about the possibility of steering a trouble-free course through the rest of his life became amplified, as he heard himself saying, *come back Martin, all is forgiven,* on repeat – you only realise how much you need someone when they are gone. It turns out this applies to good managers as well as lovers. What would he do? The vodka gave him temporary relief, the transient euphoria gave him moments of hope. He deluded himself believing it helped him sleep. But of course, this was only the beginning of the night; now he regularly spent the small hours awake, haunted by his future or the past he had locked away.

Chapter 14

Apart from a few unwelcome encounters with the more dangerous elements in his circle, Jez found enough good-hearted people through his travails to maintain faith in humanity. There was as much good and bad to be found as in regular life, once you spoke to people and understood their battles. Even though he now avoided the main precinct whenever possible, Jez got to know an assortment of kindred souls as he went about his daily routine. He occasionally spoke to people at the Viaduct, but the only real opportunity for socialising there was over breakfast. In the mornings he had a spring in his step, relatively speaking, due to the anticipation of impending escape and this optimism sparked some chatter with his fellow diners. On arrival in the early evening the imperative was to minimise the amount of time spent between obtaining a key and getting inside the room, such that conversations were few and far between. The Viaduct after dark was not a place to mingle. The night shelters were more conducive to the bonding process, being more communal in nature – and less stomach-churning – but there was always an air of tension resulting from the limited capacity and excess demand. A curfew would be in place and once that threshold had passed it became more possible to relax, knowing there was less likelihood of any pressure to make way for a latecomer. However, the cut-off times were not always strictly imposed, especially if a female or younger person arrived seeking entry. Indignance at unfair treatment constantly bubbled away under the surface … everyone felt at risk … everyone wanted a place. Consequently, Jez often stepped back, to allow space for others – but he still had more interaction at the shelters than he ever did overnight at the Viaduct.

Ginge was his first connection, becoming a recurring yet mercurial presence, fluttering about the scene like a cabbage white in the garden on a summer's day. Ginge just *happened,* without Jez really having any say in the matter. Their subsequent rendezvous ebbed and flowed in an unpredictable pattern but each time Ginge materialised, they were always able to pick up where they had left off. Regardless of his addictions, Ginge had more or less retained his grasp on reality and so acted as a stabilising force on Jez's state of mind. Some of the other souls he came across were less self-possessed. After finding his feet, the next characters Jez willingly befriended were Robbo and Spike, in one of the few contacts he ever *did* make at the Viaduct. Robbo was a moon-faced, balding chap in his early thirties, forever in khaki great coat and army boots, despite the fact he had never been in the services. He was diagnosed with a personality disorder, such that he found concentration extremely difficult and became easily stressed when asked to follow instructions. His mother was unable to cope when he was a child, so he had been raised in the state care system. Since that time, he had drifted in and out of rough sleeping in all its various forms. He was placed in a series of hostels but had a bad track record with eviction due to his weakness in adhering to house rules. He regularly missed the deadlines for paying the rent, which were enforced to encourage financial planning … and he consistently failed to keep his room tidy. Although not a hardened junkie, he enjoyed a spliff from time to time, even when promising not to. Such transgressions were sufficiently numerous that he kept on being turfed out. The mental care services could not get traction with him and were happy to blame his lack of motivation on the weed. The other main contributing factor to Robbo's diminishing range of options was Spike. Spike was Robbo's dog.

Spike was a liver-coloured Staffy with gleaming giraffe eyes and a permanent grin of contentment that contrasted starkly with his owner's downcast expression. Jez once thought the dogs were some kind of loaned uniform, like the vests worn by *Big Issue* sellers, dispensed on request by the charities to impart an aura of lovability. He was surprised to discover they were basically just pets … only pets whose body heat and companionship assumed a much more profound role for their vagrant owners than the typical domesticated animal. Like most of his counterparts, Spike was on the tubby side. One of the many ironies of this way of living: while the human owner begged for food to survive, the share given to the canine sidekick often contained more calories than it needed, given the sedentary existence. The owner became skeletal while the pet became obese. Spike was no exception. Their combined bodies still fitted snugly inside the great coat though – Robbo had chosen it from the army surplus store specifically to accommodate Spike inside. The fact that few hostels accepted dogs made life very hard but the in-built warmth afforded by his hirsute partner-in-crime meant that Robbo was more resilient to being on the street than many, especially with Spike's bloodline acting as a deterrent to would-be attackers – a deterrent that was more theoretical than real. Spike was so good-natured, fortunately his aggressive side was rarely put to the test.

It was Spike that met Jez first. The dog was sitting by the side of the guest house annex one evening when Jez arrived, while Robbo was in the office signing in. Spike had been coached to wait patiently outside, so that Robbo could pick him up and smuggle him indoors, hidden within the coat, once he had secured a key. On the occasions Spike got bored and pottered inside while his owner stood at the desk, uproar would ensue and the proprietor would banish them both, reminding them colourfully of the 'no dogs' rule. As Jez approached the entrance and surveyed the arrangement of figures, he understood the set-up instantly and knelt down to keep the hound's attention away from the door. The state of the accommodation was so abject, Jez did not disapprove of the covert operation in which he was now complicit – this creature was hardly likely to make the rooms materially worse and he could tell from its placid demeanour it would not create an addition to the Viaduct's overall atmosphere of menace. When Robbo emerged having checked-in he experienced an initial moment of panic, thinking Jez was up to no good, but this quickly passed seeing that Spike was completely relaxed. Jez helped complete the concealment, securing the last two coat buttons such that only a dark wet nose remained visible. 'Cheers mate', Robbo whispered hastily before stealing off to climb the fire escape. He would slip away in the mornings, without stopping for breakfast, to ensure his stowaway remained undiscovered. Jez and Robbo shared a similar attitude towards the Viaduct. They both hated it, and both only went there when unable to find a better alternative. Robbo was more willing to stay outside – his favourite doorway for bedding down was in one of the shopping streets halfway between the central precinct and Jez's cut-through. After that first meeting, they crossed paths every so often and would stop to pass the time whenever the chance arose. There was usually news of the latest attempts to find Robbo somewhere permanent to live.

'Hi Robbo ... how's tricks?'

'Hello. I'm OK ... been worse. Outreach have been round ... apparently they've got this new place says it takes dogs.' Robbo spoke deliberately, in a tone of unswerving pessimism.

'That's great. That sounds OK doesn't it, Spikey boy?' Jez was rubbing Spike's chin, who returned the gesture with a gaze suggesting it might well sound OK, but no more so than other things did when his chin was being rubbed. 'It's about time somewhere went dog-friendly. I bet most people don't find it a problem ... more likely they'll be glad to have a dog around.' Jez and Spike locked eyes as if hypnotising each other.

'Yeah. As long as he doesn't go crapping on the floor. Mind you, you get crap on the floor in most of the ones with no dogs as well.'

'Will you go?'

'Yeah ... I'll have a look. We'll go and have a look-see, won't we boy?' Robbo's lack of obvious enthusiasm did not augur well.

Jez liked Robbo and wished he could help him overcome his aversion to conforming. He was deeply moved by the devotion

Robbo and Spike shared for each other. They needed somewhere in this area to adopt a more relaxed approach. A place that would work collaboratively, to help Robbo discover the benefits of structure for himself rather than imposing it in a draconian fashion. Neither of them would hurt a fly and they needed to be kept together. Robbo never bragged but Jez sensed he had spent more nights outside than anyone else he had met so far. Robbo suffered from lung disease and his feet were badly swollen, such that walking was becoming increasingly problematic. He was old before his years. Jez wished him well with the new hostel opportunity. There was not much else he could do, apart from argue the case for this inseparable duo whenever he spoke to Colin or someone from the other charities. Another one of the hazards of this lifestyle was getting emotionally involved with others on the same precipice. A trouble shared is a trouble halved. But when that trouble has infinite bounds, the maxim does not really help. Thanks to Spike, Jez had become invested in the wellbeing of both him and his kindly, yet ill-starred keeper. He was grateful to have their company but the aura of doom that enveloped them only added to the litany of heart-rending cases that kept him awake at night.

*

The other type of partnership that found itself habitually excluded from available resources, apart from *human + dog*, was *human + human*. The hostels had few available places for couples and, as far as Jez could see, the only examples on the street displayed such haphazard behaviour that they had probably become barred systematically on that basis alone. He presumed that partners or close friends that shared an enduring relationship, with both parties free from addiction, would always provide each other enough mutual support never to fall to the bottom of the heap, as he had done himself. In his experience, the paired-up rough sleepers were usually alcohol-dependent, having formed a connection in the aftermath of earlier traumas, in which each of them had been ejected from the lives they were born into. They bonded as soul mates of the purest kind. They were not seeking approval in society or climbing any social ladders, rather they had simply found a like-minded companion with whom the days felt more bearable. By spooning together in the cold, they became each other's Spike, in a survival of the closest.

The only couple Jez met on any kind of regular basis were Dierdre and Al. They were a permanent fixture in the entrance to what was once the town's largest department store, that had been closed for several years. It was originally part of a small regional chain that had been run out of business by the big nationwide beasts, with their out-of-town megastores and distribution infrastructure, in a fate not dissimilar to that of the first indigenous drug gangs. The store building sat empty and forlorn, awaiting redevelopment, but its old-fashioned threshold with diagonal recess and decoratively tiled floor was one of the prime sites in town. Dierdre and Al had made it their own. Dierdre was a cheery Irish lass with unkempt curls, who resembled an oversized Rubens cherub wearing an anorak. Al was swarthy, wiry and bearded with weather-worn black hair and a haunted look that spoke of countless ancient conflicts. They were an unusual combination.

Al had once been Ali. He was of Moroccan descent and had been itinerant for as long as he could remember; longer in fact. Colin said their theory was Ali had been kidnapped and brought to the UK as a child, but now had absolutely no recollection of his parents or native birthplace. He had somehow escaped a life of slavery and been living by his wits ever since, through a dizzying cavalcade of delinquency, casual jobs, peddling, playing drums and even a spell as a street magician … but those wits mostly eluded him now, as a result of excessive drinking, and he barely remembered a thing. Luckily, at some stage in his storyline, someone had managed to conjure up UK citizenship for him. He called everyone 'Boss'… everyone except Dierdre. For him, she had become 'Didi'. Which got him off the hook, because most people ran into trouble for mispronouncing her name. 'It's Deer-dra … not Deerdree for Jaysis sake.' She must have cried this a million times. Dierdre had taken to the bottle after being kicked out of her childhood home in Dublin by her physically abusive father when she was a teenager. She came to London to live with her sister, but her learning difficulties and alcoholism made it impossible for her to find work and settle down. By providence, Ali and Dierdre both ended up destitute and in a state of perpetual inebriation, at the same place and the same time. Their support networks had managed to get each of them a place in an experimental wet house where drinking in moderation was tolerated. However, neither of them could come to terms with the regimentation and reproach. They both tried breaking into the office where their rations of super-strength cider were held and this is how they met, bound together as unlikely co-conspirators. Eviction soon followed. It was inevitable; they were both so used to living free, the constraints of the hostel were insufferable and if they had not been forced out they would have deserted anyway. Dumped onto the streets of London together, like two cartoon characters kicked out of a wild west saloon, an indelible alliance was formed.

Dierdre and Ali clicked in a heartbeat, in a way many more advantaged couples would find enviable. Each felt as if they had entered a secret paradise for the first time, of finding someone on the same wavelength ... someone that cared, and someone to care for. Their love was manifested in simple ways only they could understand: the rescue of a discarded teddy bear, the laughing eyes during their attempts to sing, the apportion of every penny. While in many ways they could not have been closer, they never once made love and their straitened circumstances allowed no time for ceremony. They were oblivious to the paradox that by forming a double act they were now less likely to find official accommodation and fearlessly embarked on a life as a twosome, resting their possessions wherever they could and drinking together without shame. Trouble lay ahead though, in the form of the feral youth that infested the walkways surrounding their initial resting points, and who took offence at this incursion of unwanted diversity. Several times – to a chorus of Neanderthal howling – 'Paki-loving slag!', 'Towel-headed cunt!' – they were attacked by mobs of hooligan diehards, showered with kicks and worse. The ever-present anaesthetic effects of the booze played an important role in helping them recover and forget these episodes but they eventually decided to move away, to a different town, to start again. They changed Ali to Al in an attempt to make his name sound less foreign. It was doubtful this made any difference but, for whatever reason, the move was successful. Outside the department store, in this more provincial locale, they no longer attracted violent racist assaults and Dierdre and Al were left to live in relative peace, apart from the mayhem they bestowed upon themselves when exceptionally drunk. When the feeling took him, Al would get out his drums to serenade passing shoppers … and Didi might sing along. The pair became an established part of the town centre's fabric, to the extent that the police were petitioned not to move them on, despite the poorly hidden bottles and cans. Although Colin feared they were being laughed at, rather than laughed with, he welcomed the fact they attracted so many donations of bed linen that their patch turned into another form of recycling facility, for the benefit of others.

Dierdre and Al's nesting ground occupied the opposite end of the high street from the covered mall and bus station, so Jez was not discouraged from diverting their way on his wanderings. So surrounded were they by sleeping bags and quilts, he could never get close enough to sit down for a chat. They were pretty much spaced-out and slurring all the time anyway, so meaningful conversations were rarely easy, but a rapport had been established. After exchanging hellos, Al stayed mostly quiet but Dierdre would always ask about the books.

'Is it a love story Jez? Does yer man get the girl?'

'No … no … I don't think you'd call it a love story.'

'That's a shame Jez. Let me know if you've ever got a love story. I'd be interested in that one.'

'I certainly will do Dierdre … when I get a love story, I'll bring it round. I better be off … cheerio for now.'

There was no point staying for long. Jez usually carried his latest book along when he went roaming. He was sure Dierdre was unable to read but still promised to lend her any love story he came by. He could see Al smiling at his Didi when she was in full flow. He was humbled by the thought these two were already living a very extraordinary love story of their own. Sadly, most of it was forgotten … but what sagas must there be, lying buried beneath the blankets in this abandoned portal, never to be retold.

*

It had been a summer of weather lifted from the pages of romantic fiction – a golden idyll that barely seemed real. Rain as a concept receded into memory and the evening light glowed as if reflecting directly from the painted harbours of Italy. However, by mid-September, even though conditions remained fair, the night-time temperatures were starting to bite. Jez had been struggling to keep warm since his days with the tent and the period of morning sunshine was rapidly depleting as the equinox drew near. As a consequence, his gratitude to Richard, one of his regular callers who nearly always brought coffee and cash, grew by the day. Richard was a graphic designer who ran his own company creating logos and websites in a small office above the travel agent a few doors down from Izzy's gallery. While almost hairless, he looked expensively groomed and the checked shirts and waistcoats put Jez in mind of the phrase 'country gent', although he was not sure if country gents actually existed anymore. Richard was always brisk and jovial … and he understood how Jez liked his coffee … he even found himself asking for 'a normal white coffee' instead of 'an Americano with a dash of milk,' having listened to Jez's soap-box monologue several times. And he knew not to add any sugar.

'There you go, Jez old son. How's life treating you today?' Richard had popped out just before lunchtime to beat the rush. He often stopped for a word, crouching rather than sitting to protect his designer jeans from the dust.

'Hi Richard, thanks very much. Well … I'm starting to really feel the cold to be honest. It's taking much longer for the sun to come up now isn't it.'

'Agh … you poor bugger … still, I think I see a way out of that!' said Richard, arching his eyebrows in Jez's direction. Richard was another one who tried to encourage Jez to seek proper help but, like the rest, had become resigned to his stubbornness. 'Yeah

… it'll be Christmas soon … for our sins. What's it like at that B&B … is it very cold there?'

'Not really … it can be quite stifling sometimes. But you have to have the window open for the smell. I try to get away from there early enough, to get back here before I lose the spot … but it's getting harder to get going in the mornings.'

'I see … hmm … tricky.'

Richard looked more contemplative than usual. He had a question for Jez.

'You know … I came across a girl at the weekend. Sitting under the arches in the dark, down by the waterfront all on her own. Just sitting on the ground against a wall, just like you are. I'd been out on the lash and was walking home after midnight. I was a bit worse for wear, if truth be told, but anyway … I walked past this girl and she looked so pathetic, all on her own, calling out for change. Initially I just kept on walking because … well, I wasn't in the mood, you know … but then started to feel really guilty. It struck me … what if she was really desperate for help … what if something happened to her and all I'd done was walk away? So, I turned around and went back to her. I knelt down and said, 'do you need somewhere to go tonight?' Her face looked so grey. Thing is … I was surprised … she looked so normal, drained and desperate yes, but normal. She didn't look wasted or anything, you know, not like …'

'The kids are normal Richard. To start with they're all normal.'

'Yes, sorry … I didn't mean … Anyway, she just looked at me and shook her head saying, 'I don't know ya.' I tried to reassure her that she'd be safe. I thought I could take her in, that one night only. I guess because of the booze I wasn't really thinking straight. Anyway, there was nothing I could say, she just wanted to be left alone. I gave her some money in the end and simply left her there. I can't get the image of her face out of my head. Did I do the wrong thing Jez?'

'No, I don't think you did the wrong thing. But she was never going to trust you, Richard. These kids have been let down by everyone in their lives. They are so broken down they just want to fend for themselves … and find it impossible to trust anyone or anything. When she saw you, she would have thought: this man is going to rape me. She is weighing up whether being raped is better than being out in the cold. She cannot see who you are because she has never had people like you in her life. That's why Colin's so great. I mean ... obviously he fails most of the time ...' They both laughed, 'but sometimes, to be fair, sometimes he does break through and gets people to *trust* again. He really listens.' Jez then remembered something he had been told. 'Oh ... just had a thought ... the outreach team have a 24-hour hotline, call that next time. And something about an app?' When he got back to his desk Richard looked up the details.

Jez surprised himself with this exchange. For the first time he felt that he had learned some useful lessons. The fact that someone like Richard would seek out his advice was something of a revelation. A few days later, when he was down by the quayside sheltering from some showers that had broken the sequence of rainless days, he spotted his mystery man again. The hunched figure, occasionally seen, stepping in and out of the shadows as if hesitating about what to do. He started to think of this character as Harry, after Harry Lime, elusive and mysterious ... was he really there or just something of the imagination? Jez wanted his Harry to step into the light, to become real. Maybe he could advise him too, the same way he had spoken with Richard.

*

The next time he met Colin, Jez asked him how many people had been helped out of homelessness under his watch.

'That's a difficult one Jez. We can help move them on from the front-line shelters, but we don't always know what happens once they've been placed in a hostel. It's all so complicated. Every rough sleeper has got a different set of issues to deal with.'

'You're not wrong. You always said so. I really see what you mean now.'

'Yes ... well ... we try to establish a strategy based on the needs of the individual. The hostels are not simply supposed to be storage for problem people, somewhere to put them out of the way. They need to provide the support to help the guys move forward. There is such a risk of relapse if the ongoing support isn't there. The government says it's doing its bit, and yes sometimes there is more funding … but the one thing they could really do to help is to stop bloody well changing the rules every five minutes. It's so hard to give advice on benefits and tenancy rights et cetera when the bloody law keeps changing.'

'It's a great thing that you're doing Colin. You have my admiration.'

'Thanks Jez. One success makes up for a hundred lost causes. You really should try to get out of this life too you know.'

Jez paused for several seconds. His heart went out to the tragic cases. Melody, Ginge, Robbo, Dierdre, Al, the grey-faced girl that Richard had tried to help. He wished better lives on all of them. But as for himself … he was still in control, this was what he needed, this was what he deserved. Finally, he replied.

'That's not going to happen Col. I'll be fine.'

Chapter 15

When Howard Bone finally made it to the depot, he had three people to see. His journey from Sunderland had taken most of the previous day and he spent the evening at his Travelodge brushing up on their career records. His new role had been suggested by HR on the basis of his voluntary activities away from Allied Grids. He had the weathered yet kindly look of a long-serving junior school headmaster and his work for the Samaritans suggested he had powers of motivating the spiritless – an attribute HR took to be ideal. He had previously been working as a project manager, but the pressure was getting to him, so he asked for some kind of sideways move. HR decided to give him a chance as one of the new full-time people managers, in favour of the alternative option of making him walk the plank. He could already see it was a thankless task and the constant travelling was probably going to finally kill off his marriage, but at least he was no longer getting his head kicked in every day for missing deadlines. Of Howard's three reportees on site, Bevan knew of the other two but had never spoken to them. His turn was last, at the end of the afternoon.

Bevan's loathing of being managed was as strong as ever but, with the new structure, he had reached the stage of suspending disbelief completely. It was so clearly bonkers to have his performance judged by someone who was based nearly 300 miles away and had no understanding of the tasks he carried out, that he gave up worrying and just decided to try and make it as painless as possible for both of them. When his time came, he gave Howard a demonstration of CRUSOE in action and explained how he spent his time.

'Looking at your last few sets of objectives Bevsie, they don't seem to have changed much year on year, is that a fair observation?' Howard was trying to sound diplomatic.

'To be honest Howard, the job does largely stay the same. There are lots of engineering projects underway all the time and they need to be supplied with parts and materials. That's what we're here for. I have to spend a lot of time in the data and reading the projected estimates to make sure we keep up with demand.' Bevan was trying to sound patient and keep the traces of bitterness out of his voice.

'True, true … I accept all that of course. But, you know, part of the 'maximising the potential of the organisation' agenda is not just about *what* you do, but *how* you do it.'

Bevan could now see why Howard got the job. He had been dragooned into parroting the company line.

'*How* I work, not what I actually deliver. Hmm …' Bevan paused. 'Am I supposed to skip into the office every morning, slap my thigh and shout, "Hey folks, we're going to put on a show in the barn!" or something? Would that help us avoid running out of cable drums?'

Howard had heard all this before on his travels around the country. He took Bevan's sarcasm in good heart and tried to explain that he could contribute in other ways: his interaction with colleagues and impact on *their* work; his communication style and the effectiveness with which he conveyed relevant information up the management chain; his use of resources … things like that. *Use of resources?! I buy my own fucking biros!* thought Bevan. But all he cared about now was doing what Howard wanted as quickly as possible, to make him go away. After that initial meeting they co-existed for a few years and managed to tolerate each other from afar. There was no significant change in the tenor of Bevan's objectives or review comments, despite the additional page of 'behaviours for success' – the Hows as well as the Whats – making the whole process take even longer now. Bevan copied and pasted bits of text for his input from wherever he could find, to make it look like he was playing along, and Howard was spread too thinly to have time to read or amend each and every line properly, when it was time for his assessment. His summaries bore no relation to Bevan's reality on the ground, reviews were done by phone and the 'meets expected' ratings continued.

*

The one thing Bevan did take from his sessions with Howard was to muse upon the way he communicated. He had always found it difficult to put across his feelings. Fiona was the one. Only she had instinctively understood him, without the need for re-explanation. But Fiona was gone, thanks to his stupidity. After she vanished, he never hoped for, or sought, another companion. He spent most of his time alone, he took the paper to the pub and would watch whatever match was on TV. He held conversations in his head all the time but never seemed to compute the words fast enough to click with the guys at the depot in a natural way. Anyone meeting him for the first time assumed he was annoyed by the interruption whereas in fact he was usually just perplexed by what to say.

In the 90s, email had been part of his salvation. Email gave him a voice. No longer did it matter if his facial expression was not reflecting the thoughts inside, or if he failed to think on his feet. The sudden proliferation of email as an office tool meant his views could count as never before. The fact it also meant he could remain at his desk as much as possible was an added benefit. The ability to craft an email, to consider the words and re-adjust before sending, rather than having to compose your ideas in a hurry on the phone, was transformational. Since his youth he had avoided making or answering calls at all costs. When his desk phone rang, he was driven to panic … but the tactile thrump of typing and the asymmetrical nature of the flow, when exchanging emails, appealed to him. He came to respect those who always replied, but only after a gap; more so than those who always replied immediately. Time to think.

Initially he dismissed emoticons, regarding them as childish and unnecessary. He poured scorn on people who used them in the early days. The weight of pressure eventually told, however, and he reluctantly adopted them occasionally. In fact, he came to wish there was a spoken word equivalent to emoticons that could add the right body language to his real-life conversations – that way he might not have been so misunderstood all the time. Via his email alter ego, Bevan established a reputation for sanity and humour within the department (or 'business unit' as they insisted on calling it). He was a bit weird, a bit trapped in time, a bit of a stickler. But cutting through all the pedantry, he was persistent, logical and constructive, even though his tendency to email colleagues in the same room rather than talking to them in person was an object of amusement.

Bevan looked forward to checking his inbox first thing in the morning, his ritual call to prayer, his entreaty for a sensible day. This was despite the fact his long hours and rare absences meant that the number of unread messages was usually low. Overnight it was mostly automated propaganda to the masses from HQ, or aggressive one-liners from management types who appeared to work all night and would routinely send emails at three in the morning. He was sure they did it consciously as a form of self-aggrandisement. Bevan sympathised with the desire to sink all your energies into work, he did so himself, but he asked himself *don't these people ever sleep ... don't they ever get pissed in the evening?* They were not to be trusted. He was fastidious with his replies, picking up on each issue raised in the original and seeking to end with a solution rather than making the problem worse. His pet hates were correspondents who left some of his points unanswered and those that repeatedly chipped in to convoluted threads for the sake of it, without adding any value, just to give the impression of being involved. When certain individuals started lobbing in fractured and pointless little haikus from their mobile phones on trains, as a show of working on the move, he wanted to vomit. Travel is for contemplation. He often felt email should be rationed to five a month per employee.

That might make some of the idiots stop and reflect upon their nonsense before hitting *Send*. (Another staff suggestion that disappeared into the ether.)

*

Bevan had not really stopped to think about how much email had affected his ability to make contacts until Howard started going on about communication styles. He wondered how different his life might have been if he had always been able to converse in this way. He might have developed a greater number of more meaningful friendships. More people might have come to appreciate his sense of humour. He might have felt less lonely. It was too late now, of course, but he gained some satisfaction from the respect he engendered from his peers through this, his favourite channel. Most of the discussions he was engaged in revolved around CRUSOE: the planning of releases, the upkeep of support information on the intranet, the provision of access to the occasional new user. He got to know a few of the characters in the central IT department and was surprised to discover that not all of them were arrogant bastards. The curse of the phone was ever present but at least with conference calls there was usually someone else talking.

However, a more malevolent threat was around the corner. Towards the closing years of the noughties Allied Grids formally adopted instant messaging as a corporate tool. Bevan had always hated how society flocks to the latest gimmick from the tech industry like lemmings, dismissing all that had gone before as being antiquated. He despised the way IT enthusiasts were so obsessed with the 'next big thing', like Regency fops desperate to stay at the cutting edge of fashion. And now this obsession with coolness was infecting the workplace. Email suddenly became viewed as outdated and almost overnight the bulk of personal interaction switched to instant messaging. Bevan despised IM … it became his nemesis. Once more the need to verbalise before thinking. And in his view, in contrast to the IT department spin about 'enabling collaboration' or 'leading to faster decision-making', it was actually damaging. People on conference calls having micro-conversations

in the background, subverting the consensus being painfully ne-
gotiated in the main body of the meeting. A renaissance of cliques.
He noticed more and more that actions following a conference call
could be at odds with what had been agreed. He suspected the
existence of parallel discussions between the most gung-ho partic-
ipants on calls along the lines of:

'This is all bollocks isn't it ... why don't we do X instead?'

'Yeah, go for it ... it'll be done by the time the minutes are
written up.'

It meant the loss of an audit trail, the loss of accountability. In
Bevan's heartfelt opinion, instant messaging was a cancer in the
organisation and should be returned to its box. Much to his dismay, no one else concurred: 'Typical Bevsie, he never wants to
keep up ... he's always stuck in the past ... yeah just look at CRU-
SOE ... it's like something from the Middle Ages.' However, despite his misgivings and, against all expectation, this new fad and
object of his disgust ended up leading Bevan into the most touching friendship he had felt since Fiona.

*

Just like every other large user of computer technology in the western world, Allied Grids had outsourced parts of its IT function to
offshore contractors. Skilled labour in Asian countries was spec-
tacularly less expensive than homegrown resources and the outsourcing companies were huge, well organised and ultra-
competitive. They could be chopped and changed with minimal
impact to keep costs down, and to keep them on their toes. A
blind eye was turned to the working conditions of the offshore
employees themselves, but this was easy to do when they were
foreigners, 5000 miles away and their masters seemed so willing.
Slave labour for the digital age.

Allied Grids had signed a strategic partnership with one of
these behemoths in India called Vedaneo, which had large cam-
pus-like operations in Hyderabad and New Delhi, buzzing with
thousands of gifted young graduates eager for success. The Indian
resources were used for application development, system testing,

support and managing complex system upgrades. Despite his interest in the subject Bevan had never looked for career opportunities in mainstream IT, he wanted to remain working in the stores team. But he came to understand the resentment in certain quarters of the central team because of the lack of openings for UK-based computing specialists, thanks to the outsourcing. And nearly all the helpdesk guys had gone. Not that the replacements were sub-standard. Most people held a stereotypical view that offshore would be painful to work with, based on their early personal experiences with consumer call centres located in the sub-continent. But it only took a few conference calls to realise the Vedaneo teams were really switched on and well briefed. Bevan was astounded by how much they knew about Allied Grids that he did not have a clue about himself.

By the end of the decade the releases in which CRUSOE was implicated were managed from India. Even though Bevan was only required for the testing stage, he was included in all the email chains for each release. He was astonished to see just how many names were copied in. Representatives of all impacted systems were expected to join the expansively scheduled planning and progress update calls. Changes to CRUSOE itself were never involved, Bevan did all those himself, often under the radar. It was usually only an adjustment to a value in a configuration file anyway, minor tweaks that needed no downtime. CRUSOE was relatively simple (albeit the software it was built from was becoming increasingly obsolete). When Vedaneo were first brought in, a spreadsheet was circulated to all responsible contacts by Bob Groves, IT Applications Manager, seeking information on the suitability of each system for delegating the development work to the sub-contractor. Most of the information had already been filled-in; only the strategic systems would be handed over, for support and onward development. The odds and sods, the *found* systems, the spawn of the hobbyists, would remain in-house. There was a field on the form for something called 'Rationalisation Programme Status'. The options were 'Keep,' 'Rationalise' or 'Remove': CRUSOE was set to the second of these. Bevan had not been aware of this before and he emailed Bob politely asking him to explain what 'Rationalise' meant. He got a terse single line reply: *it means target to replace with another existing system*. No smiley face. Bevan suspected that he had only been sent the form as another warning shot. All he actually needed to do was confirm his contact details. He was grateful that his pride and joy was going to stay in the UK for the immediate future at least, but now the ticking of this rationalisation clock added to the sounds of ill portent jangling in his head.

*

The first conference call he joined hosted by Vedaneo was the kick-off meeting for the 2009 Q3 release. This involved changes to six major systems, with many other smaller ones impacted for testing, including CRUSOE. There were about twenty-five people on the call. Each of the outsourced systems had a project manager, development lead and test lead in India and most of them were present. Bevan found it impossible to tell who was who, apart from Deepti the release manager who was orchestrating the call with the precision of an auctioneer, keeping each participant to heel with her distinctively piercing voice. It lasted for three hours: all the relevant system leads were expected to present their plans, be subjected to the owlish scrutiny of some older-sounding voices in the background, then commit to the timelines. He listened on mute throughout, CRUSOE was way down the agenda. Fortunately, with the time difference, these calls were always in the morning, so he usually stayed awake. The others in the office wondered what he could possibly be doing, staring at the wall with his headset on, for all that time. Eventually it was Bevan's turn.

'Hello, do we have the CRUSOE rep on the call? Hello, is the CRUSOE rep there please?' If he had been nodding off, Deepti's strident tones would have brought him back to life instantly, but Bevan was ready and waiting. The novelty of working with people with such exotic names, so far away, had him fully alert and he unmuted himself exactly on cue.

'Hello, yes … it's Bevsie here … I'm the contact for CRU-SOE.'

'Bevsie? Is Bevsie your name? You are the rep for CRUSOE Bevsie?' Deepti's voice rattled like an automatic weapon.

'Er, yes that's right, I'm the rep for CRUSOE, I er …' He did not get a chance to finish.

'You are the rep for CRUSOE, thank you Bevsie. Bevsie you are test impact only, right. Bevsie can you commit for the test timelines for 2009 Q3 please?'

'Yes, yes … test only. The dates are fine, in fact I'll be … '

'You are committing for the test timelines for 2009 Q3 thank you Bevsie. Please do the needful. Hello, do we have the GLASS rep on the call? Hello, are you there please?'

Deepti continued with the call and finished on the dot at 1pm UK time, exactly on schedule. Bevan had eaten his sandwiches on mute at his usual time and spent the closing minutes looking up GLASS on the intranet, he had never heard of it and wanted to know what it was used for. He felt exhausted.

He joined the progress update calls, despite there being no great need. The discussion was mostly about problems being experienced by the development teams on the other larger systems. His direct personal involvement in the release would only come in its latter stages. He lurked in the background on mute, proceeding with his day job while listening to the cut and thrust. He found the voices hypnotic. There was one moment when a new test coordinator was announced: Sejal was her name. Sejal was introduced to the voices of the test contacts and Bevsie said hello. She sounded heartbreakingly polite, if he'd had one left to break.

*

The time came for the testing phase to start. At the beginning of the process Bevan needed to submit his test plan: a document describing the steps he needed to take in order to demonstrate CRUSOE was still functioning normally after the changes in the other systems had been switched on. There was no separate test instance of CRUSOE in the offshore environments, the technology was too old, and it was impossible to set up a replica of it on the Vedaneo servers. So, ahead of the release, Bevan was simply sent examples of the data extracts being produced by the new code to make sure it still had the right structure and would not generate any errors. Sejal was responsible for making sure all test activities happened according to the plan. One-on-one communication with India was nearly always conducted on IM and Bevan could not escape its clutches forever … eventually, early one morning, the ice was broken.

Hi bevsy

An unfamiliar icon started to flash on Bevan's screen. He had been caught unawares while buried in the database snuffling out erroneous digits. Until now he had shunned the corporate IM tool, and this was the first time anyone had 'pinged' him. He stared at the bottom of his screen in trepidation for a while before clicking the icon to open the chat window. It was Sejal. He eventually summoned the will to respond but insisted on typing his own hesitancy.

Er…. hello Sejal

It had been 30 minutes since Sejal's initial message.

Hi Bevsy. I'm calling you Bevsy is it fine?

Yes that's fine…well, it's "Bevsie" I suppose

Hi Bevsie

Hi Sejal

How can I help?

I need to check on 2009 Q3

OK

Will CRUSOE test plan be completed in the timeline pls?

Yes definitely

Thank u

Pls send me a draft when you have it

Yes, will do

Sejal's status immediately switched to *Busy* and she was off. The test plan was always the same. CRUSOE had a single interface, an import from one other system. Bevan just had to manually run the data load process with the test extract and check for errors. Then run a few queries to make sure the information in the database was not getting corrupted, then delete the dummy records. He knew the system so well a realistic plan would just say: '***test 1****: Bevan checks the data*'. But he had to be seen to be more thorough, so he had written a ten-page plan of more specific, pedantic test actions. He sent his document to Sejal the next day and received a smiley in return.

Bevan found these interactions refreshing. Most of the Vedaneo people were charming, efficient and ultra-positive. Having been initially wary, he came to look forward to the occasional pings. He wondered what their lives were like. He had become so disillusioned with his own existence, and the atmosphere in the depot had become so desultory and cynical, it came as an unexpected boost to experience moments of connection with these young and sparky souls. He was struck by their enthusiasm, especially considering they appeared to work such inordinately long hours. Despite being five and a half hours ahead of GMT Sejal rarely went offline much before he packed up for the day himself. Even if they were not chatting, he started to look out for her status in his list of contacts and silently wished her well when she finally changed from green to beige. For the first time in what was essentially longer than he cared to remember, he decided he wanted to know more about another fellow human.

*

As the release date got closer, tension increased on the progress calls. Sejal was always there and Bevan found himself thinking *go on girl* during her verbal jousts with Deepti, like he might when watching a race on screen at the bookies when he had a bet on. She always gave the impression of having everything under control. Then, a week before the release, she pinged him.

Hi Bevsie

Hi Sejal

How r u?

I am very well. How about yourself?

Am good

Glad to hear it

How can I help?

Just checking you are on track for next week?

Everything is in hand Sejal. Don't worry I will definitely be there for the post-release testing

That's cool. Thank u

No problem

Sejal, can I ask you something?

Sure

Bevan was disproportionately nervous now. He had been wrestling in his mind about whether it was worth trying to strike up a conversation. After all, what was the point? He was probably thirty years older than her, why would she want to tell him anything? And it was probably against Vedaneo policy anyway, she might get into trouble? He asked her the plainest question he could think of, and one that he thought he knew the answer to.

You're in New Delhi I think?

Um no... I'm in Noida only

Oh ok

Is Noida near New Delhi?

Yes

ok

Office is Noida but my place is in Delhi

172

I have to catch my cab now

am leaving

Oh ok

How long does it take you to get home?

About 2 hours at this time

Rush hour

Oh dear… that's a long time

Bye then, good luck, have a good evening

You too have a good one

Bye Bevsie

Bevan was shocked to learn of her commute time. He might have welcomed that kind of life himself but for someone her age, alone, after a ten-hour day… he was genuinely surprised that Allied Grids were willing to condone such harshness. He guessed that was the whole point. Employees' rights cost money, so get work done where those rights are non-existent and where competition for work is so intense that people will put up with anything. Bevan hated the thought of Sejal having to travel so late in a country where violence against women seemed to be endemic, if the news stories could be believed. His concern for her well-being ensured that her IM status became the top priority in his daily rituals, on reaching his desk.

The release was successfully deployed but not without teething troubles. One of the six main systems failed to start properly when all the changes were first made live. Deepti's conference call overseeing the whole operation became supercharged with anxiety as the teams tried to find a solution … and find someone else to blame apart from themselves. A procession of senior managers was summoned to dial-in over that Saturday morning, roused from their breakfast tables or the golf course by different stages of escalation, senses primed to discover whoever was at fault and scenting blood. With the various system support guys flat out, attempting to troubleshoot what was wrong, the release spilled over beyond its agreed downtime window and an emergency broadcast went out to all Allied Grids staff warning that the outage would leak into working hours. CRUSOE was working fine but Bevan stayed on the call anyway, just to see what happened. At one point mid-morning he nodded off and started to snore, accidentally unmuting himself at the same time.

'For Christ's sake who's that with the heavy breathing?' This was Bob Groves, who had been wheeled in to remind everyone about the consequences of not delivering a fix.

'Umm ... I think it might be Bevsie?' said Deepti, with exasperation.

Bevan sub-consciously detected this exchange and quickly came round.

'Oh, hi Deepti, er ... sorry ... er ... I'll put myself on mute.'

'We don't need you on the call now, mate. You may as well drop off.' Bob spoke through gritted teeth, calm as a gangster. He did not have time to get distracted, he was already in serious trouble due to the unplanned downtime. Bevan had been on the call since 2 am, it was approaching 10 now. He reluctantly hung up.

'*Tit!*' Bob seethed, making the word sound longer than anyone could remember hearing it expressed before. 'What was that idiot doing on the call in the first place!'

Bob could not dwell on his annoyance – he redirected his attention back to threatening Deepti and the other system leads. At last the cause of the failure was pinpointed, the problems were resolved, and the release completed just after lunchtime. Allied Grids' customers, in particular the supply companies, would have been affected by a temporary loss of capacity information and a fine from the government regulators would follow ... but no one lost their jobs. It was a near miss though.

*

On the Monday following the turmoil of the release weekend, Sejal appeared to be constantly busy so Bevan left her alone. But she showed green when he arrived the next day.

Hi Sejal

Hi Bevsie

I am very sorry about Saturday

np

Then immediately she was off, busy in another chat, dealing with the aftermath of the release. As it happened, she had been away from the weekend call at the time of Bevan's unfortunate interjection, talking directly with the offshore testers, so was unaware of his embarrassment. She had escaped any blame herself; the issues were down to an unplanned firewall change made by the networks team that they neglected to tell anyone about.

A few weeks later Bevan was alone in the office and close to leaving. It felt like winter darkness had persisted all day, ice festooned the roads and pavements and even the air looked frozen. During the gaps between the releases there was not so much to occupy him. He had run out of steam tending to CRUSOE and was feeling sorry for himself. He looked through the window at the black air, smeared yellow by sodium lamp beams and mist, thinking about degrees of loneliness. Did it matter that no one knew he was there … that no one would see him leave, or scrape the frost from his car before setting off … that no one would hear the sound of his key in the door when he reached home? Bevan was trying to ascertain whether the pain of feeling isolated was worse now, or when he was a child at school. The heating in the building was on a timer and, at that time of year, it became a battle of wills between his desire to persist at his desk and his ability to retain any body heat after 4pm. Chill seeped into the building, corralling his voices of desolation. Then he was startled by a ping.

Hi Bevsie

Oh… hello Sejal… nice to hear from you

… it's been a while

What's up

… is there an emergency release coming up?

Nooo…

I saw you online and thought to ping just like that

Gosh…

It is lovely to hear from you.

How are you doing?

Tired I guess. It is getting late here.

My cab is not due for another 30 mins

And then 2 hours home?

Not so long, maybe 1 hour now.

Earlier there is so much crowd getting out of Tech Park it takes longer

I would like to see where you work

Hmm

Do you have a wife Bevsie and kids?

Um… no… I live alone, never had kids

Ohhh… I thought you must be married

No that never seemed to happen

Sejal… can you give me 2 mins please?

np

I'm here only

Bevan broke off, he remembered there was one email to send before shutting down for the day. He loved the phrase 'I'm here only.' He nurtured the idea that, if he ever wrote a book about his life (which of course was inconceivable) *I'm Here Only* would make a good title, without being quite sure why. It had confused him at first but came to realise it was the equivalent of an English person saying: 'I'm not going anywhere.' Much to his consternation, his heart was now pounding, and his hands were struggling to type. He told himself it must be the cold.

I'm back

☺

You are usually so busy.

I always worry about you

working such long hours.

Is it quiet there now?

Yes. Not so much of work right now. And manager has gone home 😅

Ha ha… that's good to know

I am also done for the day. Got the CRUSOE data up to date and now was thinking about… thinking about leaving too.

It is very cold outside here. Ice everywhere.

Ohhh… please keep warm… and hats off to you, I would not like such cold

'hats off' – I love your turn of phrase ☺

Mind you…

I need my hat on when it's this cold!

Your English is good Sejal.

I guess… Hindi is your first language?

☺

Guajarati is. Then Hindi and English

Guajarati?

Yes

I'm from Gujarat…

a place called Rajkot

Oh I didn't know

I thought it was all Hindi over there

Nooo... many languages

Sorry I had no idea

np

different states have their own language. Guajarati is spoken in Gujarat.

Guys here in Noida say I talk funny ☺

☺

Well... you don't sound like it to me! Your English is much better than my Hindi!

I guess we speak a fourth language also... Hinglish ☺☺

Ha ha... yes ... sometimes on the calls I wonder what's going on

Yes...

So much of UK and US culture over here... we can't help using the words and it gets kind of mixed up ☺

I wish I could visit India

to see what it's like

Hmm

I wish too

Bevsie I must go now.

Oh ok... well... lovely to chat...

thank you for pinging

np

Bye

Bye bye Sejal

take care

yes I'll

you too tc

Bevan sat back in his chair, stunned. Stunned that, from nowhere, when he least expected, this young girl on the other side of the globe had chosen to send him a greeting spontaneously, without any work-related cause, timed perfectly as his thoughts had been slipping into darkness. He was also a little stunned that he had found it possible to make small talk in return, seemingly without cocking things up. He had even used smiley faces. He was now oblivious to the cold as he left the office and walked to his car that night, all trace of loneliness forgotten.

They began to chat regularly. Usually Sejal was locked in calls when Bevan first went online in the morning, but they would dip in and out during the day and often her leaving time coincided with a quiet spot in the UK afternoon, so they could wish good-byes to each other. Bevan lost himself in this private world of mi-cro-connectedness. It was almost like having the imaginary friend he had never concocted as a child. He thrived on being able to share thoughts without being judged and, while she was an ex-tremely bright girl, he knew with the language difference he did not have to try too hard. The conversations were mostly the same and he could usually guess what Sejal's replies were going to be. But she was funny and occasionally teased him. They each lived de-humanised lives, albeit for different reasons – her long, lonely hours were by necessity, not choice – so this homely companion-ship made a difference to both of them. He was inspired by her sunny disposition, which remained constant despite the punishing hours and bullying management she was subjected to … also de-spite the fact she was living so far away from her family. He rel-ished hearing her tales of festivals, street food and trips to the movies when they both had freedom to chat for more than a few minutes. From her perspective, she was glad to have found an onshore person who did not treat her like shit and seemed to be so sensitive and genuinely interested in her life. Bevan knew that nothing would come of it, of course, and he kept Sejal away from the deadness inside his soul. He doubted they would ever meet. But their delicate friendship lifted his spirit – it provided a welcome flickering of joy, like fireworks seen from a train window on the way to an unwanted destination.

*

Bevan and Sejal had been swapping glimpses of their contrasting lives for over a year. One morning Bevan decided to send her a photo. There were swathes of daffodils growing by the depot entrance and for once he noticed them, drenched as they were in watery sunshine that day. He knew she loved flowers and it struck him that this dazzling scene might be so uniquely British, that daffodils might be so unfamiliar in India, the photo might make her happy. Bevan had only ever used the camera on his mobile phone before to take pictures of different types of equipment in the warehouse and once some scratches on his car for an insurance claim. He had certainly never thought to capture an image for aesthetic appeal, let alone send it to someone else for their pleasure. Now he felt self-conscious, as he entered the realms of content sharing. Any form of social media was complete anathema to him, but Bevan was prepared to take the steps in this case. For Sejal, he was prepared to *join in*. When her name appeared online, he clicked her and attached the photo, hoping it would be a surprise. Having posted the daffodils, he began a chat.

Hi Sejal

Despite appearing online there was no reply for over half an hour.

Hi Sejal, are you there?

Hi

This is Ankit here

Oh… Hi

Sorry Ankit

I thought you were Sejal.

Sorry about that photograph.

No problem. Flowers are looking nice ☺

Sejal has gone. I have her laptop and logging in with her ID today, mine is not set up.

Gone? Gone where? Bevan's heart sank beneath the floor. He could not believe his screen. Such a simple collection of words in a chat window yet bearing such heartache on one side of the exchange.

Oh no…

Where has she gone?

Back to her native

She's getting married I think

Oh… gosh

Is she coming back, do you know?

I doubt

She's gone from Vedaneo

I'm taking over the test planning role now

Oh

OK

Thanks Ankit.

I expect we will meet again on the calls.

Sejal has gone. Once again, without any warning, something Bevan cherished had been taken away. He had allowed himself to care too much and now he could feel the stabbing pains again. His thoughts thrashed around trying to assimilate the news. Why did this have to happen now? Why had Sejal not told him about it, let alone say goodbye? All his doubts about other people's motives resurfaced: did she *ever* mean to be friendly or was it all part of the job, playing the client along? He tried to convince himself that this was not so, that a sudden disappearance was just part of her culture, part of the mysteries of the east. Maybe she had been forced into an arranged marriage against her will and was unaware it was coming … and worse, was scared about it? Bevan had no way of finding out. Their only communication had been via messaging at work and he could see no way of enquiring through Vedaneo. He wanted to cry out to her. Bevan chastised himself for being so stupid. For allowing a trace of involvement to take root once more, after so long. He had promised himself this would never happen again and now the wisdom of that pledge was laid bare by his stifled tears. He tried to rearrange the scar tissue to cover this new loss, this outlying pulse of emotion, but the feeling was too raw. He never heard from Sejal again and her absence made the calls with India become simply another thing to endure from that point onwards.

*

Bevan was transported straight back to the dark moment before Sejal had first reached out. The universe was playing tricks on him. His period of chatting with her instantly morphed into something too good to have ever been true. Maybe he imagined the whole thing, maybe he really was going mad. He returned to his buried state, plugging away at his old routine, without the drip feed of warmth from India he had come to adore. Why had it been so important? After all he could easily make similar small talk with Angie or someone else at the depot. He guessed it was because the connection was so contained. There was no chance of the discourse spreading outside the little box of the chat window into areas that made him uncomfortable. He could keep it under control, while at the same time gaining the benefit of being listened to. The sense of never being listened to added fuel to loneliness.

He also felt protective towards her. Bevan had never wanted children and perhaps Sejal fulfilled some form of parental instinct in him that had always been suppressed. (Fortunately, Fiona had never wanted children either ... or maybe she did without saying ... perhaps that's why it all went wrong?) There was a new pain now. Once Sejal's profile disappeared from the corporate directory, Bevan no longer had the anticipation of checking her status as he drove to work. He missed her – he missed her innocence, charm and unaffected humanity – although he did not even know what she looked like since her profile had no photo. He was so against social media it never even occurred to him he might be able to trace her there. Sejal had gone for good ... and Bevan's world was empty once more.

The rhythm of counting down the seasons re-established itself. Bevan sat through another year of managing CRUSOE and supporting the releases with a minimum of drama. But the ticking clock would show no mercy. The time came for a dreaded meeting request to arrive in his Inbox. He knew it was inevitable, but he put himself in denial, month after month, until the day of reckoning. At last there it was, sent at 3 am, a conference call entitled: 'CRUSOE rationalisation'. It came from Bob Groves. The IT department had targets for simplifying the technology used across the company and reducing the total number of different systems (in particular aiming to kill off the most ancient ones). The day of the call arrived. Bob and Howard were both present, along with project manager, business analyst and experts from Allied Grids' main centralised resource planning system, the ERP. Bevan joined impassively; his mind locked on autopilot. He knew what would happen but was prepared to say his piece.

'Morning, er, Bevsie. Thanks for joining.' Bob was trying to sound empathetic.

'Hi Bob. No problem.'

'Let's get straight to it. The purpose of the call is to talk through the steps needed to migrate CRUSOE into the ERP tool.'

'Um ... actually ... it can't be migrated. We have different processes here from the other regions.' Bevan was feeling no fear because he was feeling practically nothing at all. He knew there were only five users left in the depot now and he was on shaky ground … but he had nothing to lose.

'Bevsie, in case you weren't aware, there's now a standard set of processes for equipment ordering across the UK … there's no need for your area to be different. Have you not seen the briefings?' This came from the business analyst who sounded like a trendy vicar. Bevan had read something about a new procedure, but the preamble was so full of buzzwords he deleted it before reaching the end.

'We've got unique requirements in our area. CRUSOE has been adapted to handle them. Why didn't anyone ask *us* about the new set of processes. How do you know they will work in our region if you don't consult with us?'

'We did try to consult but …' The business analyst was getting defensive, but Bob cut across him, with a bigger fish to fry.

'Did you say you've adapted it Bevsie? How have you done that?' Bob had been hoping for this opportunity. 'It's only ever down for test impact in the releases as far as I knew … not any system changes.'

'I update the macros myself out of hours.'

'Are you saying you make changes to a live system without getting an outage approved?' Bob was into his notorious East End villain mode, talking slowly with understated menace. 'And what made you think it was OK to do that?'

'I know all the users, they know me. I tell them what's happening,' said Bevan after an uncomfortable pause.

Another pause ensued. Howard and the business analyst then both tried to speak at the same time. 'I know Bevsie is fastidious …' 'I assume all this is documented …' before Bob continued. He could not really care less about the detail of what Bevan did, he knew the hobbyists were all the same and had to be wiped out.

'The point is, we have now captured the full standard process in the ERP workflow, and everyone should be using it. CRUSOE was probably good in its day, but it's not needed anymore.' Bob added the *probably* in order to maintain the levels of antagonism.

'But it hasn't failed once in the last fifteen years. What's wrong with keeping it? Have you consulted with the users?' Bevan managed somehow to restrain himself from telling Bob Groves to fuck off. Bob himself showed no such restraint.

'You're not listening to me. We don't need to consult with your users. CRUSOE is a *liability*. It's not even a fucking system! It's a poxy file database in a format that went out of support ten years ago, based on code no one understands apart from you ... and you obviously haven't documented properly. It costs us more to test the fucker each time we do a release than it would to buy a fucking robot to look after the stores.'

Bob continued in similar vein. The project manager went on to describe the plan for reviewing CRUSOE's functions to make sure everything was covered in the ERP tool, with the sub-text being that if the depot had special requirements that deviated from the rest of the company, their process would have to change to match the technology rather than the other way round. Howard promised to give Bevan some support in his expected contribution to the migration project. But Bevan had stopped listening. During Bob's rant he had flung his headset onto the desk and banged his fist against the wall. He clamped his eyes shut, his mind locked into a circle of *bastard, bastard, bastard, bastard* ... A combination of his hatred for Bob mixed with his own self-reproach. The depot had become so deserted that Angie was the only other person in the office. She heard the sounds from Bevan's desk and called out to him 'Are you OK Bevsie hun?' But he ignored her and, sensing how much he preferred to be isolated these days, she left him to it.

*

Once the anguish had subsided Bevan unplugged the headset and logged off from all his windows, apart from one. He spent the rest of the day running queries in CRUSOE and checking for data anomalies. As always, he found a few user errors – he always knew where to find them. He ran the corrective scripts and revelled once more in the injustice of his efforts going unrecognised. *Single Point of Failure* indeed. It was not a failure. It was a goddamned success

… a single point of *success*. It works. And the bastards are going to kill it.

Once his weeding of the data was exhausted, Bevan returned home and opened the vodka. He reasoned that he was not an alcoholic on the basis that he only ever drank in the evenings, on workdays at least. Winston Churchill and Jack Regan both had spirits on the go all day, and they seemed to manage all right. He was doing better than them. He often reminded himself about the possibility of being over the limit the next morning, but he had a system in his head – as he often did. One hour to metabolise one unit. If he avoided alcohol between 10 pm and 6 am he should be OK on his drives to work every day. He wondered if being awake half the night made any difference.

Chapter 16

By 2013, CRUSOE had been decommissioned and the former users, the few that remained, had been inducted onto its strategic
successor. Bevan had to sit through a few galling sessions, explaining to the analysts from the migration project how CRUSOE was
used, as they nodded eagerly, agog at the prospect of another system closure, another target met. He knew they did not really grasp
why the depot was different and why certain processes had
evolved that deviated from the norm ... but the spirit of the place
was gone now and resistance to the switch was minimal. Angie had
taken a redundancy package and gone back to Scotland to make
pots, leaving Bevan alone in the office. He helped with the data
transfer, in which all existing information in the CRUSOE database was copied to the ERP. Somehow, he survived the exercise
without murdering anyone.

'I used to spend a lot of time making sure the data was accu-
rate you know,' said Bevan to the analysts, as they considered how
much of it was really needed. They looked at each other and
smirked like schoolboys.

'ERP doesn't allow inaccurate data to be entered in the first
place. And we won't be needing that Comments field, that's for
sure.'

The dismantling of his brainchild felt to Bevan like being evicted from a long-standing family home. To see everything he held dear being picked over by these disrespectful toe-rags was an excruciating experience. He willed them to catch some disease from the water cooler – the bottle had stood untouched for about three years, a fact he kept to himself when asked: 'Yeah, it should be fine.'

With all traces of CRUSOE now obliterated Bevan had to learn the new system. His role reverted to overseeing the goods in and out of the store, he was no longer required for any system maintenance or testing. But with so much work contracted out and the supply chain so diversified, it was only the larger items that now passed through the depot. Fewer deliveries, fewer collections. There was hardly any work for Bevan to do. Howard had tried to encourage him to look for another role, or take a package, but he preferred to stay where he was, still drifting on the stream. Some-one would have to physically drag him out of the office; either that or demolish the whole site. Predictable as the tides, HR policy changed and full-time people managers fell out of favour. Howard disappeared and Bevan fell under the regional management team. The cost cutting had removed all the excess fat from the organi-sation and was now eating into the muscles and bones. No one really had time to act as Bevan's manager, so his isolation was al-most complete. As long as he kept doing what was left of his job … he was now barely perceivable.

Despite the reduced workload Bevan kept to much the same timings. His pattern was too well grooved to alter. He wound down the clock at his desk, maintaining the habit of residing there much longer than was necessary, while only recording the standard seven hours twenty minutes on his timesheets. What difference did it make … he could record twenty-four hours a day and no-body would notice? He knew his behaviour might be derided by some as *presenteeism* … but he found the term disrespectful – as far as he was concerned he was not merely there for the sake of it, he was providing a service by manning his station in case of emer-gency. Bevan sometimes wished he could stop falling asleep though. With so few people about, the lack of distractions meant his slumber could fill an alarming proportion of the day. He wondered how he would have fared during wartime if relied upon as a lookout. Would he have been able to keep his eyes open with the heightened atmosphere of peril? Or would he have drifted off just the same, only to be woken by the sound of bombs falling inland, as unalerted fighter squadrons sat idle? Bevan assumed the latter, the compulsion to doze was irresistible whatever the situation. He felt reasonably secure that no one would find him asleep, he would hear if anyone came through the door and with his head on the desk he could not be seen from the window. However, he disliked not being able to control himself and would have preferred to save it all for night-time, to help block out the voices.

Although he was steadily losing his sense of reality, he retained enough appreciation of the various policies not to transgress his terms of employment. He would have loved to spend time following the horse racing online but knew this would be detected, if not blocked. He read all the internal communications' emails and intranet updates that spewed forth incessantly. He spent a particularly long time researching all the information broadcast about the pension scheme and decided to cash his in, having just turned fifty-five. The usual concerns about being afraid of having nothing left for very old age were not a factor for him. He pictured himself just fading away once his work at Allied Grids was done. He sat with glazed eyes through a couple of interviews with HR minions, there to make sure he was doing the right thing, while they glanced nervously around the office wondering why no one else was there and how anyone could tolerate such a filthy building; unclean mugs stood on windowsills, accumulating mould, as memorial shrines to departed colleagues. The high point of his self-delusion at that time was the assumption he had another ten years to go; ten more years to hide from himself, despite no longer having any real motive for being in the office. Bevan decided the money was better spent now, while he could make use of it. He started to go on long train journeys at weekends, hoping the changing views of scenery truly would erase some of the thoughts he could not shift. He would spend entire Sundays on the rail network, collecting nondescript towns and cities, sampling pints of the indigenous beers along the way. And he bought more expensive brands of spirits just for the hell of it.

There was a major project up the coast, laying cables to connect one of the vast new offshore wind farms to the grid. One Sunday Bevan drove up to see for himself. He looked out from a stretch of low cliffs, the impermanent cliffs of East Anglia that bore sole witness to entire communities lost to the sea. As caterpillar ships inched along the horizon, in their path the ghostly figures of turbines faded in and out of view like a mirage. Breaks in the cloud allowed shafts of light to illuminate them in groups, like distant ballerinas picked out on a stage. And then, in an instant, the graceful ranks would be shrouded in haze again. He watched them wax and wane for an hour or so, dumbstruck by the sheer scale. Noticing a lighthouse on the next arc of coastline, the thought occurred that his existence at the depot had become akin to that of a lighthouse keeper. A purpose simply to be there. To keep the lights on, maintaining a token human presence in an outstation of geographic significance, on hand in case of … in case of … here his thoughts ran aground. He was unable to think of any eventuality in which his presence would be absolutely essential.

The cable drums were now self-tracking. They had electronic tags, as the delivery lorries had satellite positioning. The larger items in the depot *knew where they were* and transmitted their current location back to the central computer system automatically, like teenagers taking selfies. This further eroded any value in the stores controller function. Bevan wished he could be involved in creating the vision for these great engineering extravaganzas. Surveying the maps to decide the best locations; planning the infrastructure required and the quantities of plant; building alternative models and assessing the cost and environmental impact. But these tasks were all done by external contractors now, the part played by Allied Grids was more as a hiring agent. He liked seeing pylons from the train and felt sorry these new cables would be hidden underground. He had once enjoyed tracing all the wires to the hi-fis and TVs his Dad had installed at home, to see what went where. Now it would all be hidden behind trunking. It was impossible to tell how things worked these days.

Returning home, Bevan reflected on the scope of human achievement, even in such a hateful age. How could there be so many people whose lives had steered a course free of self-doubt, with the confidence to even think about placing windmills in the sea, let alone making them work to create power on land. Most people must be wired differently compared to him. Had he always been psychologically disabled in some way ... had he always lacked some key ingredient in being an effective individual? Had he always been denied any capacity to contribute to the progress of mankind, trapped as he was in a perpetual loop of introspection ... or was it just his own weakness? Could he have lived his life differently, or was he hamstrung from day one? He stopped for provisions before reaching his flat, hoping that a better class of vodka would refine his insights and bring him more answers than the cheaper stuff he had relied upon until now. His evening passed through the usual stages of mild, transient euphoria followed by the dimming of all feelings. As dusk fell, he watched the lights of the town gradually outshine the sky. He marvelled that those lights would one day be fuelled by the twirling of phantom ballerinas, dancing to their music box tune at the edge of the ocean. Maybe the lights' brightness would rise and fall in harmony? Before any questions could be resolved, he was off and dreaming.

*

The following day Bevan set off for work as normal. Being not long past midsummer, the sun was up, and the natural world was in full swing well before commuter traffic started to build. He had to park in a lot surrounded by low-rise office blocks a hundred yards or so from his flat. For a few weeks each year he would be dive-bombed by over-protective herring gulls that were nesting nearby, as he approached his car first thing each morning. They often came out of the sun, yapping belligerently as their fluff-ball chicks wailed on the grey rooftops. It was an alarming experience, but he admired the gulls' determination. He had forgotten what it must be like to feel such vitality, such passion about anything.

They looked for all the world as if they wanted to peck his eyes out but just swooped as low as they dared. The frisson of danger gave a kick-start to the day. He had to watch out until being safely behind the wheel … and his thoughts were still partly in the sky as he turned the engine.

Bevan reached the dual carriageway, which was quieter than usual due to the school holidays, and slipped into his usual trance, riding the curves through muscle memory. The fields shimmered and the haze of the previous day still lingered. The ground held enough warmth for thermals even at this hour. He spotted the circling of a buzzard and wished he could hear it cry, this being one of his favourite sounds. The bird soared upwards and he turned his head, trying to keep it in vision as it glided above the dusty terrain. Bevan should not have allowed himself this lapse in concentration – by the time he noticed the line of stopped cars that he was speeding towards, there was no time to react. He tried to brake but he was too close and slammed into the back of the queue. The slip road of his normal exit had backed up due to roadworks at the roundabout. There was damage to the two vehicles immediately ahead, though all including his own were drivable. The young woman in the car he struck was called Amy, a nurse on her way to work at the hospital. She already knew she had suffered whiplash damage and was in too much shock to lambast him when he dashed to her door. The sales rep in front of Amy was apoplectic but held back from seriously assaulting Bevan having instantly computed the potential for compensation while calling 999. He just grabbed him by the throat and called him every expletive under the sun.

When the police arrived Bevan's flashbacks to an earlier time, prompted by the sight of the uniforms and the memory of his previous experience with the emergency services, added to his feeling of nausea and he leant on his car to avoid passing out. He apologised profusely, explaining that he had been distracted and taking full blame for the accident. The sight of Amy shaking with fear, clearly in pain, was another knife to his heart and he was glad the ambulance arrived quickly to take her away. He felt physically undamaged himself, but his thoughts were racing once more. Had he committed a crime? He was soon left in no doubt when he failed the breathalyser test. There was still too much alcohol in his system from the night before; his carelessness could be pinned to inebriation. Hypnotised by the lights, he had failed to stick to his system. As a consequence, he caused a crash while driving illegally and now was in trouble.

*

Bevan's case was dealt with by magistrates, he narrowly escaped the crown court due to Amy's reluctance to press charges and her unexpectedly quick recovery. He was fined £10,000 and given an eighteen-month ban. It could have been a lot worse, but Bevan was cooperative, remorseful and his blood alcohol had only been just over the limit, his method for calculating how much booze he could safely metabolise nearly proving successful. (His mother had unwittingly made a similar mistake, albeit under different circumstances and with her paying a bigger price – this was another example of symmetry that later played on his mind). Being a first offence, he evaded prison. Although drivable, his own car was written off, as was Amy's. The sales rep's protestation soon dampened down once he recalled his backlog of unpaid parking fines – his car was only slightly damaged, and Bevan's insurance paid him off. The entire episode lasted six months, at least giving Bevan something to focus on while being kicked out of his job.

In the aftermath of the collision, several weeks passed before Bevan realised his biggest problem was not going to be the fine – or the loss of his licence – or even the loss of his car. That there was a threat to his tenure at Allied Grids only sank in after a discussion with his latest line manager about taking time off to attend to his hearings. As soon as the full implications dawned on him, the possibility of a fine and its magnitude became irrelevant. Bevan was suddenly on death row. If they sacked him he could see no future. He would enter a void, with no means of survival. He prayed it would not happen, but his gods were not listening. When the verdict came, Allied Grids were able to terminate his employment on the basis that his responsibilities still included driving, on paper at least. HR had been looking for ways to manage him out of the business anyway – when this opportunity fell into their lap they swooped as quickly as the herring gulls. The absence of any compassion was breathtaking, the dismissal letter being dispensed with ruthless speed. No one spoke to him face-to-face in parallel, he was just given his marching orders. Where once he had jumped for joy to see the word 'confirm' in a letter from the National Electricity Board, now the only words he saw were 'terminated forthwith'. Not that there were many other words to read. It made his heart shrivel. The people that write this stuff, the HR demons, clearly had no heart at all. Thirty-seven years of dedicated service, one mistake and all he got was a decree of execution, a single paragraph long. All they saw was another tick on a whiteboard – another step towards a staff reduction target – not any actual impact at a human level. These people disgusted him … could they even be real? 'So many plastic faces,' as Sejal used to say.

Bevan had been made redundant and, thanks to the fine and the reparations sought by his insurers, a sizeable chunk of his pension money had been cleaved off, all as a consequence of his thoughts being transported for a moment by a bird of prey, instead of being fixed on the road. He still had his flat and the remaining money, but everything else – *everything else* – was gone. He was given permission to make a final visit to the depot to retrieve some personal items from the locked drawer by his desk. HR had agreed, assuming this meant artefacts of sentimental importance like family photos. But the haul only amounted to mugs, a cardigan, a hole punch and the pens Bevan had grudgingly provided for himself. That itself felt like a minor victory but his main objective was making sure he had not hoarded any data CDs that should have been destroyed when CRUSOE was shut down. He could not remember. Fortunately, there were no such incriminating remains, he must have done what he was told at the time. All he left behind in the drawer for them to find was a collection of T-cards.

Again, as with Martin approximately ten years earlier, a security officer was despatched to oversee these last acts, accompanied by an HR henchman. They could not spare the time to counsel him about unemployment, but they *could* spare time to see him off. Bevan pictured this duo spending their lives travelling the country purging the unwanted remnants of Allied Grids' workforce, clearing the corners of the organisation of all errant individuals who strayed from the path, like witchfinders. Once he had his biros, Bevan was hauled from the building by the impatient eyes of these two watchmen. As he walked across the car park, carrier bag in hand, the only vehicles present were those belonging to his overseers. He did not look back. He held no fondness for the depot's physical structure, but it was the rock he had clung to – he had no desire to watch it fade into the distance, his only choice was to let go. He walked back to the station via the Railway Tavern, one of the pubs the old gang had frequented and felt the pangs of passing time. It would not have been out of place to see a photo of the electrical fitter crew on the wall, an antique memento of former ways of living, like the sepia images of draymen that hung alongside the horse brasses in the Three Tuns before it closed. Bevan continued on, to catch his train home. Within a year the depot was bulldozed and turned into flats.

Chapter 17

The passing of the seasons was catching up with Jez. As the year ground on, he was not anticipating the arrival of autumn with bated breath. It did not seem like an arrival anyway ... more like a decision by summer to pack up and leave, restoring England back to its native leaden countenance. The circus was moving on, the merriment and colour were stowed on pantechnicons bound for another country and the true complexion of the outside world was revealed again in all its true dourness. Emerging from the dankness of the Viaduct into a morning of cold, blustery drizzle – conditions that would raise a grimace from even the most pampered individuals – was a withering challenge to the spirit. At night, in the rooms at the guest house, Jez would feel his body tense inside the sleeping bag, willing every sinew to avoid contact with the bedclothes. He would use the stinking bathrooms for the absolute minimum – the idea of using the (at best) tepid showers, in cubicles with no curtains, in a room with no lock and filth encrusting the floor, tested his resolve every time. Sometimes he had to, sometimes he went without. When the days were bright, it felt like a redemption to be back on the road, heading past the station, back towards the more salubrious parts of town. When the weather was bad and especially as the mornings got darker, it felt like a successive stage of purgatory.

His usual alcove was losing its lustre as the first port of call. It was becoming permanently damp and the lack of morning sun meant there were better places to get warm. As his arrival times got later and more variable, soon enough an interloper appeared, filling the space that was normally his. Jez knew protesting was futile. He had only left a pile of cardboard behind, which was saturated now and would not have withstood any kind of tug-of-war that might have ensued, if trying to reclaim it. He had to accept the loss, concede the ground. His attempts at pleasantries were ignored, as the stranger appeared to have no English. Jez sat down, further along the path, nearer to the car park where the sun was now pitching, contemplating his options. As his numbed mind chugged into life, he noticed a crow on the rough ground opposite his feet, wrestling with half a sausage roll. The bird was struggling to control its quarry, which kept sliding down the slope towards the footway, where danger lurked in the form of passing humans. After some deliberation it knowingly impaled the pastry with its beak, pointing its head to the heavens like a performing seal and flapped carefully up to the roof of a nearby Land Rover, to make use of the hard, flat surface as a dinner plate. As the crow triumphantly pecked away, Jez marvelled at the display of intelligence, strength and agility he had just witnessed. He was reminded, on an earlier occasion in the same car park, that he'd seen another crow dart across his vision to grasp an unsuspecting pigeon by the neck, throttling it to death on the ground with incisive brutality, as might a peregrine falcon on the wing. That was a shocking sight – he had previously assumed crows to be much more passive foragers. What struck him now was the sophistication of their actions, the different methods in their armoury for obtaining sustenance. (*Unless the pigeon had been a vigilante killing rather than one for food,* he mused, wondering what transgression a pigeon might be capable of to warrant such a punishment ... *adultery perhaps?*) Whatever, it was complex and decisive behaviour, leaving him to doubt whether homo sapiens truly was the master species after all, when he was failing so miserably to adapt to the same environment.

Izzy suddenly appeared from the archway onto the street, whisking along on her way to an appointment. She did a double-take, initially only seeing the stranger again – he had sat there for a while, prompting her to entertain the hope Jez might have moved on to somewhere decent. Now she realised he had merely been displaced.

'Hello Jez, my darling!' She beamed her soothing smile. 'I nearly missed you my lovely ... what's going on here then? Looks like you've been gazumped!'

'Looks that way doesn't it ... goes with the territory I suppose. Not much I can do about it I don't exactly own the land.'

'Ahh ... you poor thing. It's about time you got yourself something sorted my dear.'

'Hmm.' Why did they all always have to say the same thing? As usual Jez wanted to talk about something else.

'Izzy, do you see that crow over there ... on the car roof? You see what it's eating, you know it carried that up there by itself. It flew onto that car with a sausage roll in its beak.'

'The cheeky bugger! I bought that! It was meant for you actually. I was surprised to see matey here sitting in your place just now. Bugger it, I thought ... but then I thought ... I may as well give it to him instead, I didn't want to waste it. I didn't think you were coming today ... obviously not good enough for him, the ungrateful sod.' She looked back towards the alcove with accusing eyes.

'Was it the artisan herbs and apricot?'

'Of course it was honey. Only the best for you.'

'Hmm ... maybe he prefers a Greggs. The crow obviously appreciates it though.'

Jez smiled ruefully as Izzy laughed ... and then she was off. As usual, he basked for a moment in the mellow glow she always left behind in her wake, wishing he had been there before to receive her gift, but soon reality kicked in again. He knew he had to find somewhere else to go. Maybe there was somewhere he could sneak into, in another part of town, that no one had thought of before. An undiscovered oasis that could save him from any more nights at the Viaduct. Reluctantly accepting that his pigeonhole was no longer a dependable haven, Jez decided to go on a voyage.

*

Walking had become agony. The blisters on his soles and toes had evolved into permanent sores while his ankles and calves cried with pain because Jez had been treading unevenly to reduce the abrasion. Bandages and dressings could be obtained from the Caravan and he would observe the ritual of re-binding his feet in the cubicles at the drive-thru approximately once a week. On this morning, fuelled by a new sense of purpose, the discomfort was barely perceptible. Jez had been reading Primo Levi. Initially, he was affronted by the suspicion the donor intended the gift in a spirit of: 'if you think *your* life is bad.' But he persevered anyway and found himself both riveted and appalled by the accounts of wooden shoes – how longevity in the death camps was directly proportional to the fit of the rough-hewn clogs bestowed on each prisoner. The further they could walk, the more enforced labour could be heinously wrung from their pitiable frames. The sooner movement was made completely insufferable by the hard, unforgiving wood clamped around their feet, more quickly came the final murderous dispatch. Jez was unsure which outcome was preferable but was thankful not to have been subjected to such random life odds. Colin had found him a pair of suitably-sized leather boots. He was reasonably well equipped but nevertheless the constant need to stay on the move was taking its toll. On this day however, he was blessed with a reason to ignore his hurting limbs. He was going house hunting; he was going to find a new home.

Jez turned away from his familiar circuit of the inner ring road and headed for the more unexplored reaches of town beyond the docks and the old power station site. As he gathered steam his mind took flight, fantasising about potential hidden spaces in abandoned buildings. Perhaps a remnant office block attached to one of the dismantled factories. If such a thing remained intact maybe an electrical supply might magically still be in place, on some long-forgotten account, with heating on a timer no one had bothered to switch off. He convinced himself a secret treasure trove lay waiting to be revealed … and through his ingenuity he would get inside and lay claim to its sanctuary. The sprawling works surrounding the former turbine halls were preserved, motionless and largely untouched since the fires had stopped burning. Developers had thus far shied away, scared off by the costs of decontaminating the land. The streets running downstream from the gentrified quayside had to divert inland to bypass this wilderness of silos, buddleia and barbed wire. Jez plodded on, following the main coast road that skirted the site, ascending its gradient stoically, into an increasing headwind. Rain began to fall to a steady beat, whipped into crescendos by the breeze. Life on the street encouraged the revival of ancient skills, like forecasting the weather solely from signs in the sky and the direction of the wind – the use of TV showrooms in the high street as a means of keeping in touch with events of the day being a far distant memory. But today Jez was oblivious to any rain – he did momentarily consider it was not the best day for roaming but was too driven by the object of his quest to be deflected. He carried his backpack, with rolled-up sleeping bag strapped on top, and with the seams of his waterproof coat starting to fail, everything he owned was being gradually saturated by the horizontal downpour. It did not matter, the heavens could open to their heart's content, he did not care. He was on course for somewhere dry and secure, somewhere that would provide a shield against the casual cruelty of the British climate for good.

As the road levelled out again, a view of the whole docks area was unfurled. Low clouds skimmed the trees in the distance beyond the estuary, merging town with sky in watercolour grey. The arches of the viaduct were just about visible through the mist, as they curved across the flat valley, marking the target of his loathing. They looked so distant, the prospect of ever returning to the lodgings that festered at their root seemed unimaginable. A morass of industrial wasteland filled the foreground, sullen, in perpetual mourning for the loss of the power station building and its monumental chimneys … a fossilised landscape, frozen in place when the throb of the generators ceased. The vast expanse was enclosed by a single, ten-foot-high steel fence, with tops twisted into jagged shapes designed to rip flesh. Jez could see a small rectangular building close to the perimeter, featureless apart from the 'Danger: Asbestos' signs on the side, but could tell there was no way in. Even if he had somehow been able to vault the fence, the doors and windows appeared so fiercely boarded up, an assault would be futile. He tried to perambulate the entire boundary, as much as the right of way allowed – some stretches of fence that abutted onto back gardens or allotments, were impossible to follow. The constructors of this barrier certainly meant business. Jez failed to find a single flaw in the defence and eventually was forced to conclude the power station site was impregnable. He had to look elsewhere.

*

Jez looked to the sky for inspiration. He knew people often referred to the big skies in this part of the world. He failed to see the attraction. He wanted small skies. Small skies that could easily be sheltered from. No inspiration was forthcoming but at least the wind and rain began to die down. He had to keep moving, in the conviction his body heat would drive off some of the dampness that now enveloped him. Rather than retracing his steps back towards the town centre, in desperation he kept going outwards towards the periphery, investing his faith in the munificence of the unknown. Beyond the docks the road gradually lost any trappings of commercial activity, the mixed nature of its layout replaced by an uninterrupted procession of semi-detached houses. Daylight was starting to fade, allowing Jez to catch glimpses of domestic normality through illuminated windows – vignettes of other lives, mysterious and unattainable. Soon the early vanguard of Christmas decorations would begin to appear, reminding Jez once more that winter was nearly upon him, precipitating a shiver, part from cold, part from panic. This avenue was leading him nowhere, but he continued to march.

He arrived at an unexpected junction. The town spread radially in lobes of urbanisation, with self-contained networks of crescents and closes blooming from a series of main thoroughfares that sprouted like branches from the ring road. There were few concentric streets linking these suburbs together, but here was an intersection with promise. The destinations described on the blue cycle route signs suggested a slice against the grain … a traverse through the pith, cutting across the clutter that grew between the orderly segments of residential property. Jez turned left with renewed optimism. Houses soon gave way to scrubland as his new boulevard of hope sloped down towards a possible final reckoning. There must be *somewhere*. His heart soon skipped a beat. Sure enough, out of the gloom beyond the barren incline emerged the characteristic shapes and motifs of a string of small businesses. Anglia Clutch Centre, Baileys Water Softening Supplies, Vijaya Food Wholesale, Toshi Boyz Martial Arts, Poppies Hospice Furniture Depot, Go-Parts Reclamation, Tag-Me Bulk T-Shirts. An array of sheds too haphazard to be called an Industrial Park but to Jez's eyes a cornucopia of opportunity … surely there must be some units here that were out of use? He decided to scout the whole row before delving more deeply, time now being of the essence as darkness fell. He did not want to waste his energy exploring every dead-end. The food wholesaler had a gate open at the side but there were still too many people about for safe investigation. The car parts reclamation yard was more deserted and had a couple of open garages visible towards the rear, but the fencing looked forbidding and warning signs implied the presence of Dobermans, albeit Jez thought it unlikely any were actually on duty. He made mental notes and moved on.

The final plot in the sequence was completely idle. Its former use was not clear, just a featureless, two-storey block set back from the road, with an empty flagpole stuck to the front wall. No signs, no logos. The broken venetian blinds – one of which trapped a faded Garfield beanie baby halfway up the window, left stranded when the place was evacuated – suggested office use rather than light industry. Jez allowed his mind to run riot. There might be carpet tiles, kitchens, insulation? The piles of planks and a Portaloo in the corner of the forecourt suggested some aborted refurbishment. The Portaloo added further to the allure. Phrases such as 'all mod cons' and 'viewing highly recommended' burst into his mind, as he felt transported into a role as reality TV star, fronting a down-at-heel off-shoot of some property development show. Jez was feeling giddy now. The fencing was just normal chain-link, supported by concrete posts, with an extra layer of fine green mesh around the outside. He was sure he could clamber over it somehow, but an attack from the front would be noticed. The rear backed immediately onto the steep upward slope of an old railway embankment, now overgrown with trees. To the right, the plot was bounded by the brick wall of an active premises that offered no hope of entry. To the left, it adjoined the back gardens of a short straight row of terraced houses, at ninety degrees to the road. At the end of that street he found a small gap between the side of the final property and a fence at the bottom of the embankment. With heightened anticipation, Jez squeezed along this fissure to re-join the margin of the site he had just been viewing from the front – his would-be Shangri-La. At this furthest corner from the road, there was just about enough light left to see along the back of the building. Jez could discern what looked like a partially ajar window in the shadows. *He knew it!* His chance was in touching distance. The same defences that blocked off the main entrance also extended to the rear, to meet another impassable steel structure lining the foot of the embankment, at right angles, with no space in between. But although there remained an obstacle to climb, he had found a weak point. He could gain enough traction into the chain-link pattern to lift himself into the compound ... and crucially, in the shadows, hemmed-in between the slope and the larch lap panels that bordered the end-of-terrace garden, he could not be seen.

Jez paused to gather his senses. Despite being sodden and chilled to the bone, he was fired-up inside, feeling sure he was about to take control of his destiny. Here was a refuge away from the turmoil of the centre of town. He could come and go as he pleased, through this hidden passageway. He might even be able to cadge a gas stove from somewhere, for a bit of warmth. There were many options to think about. First, all he had to do was scale the fence and scramble through that window. The top wire bit into his hands, even with gloves on, but he was able to take hold. The toe-caps of his boots would not penetrate the chain-link diamonds

203

but by pressing his foot against the diagonal concrete buttress that supported the final post there was enough give in the body of the fence to enable Jez to pull himself up. His right foot and right hand now clung to the top wire, his left hand grasped the top of the concrete post. From this position there was no way of finding a foothold on the way down. He just had to launch his body over the top and hope for an even landing. As he pushed upwards from the post with all the strength he could summon, his left foot caught the wire, tilting him head-down on the other side. He was able to break his fall momentarily with his hands on the ground but when the weight told and he became unsnagged at the top, his body slumped down into an ungainly heap, making him shout out loud at the sharp stab as his knee twisted. Jez lay on his back on the wet tarmac like a stranded beetle, temporarily unable to move. Dogs began to bark in the garden of the end house and security lights on its roof sprang to life, pinning him to the ground like a captured convict. All that was missing were sirens and shouts of 'Achtung.' He knew the game was up straight away. Even if he could get inside the building now, he could not simply stay in there forever. He needed a viable access route to and from – and the damned dogs here would sense him every time, irrespective of whether he could learn to negotiate the fence without falling. Despite coming so close, the folly of his adventure was laid fully bare. The shock of his awkward landing snapped him out of his pipe dreams. All the voices that had pleaded with him to seek proper help rose out of the shadows to cat-call from every direction. His quest had come to nothing. Alerted by the barking, real voices were threatening him now too. His hopes for a better place to stay were shattered in an instant and now, somehow, he had to retreat back to the regular haunts he knew and hated.

Chapter 18

You have to make your own reality. This was something Angie had said on more than one occasion in the office, to no one in particular. *You have to make your own reality guys*. She tired of hearing them blame other people for the dissatisfaction they felt about their own lives. Bevan had never understood what she meant, it was probably all bollocks anyway, she was a bit of a hippie after all. But this was his crucial failing. He simply did not have the wherewithal to forge his own destiny. Since the day he had applied for an apprenticeship as an electrical engineer he had followed a path of least resistance. Every step in his life had been the next most obvious thing to do, perhaps with someone there to sow the seed in his mind, or to push him down the next tunnel. There had always been an obvious signpost. After leaving Allied Grids there were no race stewards on hand to point the way. He had bounced and clattered to the bottom of the board and now was reliant entirely on a momentum he had no capacity to generate.

Since the point when he tried to end his own life after Fiona left him – and his subsequent vow never to try again – Bevan had depended on work as the minimum source of fulfilment to go on living without disturbing anyone else. Its removal left him stranded, at the mercy of his inner voices and his inability to make rational decisions. He had been functioning in neutral for so long, each daily act part of a pre-programmed ritual designed to deliver him to the office at the same time each day, he was not even aware of the material expression of his existence, the footprints he was leaving behind. Having returned home after his unceremonial eviction, all his possessions and routines revealed themselves to him as if for the first time. Bevan looked at his flat as an archaeologist might view the remains of an abbey, trying to piece together a reason for the arrangement and a narrative for events that had taken place. In order to survive, to continue his downstream passage, he needed to build some new motivation from the ruins. He needed direction and he needed it fast.

*

Bevan might have stood more chance without the money. In that initial period after being released he might have salvaged sufficient reserves of good sense to make him seek help, had he been instantly faced with financial ruin. He *was* capable of good sense. The way he administered his duties at the depot clearly proved he was no idiot. However, because he still retained a reasonable proportion of his lump sum and was able to pay the rent for the immediate future, he could afford to take his time before any urgent action was required. As the months passed, the judgement he had once exercised as the regional stores controller for a major national utility increasingly fell out of use. His lack of meaningful activity caused this good sense to atrophy, a process accelerated by the new ability to fuel his alcohol addiction at all times of day. The loss of his car caused him no inconvenience. He no longer had reasons to drive anywhere, everything he needed in town was within walking distance and he could still disappear on the train when the urge arose. He did not succeed in finding direction. All he found was a way to live without thinking too much.

Bevan suspected that others in his situation might be eligible for state support of some kind, to rescue them from hardship. The social care services, whatever they were. He paid his council tax, maybe he should speak to someone at the council about benefits? He knew where the local council offices were and had wandered past them a few times. A glass-fronted reception centre with leaflets in a thousand languages and a queuing system like Argos. He had never set foot inside though ... after all, he had money ... it was probably not meant for the likes of him. And furthermore he was a criminal. They would question him about his life and the choices he had made. He would have to dredge unthinkable memories and submit them to what would no doubt be a huge pile of forms. This was a path he would never feel able to take. And anyway ... he had money ... he did not need any help.

*

Despite his spiralling delusions Bevan did retain a degree of self-preservation instinct. He did not want to see himself as an alcoholic. He never took to drinking in the mornings. Only those who started drinking from the moment they woke up could be classed as real alcoholics, in his view. He did not want to drink until passing out in public either ... he did not want to fall. Contrarily there had been many times in his past when he *had* wanted to fall. While he was working he often caught himself envying those people who were affected by illness or injury. It gave them an excuse to drop out. They had a reason to switch off and be looked after by others who were paid to care. No need for emotional ties, just a means to have all your necessities attended to without suffering any guilt about not being capable yourself. No need to make an effort. Now Bevan's only goal was to hide from reality, rather than making his own. The debates in his mind continued to rage but a new shout could be heard when he was most in charge: *I do not need help.* He did not need help. He was not an alcoholic and that thing with the car crash was pure bad luck, he was not a drunk driver. He would be OK.

You make your own luck. Another one of Angie's mottos. In this case Bevan understood what she meant but he still thought it was balls. Luck is luck, by definition. You cannot skew the dice in your favour simply by positive thinking. All you can do is ignore the failures and keep hoping. This became the credo for his new unwelcome situation. Ignore everything that has gone wrong before and nurture a tiny flame of belief that one day something will happen to save you. He had been unlucky in his journey so far, therefore payback must be waiting just around the corner. He was not exactly reciting this mantra in his head all the time, it was more of a sub-conscious backdrop – one of the loudest voices in the foreground was actually saying: *idiot, idiot, idiot*, on repeat, but he did his best to suppress that one.

Somehow Bevan convinced himself he would manage ... somehow a new pathway would be revealed, he would be returned back to mid-river and the flowing current. While waiting, he would contain his spending to sensible limits and bide his time, ignoring any temptation to throw money at 'get rich quick' schemes. He was smart enough to know that any promise of money from nothing would prove to be a scam and make his life worse. In the new logic that was forming in his head, gambling was not the answer either. He was not hiding from reality to that extent. Bevan understood, to begin with at least, that backing horses was not going to be his vehicle for salvation. But he enjoyed the challenge of sifting through the form looking for patterns, just as he had done before when scouring the information in CRUSOE to identify anomalies and trends. He scanned the race cards for course and distance winners carrying top weight ... for leading trainers with just a single horse at a meeting many miles from its stable. He had his pet systems and liked watching the statistics play out, never expecting to win a fortune but happy to see the frequency of successful wagers belie the odds. Making his own luck, not by blind positive thinking but by understanding the data.

*

While Bevan was working he had lost the habit of setting an alarm, he was always awake in time anyway. Now there was nothing to rouse himself for, he started sleeping longer. *Maybe this was some kind of natural response to reduced stimulation*, he wondered ... *maybe he had started to hibernate?* He would peer at the clock when his eyes finally decided to open in the morning and note the time with detached curiosity, reflecting on the randomness of his current state. He rose, washed and staggered into the kitchen-living room. He had no solid recollection of performing simple chores before, for years his early morning thoughts were focused solely on reaching the moment of starting the car and commencing his drive to work. The acts of opening the car door once in the morning and once in the evening bookended his day. Everything else, before and after, was just filler. And now filler was all he had. Making a cup of tea became an act of observance; he started to take note of the colour, the taste, the difference made by the length of time the bag remained in the mug. He had no particular preference: *as it comes* he would say to himself, as if summoning an alter ego to make the tea for him … his domestic help … another voice with whom to share the day.

Bevan would stare out across the town for ages, watching the seasons change through the quality of light and turning colours of the leaves from this fixed and elevated view, rather than from the undulations of the dual carriageway. He watched couples laden with carrier bags arguing as they walked along the pavements below, speculating on how it would end. He studied the cars queuing at traffic lights looking for unusual makes and models. He marvelled at the dogfighting gulls and crows that cut across the sky. He could lose himself in the search for new details in this scene, each time enjoying the challenge to spot something he had not discerned before. In winter evenings this quest gained an added dimension as the lights came on. His fascination was not prurient, he just liked to make mental notes on the regular facets in this kaleidoscope of artificial illumination: the glow of car park stairwells, the living rooms with flashing TVs, the bedrooms with half-opened curtains that always had a lamp on but no movement, the kitchens where people stood and waved their arms.

Was he lonely? Bevan often thought that loneliness was an irrelevant concept as far as he was concerned. He had never craved company, therefore presumably he was happier to be alone. Socialising felt like torture, he felt rejection from everyone he met and had found personal interactions impossible to navigate (with a couple of notable exceptions, both of whom vanished into thin air). But he did wish he could share his thoughts. If something out of the ordinary occurred within his field of vision, something that caught his interest – a minor shunt on the ring road, an unusual bird, a rainbow – he would feel an urge to say: *wow, look at that* ... But it would be snuffed out, there was never anyone there to listen, never anyone to validate his thoughts. He could only look at the rainbows in solitude and guessed he must have been lonely all his life.

*

Bevan's professional career had lasted thirty-seven years. Throughout that period he had never stopped to think about how the rest of humanity occupied themselves during the day. Now that Allied Grids had taken his purpose away, leaving him with nothing but empty expanses of time to fill, whenever he set out for the shopping precinct he was surprised to discover a parallel world of activity that must have always existed without his knowledge. People bustled around the streets and malls in greater numbers than he ever imagined: why were they not at work? He wondered how they made a living. It gave him some reassurance that he was not the only person free to roam on weekdays, unconfined by the discipline of office life. Jobless, he was rendered uncomfortable and exposed, but the numbers around him at least made him feel less like a pariah than he expected. He took satisfaction from walking and exploring the various byways of the town centre although he was keen to avoid the typical hang-outs of the homeless that blighted certain sections. If he saw them from a distance, sometimes he would stop to see if he recognised the individuals concerned – some were not as objectionable as others, some he did not mind passing in close proximity. He hated hearing their pleas for money though – keeping his money in his pockets when confronted with a beggar was one economy he found easy to stick to. It would no doubt only get squandered on drugs after all. He was perplexed by the apparent scale of the drugs problem that frequently blared from the headlines in the local newspaper. Bevan was aware of the basic existence of drug dealing but nevertheless he still could not picture the human interplay needed to arrive at the final transaction. Where did you go? How did you find out the right people to speak to? A further and positively beneficial manifestation of Bevan's social ineptness was the fact that he was never likely to acquire a habit for illegal drugs. He had experienced enough brushes with the law for his liking and his legal drug – the drug he acquired entirely respectably alongside cabbage, sardines and washing-up liquid in the baskets of his regular supermarket – was the only one he needed.

Bevan felt in control of his drinking. Hitting the bottle was not the only thing to occupy his mind. Nearly, but not quite. If pressed, he would be drawn to admit his favourite pastime was watching the racing. That is to say, if pressed, he would admit that watching the racing was the one thing that provided any entertainment, aside from visits to the pub. There were no other sources of recreation, the fascinations with computing and home electronics were long gone, but the horses gave him at least something to fill the void. One of his many systems – the rules he set himself – was to never bet when drunk. He was generally prudent enough to realise that alcohol impaired his function. He was not stupid and knew he would only make stupid choices if trying to select winners after a few pints. In a typical day he would buy the racing papers first thing, devour the form for at least an hour, then go the bookies to place his bets. He preferred to read about the runners and riders at home rather than risk interaction with other punters – thereby avoiding that awkward gavotte sometimes necessary to keep reading the pages on the wall in the betting shop when two people are interested in the same race. He would then retreat to the pub to bathe in the luxuriant pleasure only beer could bring, albeit aware he was only quelling the voices momentarily and the amber glow would again be replaced by anxiety.

*

He would shuttle back and forth between bar and bookies throughout the afternoon, watching the races then returning to his favourite nooks of padded seat and sticky table to review why his horses had underperformed, to revisit the analysis and work out how on earth a different creature had won. There were enough tolerable pubs and betting shops to allow Bevan to alternate, thus never becoming a sufficiently permanent fixture to require any conversation with staff or customers beyond a cursory greeting. When a bet was successful he inwardly gave a knowing smile, smug that his systems were valid. He had enough winners to create the illusion he was breaking even and enough pints to convince himself the days were worthwhile. His gambling never escalated to outlandish levels, but each day began with a visit to the cash machine unless there had been a particularly long odds payout the day before. Even on those rare days of plenty, if he forgot to bypass the more sheltered footpaths where homeless people hunkered down, he continued to be unmoved by their paltry collections of coins and walked briskly past. There was the occasional vagrant who kept themselves apart from the rest and appeared less intimidating, but generally they disgusted him with their ragged appearance and boorish conduct. If he could hold his drink, why could they not do the same? He sometimes considered what separated himself from these lowlifes. They had probably suffered similar bouts of misfortune. He could identify with the willingness to fall outside society but not in such a way that would impinge on other people in their vicinity. If he felt uneasy about their presence, surely the majority of respectable citizens must too. Where was their self-respect? What made them think it was acceptable? He often inspected himself in the mirror when he returned home, looking for the same signs of disintegration and substance abuse. He convinced himself he was not like them. At least he only drank enough to become comatose when he was alone in his flat in the evenings and caused a nuisance to absolutely no one. He was not like them, he would never sink to their level.

In beer and gambling Bevan had adopted a new routine of sorts. It was fulfilling to the merest degree, but it made the days disappear. He drew comfort from the fact that he no longer had any ties whatsoever. No one was ever likely to contact him, least of all his brother and sister. He was on nodding terms with a couple of other inhabitants of his building, but the turnover was so frequent that there were always new faces to ignore. He had no idea where any of his former colleagues from Allied Grids lived now and had no interest in finding out. He sometimes thought about Martin. He pictured him flourishing in retirement, attending gigs and staying up late with friends. He occasionally allowed himself to remember Sejal and pictured her looking like a princess in exotic dress surrounded by sisters-in-law and babies – having never actually seen a photo of her, perhaps she had only been in his imagination anyway? Alternatively, for all he knew she could have died in a train crash between Delhi and Rajkot the day after their last ever chat. It was impossible to find out. As for Fiona … it was too painful to think about her now. There were so many ghosts, so many unanswered questions.

This routine was his last throw of the dice. Bevan knew that he was making no attempt to secure a future and all he wanted was to fade away. While he had promised not to deliberately make it happen, all he really wanted was to not wake up one day. He subsisted like this for a few years, on borrowed time, like a trapped miner sustained temporarily by a pocket of air. No great shaft of luck pierced into his darkness to reverse the loss of his regular income though. His pension money dwindled on the essentials of rent, bills, bets, booze and the supermarket where he would buy what he needed each day. He drank in the evenings to minimise those waking moments when he could see what was ahead. His choice of brands went down-market again, having concluded it made no difference to the shrewdness of his internal dialogues. Fortunately there was a glass recycling bin downstairs and he was able to dispense his empties in a gradual stream that prevented a confrontation with how much his intake was increasing. It was under control. He did not need help. He would be OK. But the money was running out and Bevan would soon have no choice but to break one of his promises.

Chapter 19

As Jez lay on his back, marooned inside the chain-link fence where his voyage of discovery had run aground, immobilised in the dirt by embarrassment and pain, he listened for the voices that ricocheted just out of sight. Were they coming to get him? He chastised himself for ever thinking this place held any prospect as a safe haven. How could he come and go without fear of these confounded dogs raising the alarm? What he craved was the *removal* of fear, that was the whole point of making this journey. Even if the noise died down and he could get to his feet, he no longer saw any point in trying to get inside the building. The potential entry point he had spotted was now so obscured in pitch black shadow he had lost the nerve to approach it. If he did make an attempt and by chance was able to squeeze inside, how could he ever leave? It would be like climbing into your own coffin. Now he just wanted to flee, but was transfixed, listening out for the voices.

Through fevered concentration he divined the human sounds as nothing more than an appeal for the dogs to shut up. As the seconds passed his panic subsided – it began to dawn that the barking might be a routine event. They probably made this racket all the time, in response to foxes or squirrels, with sufficient frequency that their owners no longer bothered to investigate every cause. The existence of these unruly beasts had ruined the chances of this outpost becoming his refuge – the likelihood of the same reaction happening again would make it impossible to come and go unnoticed – but at least he might be able to escape the scene now without being mistaken for a burglar and beaten up. Jez gratefully concluded that no one could see him from the upstairs windows at the back of the terrace. Tufts of hedge were visible, silhouetted by the security lights over the top of the wooden fence panels, affording him some extra cover. He willed himself to believe, despite being caught in the beams, that if anyone *was* looking out from those top floor bedrooms he was close enough to the fence to remain hidden from view. He cursed them anyway – if only the houses had been unoccupied, his plan might have worked.

Once the hounds' baying had finally ceased, Jez carefully rolled onto his side on the slimy weed-covered tarmac, then onto hands and knees. The pain stabbed again but he managed to stay quiet this time. He was reduced to primal instinct now, crawling along the potholed sideway of the building on all fours. The surface was littered with puddles and discarded paint cans and an odour of solvents penetrated the cold, damp air. It was risky to crawl too far, with the searchlights now dimmed he did not want to press his palms into anything sharp. He slowly hauled his body upright, against the grating of his joints. His feet were numb and bearing weight on his left leg was intensely uncomfortable, where it had been twisted in the fall. Jez felt behind himself as best he could, to check his snail shell of possessions was still attached, then began to hobble towards the front of the compound. He decided he may as well climb the fence where it faced the main road rather than the corner where he made his incursion, now feeling he had nothing to lose. The concrete posts were on his side now, making it much easier to scale. He reprised his recent exhibition of scrambling technique and, while the vault was equally inelegant, at least he was not tipped upside down on this second attempt. He crumpled when landing on the pavement, letting out another cry that prompted the dogs to start barking once more, but he was clear of danger now as long as he got moving. He began the disconsolate trudge, returning towards town along the reverse route of his epic walk, without a single glance back. The sheds paraded past him again, their frontages now leering and goading him for his failure. Tag-Me Bulk T-Shirts, Go-Parts Reclamation, Poppies Hospice Charity Depot, Toshi Boyz Martial Arts, Vijaya Food Wholesale, Baileys Water Softening Supplies, Anglia Clutch Centre. He felt them taunting *as if we had room for scum like you!* Less than an hour ago he had wished this setting to become his nirvana. In reality it merely acted as an amphitheatre for his inadequacy and shame to be brutally exposed. Crestfallen and exhausted, Jez's ageing body limped on through the gathering mist, away from his false paradise and back towards the surroundings he had tried to break away from – the surroundings he had come to detest, yet the only environment he could realistically call home.

*

Jez had always hoped he could stay ahead of the pack. Now, as he laboured back to his original patch, his whole body hurting and his throat constricting with the bitter air, he felt all the vulnerability of a wounded animal in the sights of the hunter. The roads peppered him with the splashes and reflected lights of the evening rush-hour. The gradients that he had taken in his stride earlier in the day now felt like chasms. He lost all track of time and had entered a trance-like state when he eventually shambled towards the main night shelter at the end of his fruitless expedition. On this occasion, he was in such a terrible state there was no way he could be left outside. The entry fee could wait, he was too cold to speak, let alone rummage into his backpack to extract his collection of coins. They knew him, he would only call for help like this in desperation. He was steered to the warmest spot available and his worldly goods were placed near heaters to dry out. Through fitful sleep his dreams held him poleaxed where he had fallen from the fence, lying on the rain-sodden ground in the dark as foxes tiptoed by, sniffing him on the way. He was practically paralysed but could turn his head enough to see light and movement … and hear the sounds of muffled laughter coming from the window at the rear of the building … the building he had nearly conquered on his heroic odyssey. Some people were in there! He was determined to join them. He tried to get up, but his limbs were unable to respond.

As sleep ebbed and flowed the dream pattern was repeated. In the morning his near neighbours complained about his nocturnal rambling – not that night-terrors were a rare occurrence in the shelters, it was something they were used to, but nevertheless was frustrating.

'What was you going on about? *'Please let me in … Please let me in'…* over and over. You already was in, you prick. How else do you think you ended up on this floor if they hadn't let you in? You wouldn't shut up … kept us awake all night … you stupid tosser.'

Jez looked up towards the skylights and mumbled an apology. He did not bother trying to explain the real meaning of his visions – he was stunned by how vivid they had been. He felt he would be haunted by the preceding day's events forever. Was his nightmare trying to tell him something? Should he have continued with his plan and tried the window, despite the cacophony from the back gardens? Reality became blurred with the imagined version of the experience in his dream, but the pain and fear were imprinted on his consciousness firmly enough that he pledged never to explore those outer regions again. Jez wanted to grab some more sleep but was chivvied out of the shelter, once they were convinced he did not need A&E, despite his sore knee making it tough to walk normally. It was raining again, so he decided to head for the quayside, to find a dry pitch under the warehouse arches. He stopped at the Caravan on the way, hoping for some new blankets. Colin was away on his rounds, but one of the regular helpers was on duty. She was shocked, if not surprised, to see the haggard condition of her visitor.

'Jez! Well hello there … long time no see. Are you OK? You're looking proper poorly pet.'

'I'm all right. Just got a bit soaked yesterday. And my knee's playing up. I could do with some new blankets to be honest.'

'You're in luck pet, we had a new load of donations in … I'll pop round the back and sort you out with something.'

Revived by soup and a new bundle of soft furnishings, Jez set off for the docks. There was always demand for the covered locations by the waterfront but today Jez was feeling more resolute not to be intimidated by any potential rivals than he might have been before. As the remnants of decent weather retreated there were fewer visitors to worry about, so the security guards were less motivated to move the street life on. The area was mostly frequented by local townsfolk now, on their way to work. The presence of a few homeless wretches skulking in the shadows during the day made little difference to businesses in the vicinity at this time of year. Jez picked a spot without much deliberation, backing onto a hoarding that screened one of the derelict old buildings yet to be converted. The pavement here was wide enough to avoid obstructing pedestrians and was completely dry, despite the morning's constant drizzle. He gathered some cardboard for a base, arranged the blankets as swaddling clothes, donned the nearly dry sleeping bag and wrapped himself up snugly. The ice-cream carton was in place in case anyone was moved to give him anything, but primarily he just wanted to switch off. He kept his books and candles free from water damage by tightly packing them in plastic bags inside the rucksack and they had more or less survived the deluge of the previous day. He stood the candle on an upturned box, lit the flame and began to read. As the shivering stopped he felt a rare moment of contentment – that feeling of being sealed off from the worst effects of conditions outside. He *was* outside … but he was sufficiently less saturated, sufficiently less freezing than he had been recently, that the difference enabled him to feel a benefit. His latest reading matter was *Catch-22*, which he was getting through avidly. The idea that if you seek to escape a difficult circumstance on the grounds it is turning you crazy – but the very act of seeking escape itself demonstrates that you must be sane, thereby negating the request – appealed to his fatalistic instincts. He wanted such a clause to apply to his own situation. Jez did not want to accept that he could unravel his current predicament by submitting to the agencies that were pleading to help him. He wanted to have no choice. And at moments like this, why should he worry. He was out of the rain, comfortable at last … and lost in a world of stories.

*

After reading for a while Jez nodded off, basking in the cosy be-fuddlement of oncoming sleep. On waking, he blinked out to-wards the water, with its facets of slate and white cut by the breeze, just beyond the railings on the opposite side of the path where he sat. Irritable gulls fidgeted in the air as if they too were tormented by the search for an acceptable place to land. They kept plopping into the water then immediately lifting off again like jump-jets, un-able to settle. Was this their equivalent of testing the water; getting used to a temperature lower than they would choose, bit-by-bit? He sympathised – it was bad enough on the pavement.

There were two pound coins and some silver in his collection box – someone clearly had been moved to hand over their loose change at the sight of this candlelit man asleep with paperback still in hand. Jez had been unaware of the gesture. Without making his gaze obvious, he watched the next few passers-by, musing on what kind of person would be strolling this way by the marina in the middle of an early winter morning. Office workers would already be cloistered away in their meeting rooms. Full-time parents would be filling their cars with an abundance of shopping bags or catch-ing up on household chores … certainly finding better things to do than idling away down here, in such unfriendly weather. There would have to be a specific purpose for being here. A well-groomed estate agent, clipboard clamped to bosom, hotfoot to an appointment to show prospective buyers around one of the luxury flats – she was miffed by the wind and rain messing up her hair, but her eyes were fixed on the commission. A couple of online daters who'd pulled a sickie from work, now heading for a rendezvous at one of the cafés. A gangland fixer suited and booted to project a veneer of respectability while en route to demand pro-tection money from an unsuspecting restaurant owner. He in-vented a back story for everyone that crossed his field of vision – if only he had seen the donor of the money … what had been their reason to be prowling the waterfront at this hour?

Would someone sit and talk today? He hoped not. His brain was still frazzled from the day before – he needed time to recover his senses, not least from the nightmare. He was glad it had not returned during his recent snooze. (*It was a dream … yes, it must have* been a dream ... *surely there had been no actual foxes at the time?*). His thoughts meandered towards the random encounters in life. The books he had been given. The trains of thought that would never have occurred without chance meetings with particular people at certain moments in time. If the enforcer who passed him five minutes ago had stopped for a light, would they have chatted? Might Jez have said something to strike a chord in the man's conscience that, by accident, would make him relent from a life of crime? If the couple had stopped and the guy declared his passion for *Catch-22*, reeling off a humorous and insightful critique, entertaining Jez in the process, would the lady have fallen in love on the spot with her ten-minute-old acquaintance? Jez wondered if there was anyone out there capable of influencing his own destiny in a similar way. How much of life follows from pre-determined action and how much from coincidence? He had no answers but somehow the sight of the water, while sheltered from the rain, plus the flickering of his candle in the gloomy daylight made his mind run free. All he knew was to live life day-by-day, following his nose. He was still in denial about the polar weather yet to come, let alone his old, failing body. Jez concluded he must be crazy, given that he was succumbing to his fate without trying to change it. But he also concluded he liked being by the water and would try to keep going for as long as he could.

Chapter 20

The final tick of Bevan's clock was his bank balance, which he'd watched eroding steadily on each visit to the cash machine. He tried to delay the inevitable by cutting back on spending wherever possible, but the drink had its own momentum that was hard to contain. The flat was furnished, there was hardly anything that belonged to him and what he did own was practically worthless. He managed to sell a few articles including the computer – the final tangible relic of his one-time technical exploits. *Making good use of resources.* The thing only had scrap value now. The amount of money he could raise from the disposal of his possessions was negligible and their removal was more about clearing the decks than generating useful funds.

Bevan was keen not to leave any loose ends behind. He gave notice on his tenancy and cancelled all payments from his bank account. He lived out the final weeks in his flat, toying with options. He was reaching the inevitable conclusion that the key principle that had sustained him for so many years could no longer be upheld … a pledge sworn to himself would have to be discarded along with his excess clothes, bedding and CDs. Had he finally reached the right moment; the moment when ending his life genuinely was the best course of action? While no single person on

the planet would be affected in the slightest if his light in the fir-
mament became extinguished now, his thoughts turned to the random strangers who might happen upon him after the event. The
determination not to cause grief to any other fellow human beings
was dusted off and played again in his mind. Imagine the horror
of seeing someone plummet from a multi-storey car park, the concrete pavement cracking on impact, in concert with their skull? He
was always appalled by stories of those selfish bastards who
stepped in front of trains. *If you're going to do yourself in, at least choose
not to ruin the life of another blameless individual in the process. Good rid-
dance to you, if you're capable of inflicting such distress on someone else, in
addition to yourself, even if you are at your lowest ebb.*

No … it would have to be done out of sight somehow, without witnesses; certainly without being witnessed by the pleading
eyes of a train driver the moment before you're squished into the
tracks. It had to be enacted alone … *but what about the effect on the
first person to stumble upon your lifeless form … how disturbing would that
be, how traumatising?* A repeat of his prior attempt to take an over-
dose was out of the question, the method needed to be foolproof.
Maybe water was the answer? Could he really live out the final act
of his imagined journey downstream, flowing out to sea and van-
ishing into the deep? But then his body would be washed up on a
beach somewhere, to be found by an unsuspecting dog walker, the
ghoulish appearance of his bloated corpse would presumably give
them nightmares for life too. Bevan considered jumping off a
bridge, or capsizing from an inflatable dinghy, with lead weights
strapped to his body, making him sink without trace. *Swimming with
the fishes.* He liked the idea but could not envisage a sure-fire means
for self-drowning, entombed in concrete or otherwise. He was
struggling to find a solution for the perfect way to die.

Where once Bevan had lost himself for hours, gazing into a
pint of beer, mulling over the various twists and turns of his life,
now his deliberations in the pub focused on the best way to disappear completely and bring those twists and turns to a close. He
always knew it was wrong. Everyone knew it was wrong and cow-
ardly. He knew it was wrong before but was blind to the impact it
would have on any bystanders. In the aftermath of the failure –

and coming face-to-face with that impact in the form of his brother and sister – the *wrongness* became fixed in his brain. But now the fixative had washed away and the reasons not to try again had flown. It was too late for counselling. He had been blocking out thoughts he found difficult to deal with for his entire life. When his father and mother died it felt like second nature to ignore the emotional anguish and carry on. The loss of Fiona, the estrangement from his siblings, the disintegration of his career and the criminal conviction for drink driving … each of these on their own were hard enough to think about, but the totality was literally soul destroying. He thought about his own reaction when reading stories in the news about people committing violent acts. A seventy-year-old woman battering her husband to death in their shed. The initial temptation was to ask why? Surely she could have controlled herself, what could the husband have possibly done to deserve a spade in the head? What you never read about were the thousand preceding instances where the same thoughts occurred, but the person concerned *had* managed to contain them. She had heard him mutter *stupid cow* under his breath too many times before, turning his back while she was still talking. Motive and opportunity. Sometimes the drip, drip, drip, catches up with you. Bevan had lost the power to contain his base instincts.

With practically all of his money gone, Bevan's detachment from reality was complete. He timed the dispersal of his earthly goods to coincide with the last day of notice on the flat, such that his remaining essentials could be carried in a solitary bag. What *do* you take with you on your final outing? He wanted to keep warm. The air was too chilly to venture outside without a coat and there was no need to suffer unnecessarily, irrespective of his intended outcome. The coat came. He had read about suicide pacts. Strangers who meet online solely for the purpose of making sure they each go through with it, perhaps asphyxiating themselves by means of a charcoal burner inside one of their cars, on some lonely rural track. The defining achievement of home barbecuing – no one used a hosepipe from the exhaust in the garage anymore, it was all silent and painless carbon monoxide from materials acquired in a poignant farewell visit to a DIY megastore on the way to the Peak District. But it still did not overcome the fundamental problem that someone has to find you and clear up the mess. Anyway, he did not have a car and certainly had no intention of meeting anyone online, even if he had kept the computer. Bevan scanned the view from his window one last time, contemplating whether he would speak to another soul before his concluding breath.

*

Before setting off, Bevan took a final look in the drawer under the bed. The previous occupants had left behind some random items all those years ago. A small box containing oriental crockery, a hairdryer, a handful of books. He had emptied every compartment of his own belongings, but these fragments remained undisturbed … to him they came as part of the property. Bevan wondered what thought process had been at play. Were they unwanted, misjudged gifts abandoned with relish … or cherished yet forgotten artefacts, abandoned in haste? He reflected on the recurring pattern. The flat as a timeless waystation where arrivals and departures map the trail of human disconnectedness. The thought occurred that he should adopt one of these discarded relics and carry it with him as a token charm. Eyes closed and with a self-conscious fumble that reminded him of the hand amongst the balls during an FA Cup draw, his grasp formed around one of the paperbacks. Thomas Hardy. *Oh great.* He always suspected his predecessors had ideas above their station, based on some of the pictures on the walls. *Thomas Hardy! Who would want to read that? What wankers.*

For once he obeyed his self-enforced rule, resisting the temptation for best of three, unlike earlier times as a child when he insisted on replays in games of throwing paper in the bin until successful, thereby proving he was not a wanker himself. What did it matter? He did not have to read the stupid thing … as long as the book fulfilled the role of object to hold, in lieu of a mobile phone, making him appear occupied and respectable. He felt the book in his hand like the comfort of a car door handle, shepherding him towards his chosen path, his ultimate descent. Bevan exited his home for the last time, allowing the front door to slam shut. He left the key in his post box and stepped into the outside world. He was more or less sure he knew what to do. The morning air was brisk and for the second time in his life he experienced the unbridled delight of knowing a release from all worry was at hand.

He had a rough plan in mind. While looking out of the window, a vision had formed of the ideal spot – a place where he might lie undiscovered for eternity. He had all day to get there though, there was no hurry. He first crossed the road at the foot of his building, to look up at the vantage point from which he had been surveying the rooftops moments before. Bevan pictured himself behind the glass, like a supposed photo of a ghost in a book about haunted houses. He dwelt for a while on whether he believed in hauntings. *Would an apparition of his last hour ever be seen?* Maybe … after all, there was no reason why ghosts should only ever be seen in ancient properties. If a ghost is the imprint of a desolate, suffering soul, modern buildings should be full of them too. Then again, that spiritual stuff was all just superstitious nonsense, which he had little time for. So no, when he was gone, he would be gone, rendered purely to inert molecules.

Bevan decided to take an elongated stroll around the waterfront, to make the most of the time he had left. Even that decision made him question himself. *Make the most of … what are you talking about?* If he was capable of *making the most of* anything, if he was capable of taking pleasure from these buffed-up surroundings, maybe there was still a sliver of hope in him finding fulfilment? *Don't be stupid, Bevan … you know what you have to do.* Even now the voices were not hushed. He realised one of the main reasons he rarely wandered this way was to avoid encountering the homeless people, who always made him nervous. They looked so unearthly, maybe they were not real at all, maybe they were apparitions of former lives? Nevertheless, one or two of them appeared to be more *human* to his eyes. Just occasionally he had paused to consider the prospect of talking to them. Maybe they understood something about life that had always eluded him? They disgusted him, but he was intrigued by what kept them going, when surely they would be better off dead? In an uncanny show of synchronicity, as this latest bout of mental wrangling swirled in his head, he spotted one of those characters he recognised, sat against a hoarding with a thermos flask. He paused again, his brain in gridlock, then almost randomly plucked up courage to make contact. What harm could it do, to satisfy his curiosity about what made these guys tick?

'Do you mind if I just sit here for a moment?' Bevan did have a few coins and handed some over – he had little use for them now after all.

'Awright geezer. Please yourself. Cheers.'

Bevan sat down, reviewing options for how to break the ice.

'If you don't mind me asking ... what's your name?'

'Everyone calls me Ginge. What about you?'

Bevan found it hard to reply and just sat there for a while. He could not believe he had started the conversation in the first place. Besides, did he still even have a name? At what point did he stop existing, at what point must his identity be surrendered? Ginge filled the void.

'You look like that Clarkson geezer off the telly!' Ginge cackled triumphantly at the likeness. He actually meant Paxman, but it made little difference.

'I'm gonna call you Jez. Ha ha ... Jezzer.' Ginge laughed again.

Bevan laughed too. He had never thought of this. He laughed out loud ... more than he could ever recall doing before. What a brilliant idea, rebirth rather than termination. Had this strange weaselly character with a tangled beard suddenly provided the alternative to shedding his past and fading into the shadows, to join the ranks of the invisible? Instead of *the choir invisible*, perhaps he could join the invisible folk he had been so wary of. Ginge was taken aback by this jovial fellow, encountered out of the blue. But it made a change to have made someone happy, so he went with the flow. He had been looking forward to a chilled-out day anyway.

Bevan regained some control after his convulsive outburst and wiped the tears from his eyes. With a new name, maybe he could seek to survive. If people like Ginge found a way to live on the streets – and see a point in doing so – perhaps it was worth a try. Rechristened, he could start from a blank page and forget. If it became impossible, the plan A that had been fermenting as he left home could be revived in an instant. Bevan impulsively resolved to adopt this new mantle ... for a while at least.

'Ginge, that's just perfect. Yes ... call me Jez, why not? Jez is just fine, it's as good as any other name.'

And they talked. Ginge shared his tea, they sat and talked.

*

It would be a stretch to claim that Ginge showed Bevan the ropes. But by talking in headline terms about their mutual life stories, Bevan came to see there was some common ground between them. He could relate to Ginge's disappointments and, although he was alarmed by the obvious drug use, Bevan began to understand why someone would make the same choices. Bevan felt as if he had leapt from a cliff, only to land on a ledge a short way down, temporarily arresting his fall. Here was another level down, separate from the mainstream, populated by the dispossessed and one step removed from the oblivion Bevan had visualised. Was it a staging camp on the way down or a rescue post from which to be hauled up? Bevan did not need an answer to that question immediately. He simply saw an opportunity to reside here for some time, to see what happened. What was there to lose? Ginge scoffed at Bevan's wish to end it all. 'You don't want to do that man ... your time will come, wunnit?'

Disguised as Jez, he found it easier to be still. The floating seed, once drifting downstream to the sea, now becalmed in eddies by the riverbank. He did not try to seek help – he was not the neediest case and his aversion to officialdom was firmly entrenched. He was scared ... but there was always the backup strategy that Ginge had distracted him from, his nuclear option, his ejector seat. He had eked out his funds through the first few months of the year, like a car running on fumes with the warning light on. If he had spluttered to a halt in January the situation may have looked different. Now, as spring beckoned, biding some time in the open air was not unconscionable. And it was possible to keep drinking, as Ginge gleefully attested, so long as you were discreet when the police were around. Ginge eventually became restive and moved along. But by then Jez had gleaned the basics of economic survival from his unconventional mentor and, with the last of his money in pocket, turned away from his originally intended direction and began to scout the area, looking for suitable resting places.

As Jez, many of the inner torments were blown away like a pile of autumn leaves scattered by the wind. The world appeared in a new light. Bevan had been trying to stay afloat while out of his depth. Jez was sitting on the shore. When he met the likes of Colin and Izzy … they could see the essence of the good person inside and made allowances for his failings. Through those interactions – and the perspectives he gained from reading, once his scepticism about literature and reluctance to leaf through a single page were worn away – Jez found a way to quell the voices. The physical challenges were exacting but emotionally he felt liberated in this unforeseen state of limbo. There were no expectations, no regrets – none of the agonising about Bevan's life – he just had to *be*. Finding a favourable spot to perch in the sun, Jez sat alone outdoors for the first time, examining his book with suspicion. He stared at the cover and agreed to last another day.

Chapter 21

Jez lasted more than one day. In fact, it felt more like half a lifetime when he found himself recuperating by the dockside after his abortive mission to the outer reaches of town in search of a safer retreat. Immersed in his daydreams, as he watched the hammered-pewter surface of the sea skitter and sway, the thought occurred he was close to the spot of that pivotal encounter with Ginge, where it all began. It was well over seven months now since he had been lured into this precarious way of life. There had been good days and bad days … and an unwelcome series of scarcely bearable nights. However, despite being physically shattered, to his surprise he felt more at peace with himself now than when first alighting here. Perversely, there was an extent to which, by abandoning all self-respect and accepting the privations of life on the street, he had regained a degree of contentment not felt for many years. Jez was surprised how far he had come and was proud of having coped this long. Word was that ice and snow were around the corner but for now, ignoring the weather warnings and the pain in his limbs, Jez escaped back to his book. The next few pedestrians were allowed to pass by anonymously, without any conjecture about their destination or motive.

After a few pages, he glimpsed a familiar figure in the corner of his eye, standing by the railings, looking quizzically in his direction. It was his would-be Harry Lime again. Jez chuntered a silent monologue in his head, *Oh for goodness sake just come over here.* For once the man did. He sheepishly progressed along the quayside, tentatively squinting into the cavern of arches from a distance. Jez recalled his own feelings when he first spoke to Ginge and wondered if history was about to repeat itself. As Harry drew near, Jez recognised something of himself in the hesitant fellow ... for once he openly returned eye contact and reeled him in. Reaching the collection box, Harry leaned forward slightly and spoke.

'Excuse me ... do you need any money?'

Peering out from his igloo of blankets, Jez glanced down at the modest accumulation of coins in his pot, then back up again at his visitor.

'I'm not going to say no.' He didn't want to appear sarcastic; he understood the awkwardness. Harry placed a five pound note in the container, then added an extra couple of pounds to stop it blowing away.

'That's very kind of you, thank you,' Jez responded.

Harry stood over Jez, clearly determined to make conversation without knowing how to start.

'You're welcome. By the way ... can I ask you ... have you been doing this long? I really don't know how you survive out here.'

Jez was never keen to speak about his past, but the vividness of recent experience was beginning to mask what had gone before. At least he managed to say something, rather than change the subject.

'I've been out here all year. It's not great but, you know, I basically lost everything. This was all I had left.' Jez had almost erased the thoughts that drove him to leave home for the final time. He banished them again as he felt his eyes prick, under scrutiny, and had questions of his own. 'I've seen you around here a few times before haven't I? Do you live nearby?'

Now it was Harry's time to pause. Jez had all the time in the world and was happy to wait. Presently the man spoke again.

'No, I don't live here, but I've visited a few times. In fact, I've been looking for you.'

'Looking for me?' said Jez, instantly bewildered.

'Yes. I needed to be sure it really was you. It is Bevan isn't it? ... I think I'm right ... you *are* Bevan aren't you?' At the utterance of his old name Jez's head began to spin, up into the air with the drizzle and gulls above the water.

'Who are you? What do you want?'

'I'm your brother.'

'What? I don't have a brother. Well, I do, but ...'

'I'm so sorry to spring it on you like this, out of the blue. I know you must be shocked. I've been trying to find a way.'

Jez just stared at the figure above him, unable to fathom why his peace had been disturbed so unexpectedly by yet another madman. Harry's voice was breaking, as their mutual disbelief in what was happening held their gaze together like a magnetic force.

'Please try to believe me. I share part of your nightmare, Bevan. My parents died when I was two years old. My mother's name was Sandra, Sandra Mitchell. And Robert, your father Robert, he was my father too. I've been looking for you Bevan. I need to understand what happened. I need to understand more about who I am.'

The stare was eventually broken when Jez lowered his eyes to the ground on one side. Harry crouched down, put his back to the hoarding and sat on the flagstones beside him.

Acknowledgements

I first have to thank Karen Ralph, whose persistent badgering finally forced me to write something. Others tried in the past, to no avail (I must thank those distant voices too - if you are reading this, you know who you are). Without Karen hollering from the side, with encouragement and insightful feedback, I would have spluttered to a halt long before halfway. She also did the pictures for the cover art.

I am extremely grateful to Mary Elgar for her editing excellence. And to Ian Hooper, Julie Rick and the Book Reality team for helping The Levelled escape into the outside world.

Huge thanks to Gemma Osei for setting me off on the right path. Gemma, Nicki Porter and Rachel Wood provided honest and constructive review comments that shaped the final outcome, for which my appreciation is boundless. Thanks also to Geoff Cole and Jacqueline Pashill for taking time to read the full manuscript and making me believe. And to my family for their support in everything I do.

And to Shaheen, for love and for showing that fairy tales can come true.

About The Author

Jon Bryant was born in Harlow, Essex in 1964 and now lives in Ipswich. After graduating from Southampton University with a BSc in Biochemistry and Physiology he took the obvious next step of becoming a cartographer. A career spent working for various large institutions led to Jon's current existence as a freelance IT contractor specialising in digital maps. While bluffing in regard to technology, Jon is most content when writing reports, or notes in slide presentations that no one ever reads.

The Levelled is his debut novel, inspired by reflection on the fine margins between staying on-board and falling adrift.